THE LAKE WOMAN

For Kevin
& Rita,

Hoping you come
under the spell of these
combes.

Best Wishes

Alan Gould

Muse of the unique
Historical fact, defending with silence
Some world of your beholding, a silence

No explosion can conquer but a lover's Yes
Has been known to fill.

W. H. Auden, 'Homage to Clio'

THE LAKE WOMAN

A Romance by **ALAN GOULD**

ARCADIA

This Project has been assisted by the Australian Government through the Australia Council, its arts funding and advisory body.

First published 2009
7 Lt Lothian St Nth, North Melbourne, Vic 3051
TEL: 03 9329 6963 FAX: 03 9329 5452
EMAIL: aspic@ozemail.com.au
WEB: scholarly.info

ARCADIA

is the general books' imprint of Australian Scholarly Publishing Pty Ltd.

ISBN 978 1 921509 34 6

Copyediting by Rhiannon Hart
Design and typesetting by Sarah Anderson
Printing and binding by BPA Print Group
Cover, colour etching, 'Wellen' by Jörg Schmeisser

ACKNOWLEDGMENTS

I would like to acknowledge the following people who assisted me in the research for this novel: Sophie Masson, Marion Halligan, Heather Gould, Major Richard Gould particularly, Les and Valerie Murray, Alan Brown of the Airborne Museum (Aldershot,UK) Ursula Langridge, Grant Nutthall particularly, Hannah Kovacs, Dr Michael Shihoff, Anton Muller, Richard Frith, Natalie Bailly, Phil and Jenna Mead.

BOOKS BY ALAN GOULD

www.alangouldwriter.com

CONTENTS

1

THE LAKEWOMAN

With his eyes closed against his death, his fists tight shut like an infant in its first seconds, Alec sucked at the good air. And for the moment, it seemed, the treacherous terrain of Normandy, having pushed its black waters into his ears, his nostrils and down his windpipe, would permit him to live just a little further into his promising future.

He opened his eyes to the roaring, flooded dark, but could not prevent the vivid scenes of his last five minutes from compelling themselves on his mind's eye. They whelmed. From the fuselage tangle of limbs he had managed to kick free. His leap into the streaming dark had been his best choice in the circumstances, the subsequent rescue from this transformed, waterlogged land, must count, he supposed, as rather extraordinary. He stared into jags of blackness, the glint of the pools like knives glimpsed in a drawer.

I'm alive, just, he might have concluded gratefully.

But he could not stop blubbering. It came from some depth in his being and with the woman watching him now, as though he were a repellent thing, he felt ashamed. He also trembled helplessly, again as though from the core of his being.

Are you sure you're up to the business, old china? offered the severe voice of his parachute training.

Give it my best shot, he wanted to say if his body would but allow it.

Your near-death recedes from you already, Dearborn. Eye on the job.

Ah, but he could not compose himself. Some old trust had burst its banks in him, taken his self-possession by surprise.

'Winded me,' as his good nature used to say when he copped one on the playing fields.

He was a young man, large of frame, amiable and appraising in his manner. The military regimen of the last three years had toughened the physique of the school rugby player and long-jumper, and never before in his life had Alec Dearborn reason to believe he was given to nervous bodily reaction.

So! Are you sure you're up there, old man?

'Haacch!'

As he vomited he also wondered why this sudden young *Mamzelle* happened to be present at the exact, unlikely spot in France where his foolish body had come to earth. It was a question that would usefully occupy his mind later, when he was behind the wire with the austere leisure to brood on the magic that settled into his life following this, his fluky rescue. Magic? He was not a fellow given to outlandish notions, and would interrogate the dubious word, looking for its sense, not in mumbo jumbo, but as some friable quantity existing within the very crevices of everyday occasions.

Rescuer and rescued now dripped from their struggle with the deadly waters. *Mamzelle* stood hugging herself for warmth, peering as though to determine what it was exactly she had fished from the glinting flood. Spread at her feet, Alec retched with small, yelping gasps the oily mire he had swallowed. His jump smock and the outgrowths of his kit gleamed with the ooze, giving him the outline of some gross reptile. All about the pair were the half-drowned trees, hedgerows and stiles of the inundated country, presenting hobgoblin profiles, infiltrated by the steeliness of the torrent whose shallows made insistent, plapping waves around their tuft of high ground. The pale parachute, still snared around the sapling, resembled a discarded birth-sac while the wind, that treacherous Invasion night wind, dishevelled the surfaces of floodland and grassland alike.

'Harrugh! Aaahh.'

Again his insides turned on him and the shaken young Australian tried to communicate what may have been an apology to this apparitional *Mamzelle* for the nuisance he felt he must have been causing her. From the cloud above came the tumult of the aircraft armada, immense in its claim on all attention. It thrummed as though it were the slipstream note of the planet itself, wave on wave of the Airborne going in, each to their drop zones, each to the fatal schedule of strategic bridges and gun emplacements, to that intent existence of hide, shoot, sprint, seize, dig, hang on until …

Alec glanced at his watch and saw the dial had been crushed by someone's boot during the fearful scramble inside the plane. So much for the grand schedule. Unbelievably that fuselage havoc was not yet even five minutes behind his present, yet the compressing effect on his mind of the hit, the jump, the immersion, seemed to place it in a former lifetime. The wind went through his sopping clothes and chilled him. It had blown the other two fellows to buggery across *Basse Normandie*. He had no idea whether anyone else managed to follow him through the stricken Dakota's doorway.

He trembled, he sob-breathed, while within some lucid sanctum of mind he instructed himself to take stock. Could he say where he was? No. For all his study of maps and scale models during the months of rehearsal, he could not now place landmarks, nor say in which direction lay his intended drop zone. Was he near enough to hear the relevant shooting when it started? There was a generalised thunder, like a distant storm, coming from somewhere—the coast presumably. Ah, it was too easy, in his present frame of mind, to recoil from the whole forthcoming show.

Up to it, old man?

Mercifully his vomiting had stopped, though mouth and nostrils were foul with mud and stomach acid. He was aware the woman was studying him and under her gaze he tried to collect himself sufficiently to try speaking with her. But it was vain, for his sodden nuisance of a body must shudder, *must*, and his voice quiver, like some delicate fabric caught in a corridor draught. Ridiculous. Fervently he wished he could have appeared more self-possessed in the presence of the woman.

For his conduct was a matter of nicety to Alec Dearborn. If the war were going to put his conscience in the way of doing jagged things, he would at least try to defend that debonair part of his nature where he sensed his good lay. His sister Bell had given him the nicer judgements on that in the days before Cambridge. After that, one or two of his Pom colleagues had observed that Alec's was your Down-under species of chivalry, hesitant, cheerful, somehow natural if you have three thousand acres of tableland pastures to gallop about on and two sisters to grow up between, an elder who, on the evidence, he could tease and adore, a younger who was dotty and must be heard out.

Indeed Alec's first twelve years, largely isolated in the small community that comprised Bell, Nance, Ma, The Dad, a governess, the station hands, had allowed him a place and a pace by which his nature could grow sure of itself. Boarding school with its free-for-all, Cambridge with its common rooms, could not disarm the amiable sovereignty of that nature.

Perhaps when the war came Alec should have taken the steamer home and enlisted with his own tribe. But the times were sunset-of-empire. They permitted a generous and far-flung errantry for those with promising futures. That errantry had got him here, in the mud, and it was too late for him to be anywhere else. He had been dropped into war with his Pom regiment, and was now furious and miserable because he was being watched by a woman while his foolish body compelled him to behave in a manner very much below the estimation he had of himself.

2

TO FLING THE LOVELY, FOOLISH BODY

During his last year at Hume Grammar, Alec Dearborn captained the Firsts, gained a cup for the long jumping, and won the Carson Prize for essay writing. 'An eloquence on paper to match his grace on the field.' Truffy the Head had read the citation to the assembled school while Alec had stood on stage with the masters, looking at his shoes. It was good to excel, yet somehow repellent to be made conspicuous, set up on the stage like someone's prize ram. Throughout school they had referred to him as an 'all-rounder' and in the last year or so he could not ignore the fact that Truff and some of the other masters had picked him out as some kind of golden youth. Natural therefore that they should have marked him down for Cambridge. And now he was in.

'Goose will wear a mortarboard and come back speaking like a Pom,' predicted Nance.

'We'll probably miss you a bit,' ventured Bell, as they stood at the gangplank of the big ship when the tannoy announced that visitors should disembark.

'Me you, Bell.' Brother and sister glanced at each other, suddenly awkward in their emotions. 'I could skip this whole promising future-lark, to tell the truth.'

'Don't do that.' Then she was gone quickly down the gangplank.

This was August 1937, and Alec crossed the seas in time to commence the Michaelmas term at Pembroke where, for the next three years, he studied an English literature and history mix. His hesitancy as to the promising future did not prevent him winning a blue for rugby and another for athletics within his first year. His team mates called him Teapot on account of the slight bandiness of his legs and shot the pilch out to him as often as they could because it was a joy to see the full-pelt and swerve of a chap who knew what to do when in possession of the ball.

Odd how flinging the body at a touchline could be such an impelled act, yet not entirely at one with how he might have liked to govern himself.

Alec found he was liked by the Poms, though they created in him a certain self-consciousness that was entangled with the word 'colonial'. This made him disguise what he feared was his too wide-eyed Australian manner with a certain dandyism. He wore a cravat and a well-cut sports coat, smoked a pipe, and in discussion allowed himself to appraise a fellow for a few moments rather than fire back a rejoinder.

'If that's what you reckon to be the fair thing,' he'd say, enjoying the tone of it, the casual authority.

He spent his summers with Ma's people, or went scrambling among the British mountains, and found himself looking out on half of Scotland from the summit of Cairn Gorm on the September Sunday when war was declared.

Ten months later, during the opening week of the Battle of Britain he sat in an echoing hall, scrawling in his large handwriting the essays for his finals. Scratch-scratch went the pens. A gasmask belonging to each examinee sat under each chair, there was an odour of ink from the small ceramic inkwells on each desk, and as he formulated his answers, Alec glanced occasionally at the fidgeting shoulders of Colfax who wrote rapidly at the desk in front, or Hartigan with his head resting on his left hand as he penned his more leisurely thoughts at the desk beside him, and for a few idle moments he would daydream the answers his two cronies might be composing before returning to his own.

With Cambridge behind them, these three Cambridge cronies volunteered for farm work in Kent while the Australian made up his mind whether to return Down Under or enlist in a regiment of The Old Country where, as things turned out, he had been an appreciative and successful guest.

'Decision time, Dearborn,' Hartigan told him. The two Englishmen were down for a county regiment.

The three lounged in the meadow grass, their shirtsleeves rolled, Hartigan smoking a cigarette, Colfax running the whetstone thoughtfully along the blade of his scythe. Deadly, above their heads, the incising vapour trails of fighter aircraft swelled whitely like welts on flesh before they slowly vanished against the perfect blue of the summer sky. Earlier, Colfax had remarked how, if one cared to bring a detached mind to the matter, the drone of those Hurricanes and Dorniers need be no more bothersome than the drone of the meadow's insect life, bee and bluebottle. Not that one could bring detachment to that remote fury.

'I don't need reminding, you blokes.'

Alec chewed a blade of the English grass, fleshier than that of the paddocks he remembered from Portobello. In fact he did need time to meditate his choices because the formation of his nature had led him to trust humans.

Twelve years and three thousand acres, Ma, The Dad, Bell, Nance, and then the governesses, shearers, jackaroos who came and went, this society had created in his outlook an essential world that was interior, and a rim of low hills from which the exotic visitors came.

You'd see them, a sunhat or trilby bumping along behind a Ford or Chev Tourer's windscreen or against the black of a pony trap hood. It was the way in which a straightforward curiosity about humanity can exhilarate a body whenever the life from outside turns up. This physiological reaction transformed the three siblings into eavesdroppers. Unable to help themselves, they lingered in doorways when the adults gassed-on, crept from their rooms after beddy-byes to watch beer being brought from the cool place and hear the pulses of laughter, the talk seeking gamefully to out-talk.

Born into Bell, Alec, Nance, therefore, was the deep pastoral trust that human encounters were inevitably interesting, and that this attitude was the most reasonable one with which to assess the world.

When it came to the war, Alec read the English papers in the junior common room, listened to the Pembroke chat, accepted that the foe was necessarily the foe. But at a further place in his being, he could not quite embrace the idea of wishing to bring down ruin on any particular person, no matter how hateful the substance of report. Nor could he quite believe anyone could wish ruin upon him. Such were the predispositions from which his openness of outlook grew. He chewed the grass blade as the vapour trails slashed at the summer sky and his two pals awaited a decision from the reflective colonial mind.

'Well then, Dearborn?'

Alec was no pacifist. Grammar had taught him that if a stoush allowed you no fair way round some objectionable character, you dealt with it. Once or twice he had knocked a fellow down, then stayed, wondering if the action had been excessive, wondering what the sensation of anger in a body might be, and why it appeared to be absent from his own nature. He could get stroppy, but that was irritation, not anger. With regard to the war, he knew he was going into the fight one way or another. The problem was, how to do this and still keep intact his pastoral trust to which people were mostly well disposed.

'Here's your dilemma, old man.' Colfax let his whetstone slide down his blade with a long shee-ush. 'You can get the boat home to

Sydney, enlist with your own chaps, whereupon I would lay bets the whole marsupial mob of you will be back here doing corps training on Salisbury Plain in three months.' He slid the whetstone again, then added, 'If the submarines don't sink you somewhere in the middle.'

'Or?' Alec spat a small mash of chewed grass toward the distant Battle for Britain.

'Or you can come in with us,' Colfax trumped his argument, 'thereby saving yourself a good deal of hazardous sea-travel.'

'One assumes Australia came in on our side?' This flippancy from Hartigan.

'One does assume.' Colfax swept down the blade again with his whetstone.

'My mother was born an Englishwoman.'

'There you are then.'

'There I am.'

'Pact?'

There was a pause from Alec, then, 'Pact,' the three said together. The hay lay in swathes around them, the sky above scored with its remote combats.

'We'll be required to adopt some very unusual behaviour,' observed Colfax. 'Squeezing the trigger and what-have-you.'

'To which, I vote, we each should bring a detached mind.' Hartigan stubbed his cigarette into the soil.

The three young men rose from their lunch respite and resumed their mowing, moving through the waist-high grass in an echelon line. The swing of their scythes was not entirely rhythmic, but effective enough in these unusual conditions where graduates became farmhands. Now the dogfights receded in long trails toward The Channel. The hay fell to the right in brassy swathes and as Alec swung his scythe a sprig of his blonde hair would come loose across his forehead, which he flicked back in time with his arm movements.

So what would it be like, going off to war? As children on Portobello, he and Bell sometimes used to sit on the veranda edge after the shearers had knocked off and eavesdrop on talk about the Great One. Some of the blokes were returned soldiers from the Western Front, and once Alec asked simply, 'What was it like to be there, Mister Dakin?'

Mister Dakin, whose complexion was brown and oiled like the Dearborn dining-room table, glanced quickly at the boy before winding the matter up. 'It was quite shocking, son. All right?' Then the blokes, as though collusive with the returnees among them, had inclined away from the boss' young-uns, had talked of engines, of anything neutral that would sink the evidently charged topic. You could be ten years old and sense the emotive fabric of this.

Mister Dakin's shortness allowed the child to learn his experience of life had been dismissed. Why? Because he did not yet know enough to steer clear of topics where he had no rights. The snub perplexed him as he grew older, for here was an impediment to his trust that when folk turned up at Portobello you could rely on a rich store of experience to be shared. With these ex-diggers, here was something dark. Was it also rich? Alec's bedtime reading had contained its share of King Arthur & Co, deadly fights in the exotic glades of old Europe. Which was where The Great One had been fought just outside his own lifetime. If war had a dark side and a rich side why should his question to the shearer have recoiled on him like some old brown snake having a go?

Twelve years from that now, Alec paused in his scything and voiced something of this perplexity to his two companions. 'Whatever they decide to do with us,' he said, leaning on the hub of the scythe, 'they will make us strangers to the thing we think we are now.'

'They'll dress our moral being to the nines,' declared Hartigan, who took a cigarette from his tin.

'They'll dress us for something.'

The three smoked, then resumed the work. Alec tried to adjust the rhythm of his scything so that the movement came from the entire deliberate body. But scything was not part of his pastoral education in the Tuggeranong valley of southern New South Wales, and he hopped like a townsman when the blade passed too nearly across his shins. Foolish body, as he liked to think of his physical bulk in the moments of applause after he had set down a try or gained an inch in the long jump.

'Well, let them bring it on,' Hartigan concluded when they had scythed to the end of their row and turned for the uphill.

The army had its own pace for bringing it on, and declined to take these three college lads in the same batch.

'Do you think we will ever again live in times suited to personal arrangements?' asked Hartigan, who had gone into uniform by November.

From the window of his train he shook hands with his two Cambridge chums and looked a little self-conscious in his khaki as the carriage moved away, bearing the young man toward his training at

Aldershot, then North Africa, Italy and a wholly effective sniper's bullet at Monte Cassino.

Alec and Colfax joined their county regiment three months later in the February of 1941.

Roared from his bed in the Nissen hut, bawled around a parade ground, vilified through sessions of kit-inspection, unarmed combat and weapons training, route-marched through the countryside until his foolish body was bruised by contact with the earth, chafed by webbing, weary beyond any fatigue it had known hitherto; nonetheless at small moments of illumination in the cold, the sweat, the uproar, Alec remarked how some tough little sergeant could take trouble to see that every bleeding-sod of his worthless responsibility should stumble across the line at the end of a route march, and would grab the manfully failing Colfax under his armpit, half-carry him, half-bellow him over the finish line. These infrequent glimmers of an austere pastoral care offset the rigmarole of harassment. True, Alec discovered how inventive, how base, how staged were the imaginations of NCO instructors, how practiced they were in finding the exact words to needle each man's private self for the amusement or edification of the others in the squad. But he also learned how to set these effronteries at the dispassionate remove required by common sense and by the fact of their common, outlandish, and at odd intervals, hilarious plight.

As when …

He stood to attention at dawn parade, trying to keep the foxy drillmaster in view without being seen to move his head. Tucked under his left arm this drillmaster gripped his pace-stick (or was it, in the weird, precisely-spoken world he had entered, a pay stick—Alec dared not ask). In any case, the instrument comprised two wooden arms hinged with brass, capped with brass ferrules at each end. It was folded on the march, but able to be expanded like a pair of dividers and dextrously swivelled in order to demonstrate the regulation thirty inch measure of the military step. Now the devilish man had disappeared from Alec's view. Seconds later, it seems there was a voice spitting something important a few inches below the young man's right ear.

'If you *hever* do *that* again ...'

'Uh?' The squad would be overhearing everything.

'I will h-ram this paish shtick hup your posteri-hoor ...'

Did I flinch, did I smirk?

'... in such a manner as to give you, sonny-boy ...'

Had he committed a fault?

'Brash *teef!*'

The electrified recruit tried to further rigidify his person around his imminently brass teeth, his reasoning mind already setting the demon in its place, turning the savage moment into what, years later as a schoolteacher, he would occasionally relate to fourth form as one of the hilarious occasions of his life. 'Brash teef!' You could relish that lifelong.

And here, he perceived, was the military design. The demon leapt at you, but was nonetheless a common property, disarmed when you shared the picturesque language later with the fellows. It was devious, rather impressive, this rigmarole of coarse, alarming strategies that went to create the finesse of their soldierly fellowship. And for all its frequent coarseness, it was a finely tuned affair, the creation of this *esprit de corps*.

Alec could see the change it required in him, a decent transfer of trust to the fellows in the squad, the regiment, and away from the idea that a differently clad bod wandering toward your rifle sights might be inevitably hived with intrinsic interest.

'Could it be, at the bottom of the fiery pit, we find the demon is on our side?' asked Alec, reviving the old Pembroke dandyism as Colfax shambled, grey with exhaustion, over the line at the end of their route march.

'I do not trust to it,' observed his slightly built friend, the future headmaster, and tried a smile.

At the conclusion of their recruit training the two advanced to officer training, from which Colfax went to Army Education, then a posting to Delhi, followed by his post-war career in English schooling.

Alec proceeded to platoon training with his county regiment, was able to recognise how the knack of commanding thirty-odd diverse fellows revived old strategies of tact, duress, laconic humour that he had learned as prefect and First XV captain at Hume. With his platoon sergeant he very promptly decided that if he did not know a thing, he would be entirely candid with this essential and watchful individual. Their training took the battalion to various places around the British Isles as one scheme followed another for the prosecution of the war. So Alec spent long hours on trains, sleeping upright among the fellows, waking to a view of bomb damaged railway stations, or slate roofs slicked with rain, his neck itchy from the rough fabric of the military shirt, his limbs stiff from the cramped compartment. From railway stations he marched them, or supervised their ongoing transport, dealing with the glitches in arrangements, reporting to the location indicated on his movement papers, then whether in dark or daylight, performing the tasks assigned to his command, taking occasional forty-eight-hour leave to stay with one of Ma's relations and wear a comfortable shirt for a day. Then back to field manoeuvres or garrison routines. Rumour would circulate that the battalion was off to Oran, to Sicily, to the Far East; but these whispers came to nothing and the months went by with field-craft, map-reading, night exercises. Among the hills of Ayrshire or the wooded valleys of Devon, rain dripped from the flap of his tent or the rim of his helmet, the fellows listened to his briefings with the range of their facial expressions and the qualities underpinning each now familiar to him. Mud hardened on boot and battledress, and this he brushed or sponged or polished away as the (sometimes) primitive conditions in which they lived together afforded.

Then he saw a paragraph at the bottom of the Battalion Part One Orders on the mess noticeboard calling for volunteers to join the Airborne. It was a few extra shillings a week and an opportunity to escape the round of field and garrison ennui. Alec joined.

In the parachute training that ensued, he quickly grasped the point of it, which was to bring him to an attitude of complete dispassion about the self. How else to cast yourself from an aeroplane? *Take that vanity, your flesh, hurl it along these high planks, at these grappling nets, into these quagmires the colour of toffee, fling it until the precious thing is so inured to risk and misuse you can forget you have a foolish body at all and find instead you have acquired, somehow ... What?*

Presumably that more intense level of *esprit* held in common with the other blokes as he ran, dared, roared with them (ah, but devious in how Alec must keep intact that part of himself that would not roar). He scrambled, flung himself across the obstacle courses, jumped from the back of moving trucks, first forwards, then backwards, remembering how to position his feet, how to roll so the impact was absorbed through knees and hips, trusting. He shared with his squad the atrocious burden of a length of timber, turn and turnabout, as they raced for killing miles cross-country. He was tested for airsickness by being swung back and forth across a hangar for fifteen minutes, then taken with the blokes up in a barrage balloon to 800 feet and nonchalantly directed to jump through a hole in the basket. Below him the sun shone on the land. The lanes, the cottages, the sloping heath, were all miniaturised rather charmingly. You could say it was a joy to be alive. And if, in a few moments, his parachute did a 'streamer' then, one must suppose, squelch.

'Tomorrow we push you fellows from an aeroplane.'

Flinging his body through the hatch or open door of an Albemarle or Dakota caused Alec Dearborn hardly a moment's apprehension. He had relished the high boards at the school swimming pool, the speed of a motorcycle along the Cambridgeshire lanes. The damage that an impact might wreak on his own hurtling body did not seriously make him doubt his invulnerability. The aeroplane's interior smelt of gasoline, sweat and, Alec noted particularly, farts. Then it was red light, hook up the static line, check the line of the bloke in front, shuffle forward toward the open door managing your kit, watch for the jumpmaster's nod, launch forward turning your back to the aircraft's slipstream. *Whomp!* In seconds the static line had pulled apart the parachute pack, the X chute had opened behind him and swung him down. Check the thing had flared as it should, and then, for thirty seconds or so, he could allow himself to enjoy the aerial view of English paddocks edged with hedgerows, the occasional elm tree, the green countryside, still after six years, slightly too fabulous for his Australian sense of the usual. Down there the busy sergeants were striding about the drop zone, firing off blank or live ammunition at the descending mushrooms in simulation of what 'the lads' could expect over there, wherever that zone might one day turn out to be.

It was for these charmed thirty aerial seconds that Alec had joined the Airborne, he later rationalised. Thirty seconds, an even shorter duration as they jumped from lower altitudes to prepare for Invasion conditions. Nonetheless the sensation, whether from the daylight or the night drops, seemed to stay in mind like a blissful suspension of interval. At forty feet (so the instruction stipulated for an altitude impossible to judge accurately,) unclip the weapons bag to dangle on its cord. Then up reared the ground. Contact, roll, release the Capewell buckle at one shoulder, spilling wind from the chute, hit the harness button, one of the instructors already belting over the grass to bellow encouragements in the ear ('You will, Mister Dearborn, sir, accelerate your self from your incarnadined harness, take your entire mortal bundle to the avidly copulating congress of humanity you can see at the assembly point …) And so on.

O it was harmless enough, being hurried along by this fierce, remote harassment. Concede its authority without quite believing it, that was the trick. Gather in chute, harness and kit; fit a magazine to the Sten gun as you run. Meanwhile, inhale the scent of new grass in England's late April; glimpse the sticky buds on the crab apples, the white flowers starring the hawthorn hedges. How remote Australia seemed; already eight years since The Dad died from heart, Nance married, Bell and Ma running Portobello. The hectic schedule of training left him little respite for the old life, though he had managed to get in the odd kickabout when one battalion played another on an afternoon of standby.

Alec knew himself to have one impediment to his outlook on the military business, and this eventually drew notice a few weeks before the D-Day event. He would not allow himself to utter the actual name of the enemy.

Jerry, Fritz, Hun, even the generic word enemy worried him. Obscurely he understood that to make free with these terms would intrude upon the very part of himself that stemmed from Portobello and which he wanted to keep intact. As inconspicuously as he could, he deflected the everyday pressure to express an attitude to the foe, referring to them as 'the other bloke, or 'the away team'.

This accorded with his feelings toward the actual faces he could imagine encountering in the forthcoming fight. Hateful, of course, was the Nazi regime, its persecutions and war making. But one day within the next few weeks, he foresaw, he would round the corner of some French street and find himself eyebrow to eyebrow with 'the other bloke'. Of course they'd shoot at him, try to do for him. Of course he would need to be quick if he wanted to beat them at the same trick. There were no choices; that was the unwelcome common plight and Alec accepted its claim on him. But this did not allow him, as he scrutinised his mind on the subject, to confidently detest those faces. In the briefing tent a week before the Invasion his colonel picked up this diffidence following a question Alec had been bold to ask.

'Mister!'

'Sir?

'We are speaking of The Hun.'

'Are we?'

'Not dancing partners brought in from the local girls' school.'

'I imagine not, sir.'

And for a minute or two at the subaltern's expense there was mirth in that tent of maps and officers. With that stagy formality the Poms liked, the colonel allowed his hard stare to remain on Alec for some moments.

'No room here for the squeamish!' Then more of that hard stare.

Alec smiled back wryly, hoped his level gaze communicated he could shrug off these thrusts at the part of himself he wanted to keep intact. Two days previously he had got the news about Hartigan. Bugger rank, he should have given the sod a piece. The charming Poms.

Yet the matter of an enemy continued to unsettle him. How would he fare if he were not assisted by some genuine animosity toward the other bloke? His emotion on learning about Hartigan was not to feel incensed. It was loss, the pity for his parents, the grievous inconvenience of never again locating the warm intelligence behind the dandy's hauteur.

If he composed his mind to the impending task before them, Alec supposed that when it came to it, he would manage the business of popping away at whatever movement might cross his gun sights in the rapid calculations required by battle. He would lob grenades through windows, do his best by those who depended on him. The rigmarole of the bayonet worried him, but with luck …

On the day in June when they were driven in trucks to the airfield he learned he had been gazetted a full lieutenant. Promotion, and yet everything still to be proved.

3

NOT FIVE MINUTES BEHIND HIS PRESENT

His seat in the fuselage was one near the open door. The airsickness tablets and the steady aero-drone had made the mood of the fellows passive, strapped as they were into their monstrous bulges of weapons, pathfinder beacons and provisions. The close, ovoid airframes of these Dakota transports invariably gave Alec a sense of being inside the ribcage of a medium-sized whale, and down each side of the plane his 'stick' of fellows had their appointed places, packed cheek-by-jowl, marked off in the dim light by the pale cross-straps of their parachute webbing. Their twenty faces were all blacked with charcoal paste, such that the chinstrap and helmet of each man isolated their features into a minimal wedge of eyes, nose and mouth.

They had all been rigidly confined to camp in the past days, and alcohol prohibited. But at someone's suggestion Alec had slipped a bottle of whisky into his pack, so once they had gained altitude and formation above southern England he took out the liquor, proffered it to Sgt Ferris in the seat beside him, and indicated above the aero-churr that the stimulant be shared. Ferris swigged and passed on the bottle. Some preferred not to drink. Most took a modest gulp and nodded appreciatively in Alec's direction.

He noted how their black war paint made everyone appear equally veteran. Ferris, he knew, had seen fighting already, in North Africa and Sicily. Alec, perhaps like most in this fuselage-cave, knew how untried he was.

What then, should occupy the mind of a man in the hour or two before he goes out to snuff out life or be snuffed? He had never felt more alive, compressed into this dark cylinder, glancing at his fellows, smelling the acridity of webbing, gun-oil, gasoline. At the same time he could not help his thoughts brooding on how the devilish thing toward which they droned would transform them all.

Put baldly, Alec gazed past Pte Hoyland sitting opposite, *we're on our merry way to ...*

Ah, it was fine and dandy, that habit of plain thinking in moral matters which was encouraged at Pembroke. Cromwell and the Puritan Revolution lay behind it somehow, he recalled from his year of history. That habit had suited Alec's cast of mind, having grown up on a sheep station, where one might blunder upon cook wringing a hen's neck or preparing a mutton.

But was plain thinking useful when it came to contemplating bayonet work?

In training he had yelled like the others, jabbed away at the dangling straw dummies even as he had said to himself, *This is Alec Dearborn who yells and rehearses the ghastly business of bayonets.* In his kit now he carried a bayonet, the short issue model that could be attached to a Sten gun.

… Which is a bit crook, from one point of view was how he decided to foreshorten his bald thoughts. And here was Hoyland passing the whisky bottle back after it had done the round. Still half-full, good quality liquor too. He took a swig and pushed it away into the weapons bag strapped to his leg.

Not that you could take any one view. *We are speaking of The Hun, not a team of …* and all the collusive laughter of that briefing tent. The Hun? Well, maybe. But you still had to reconcile the military business with the business of the self. Would he push a bayonet into a fellow's midriff with no more thought than shoving out his arm to fend off a tackle when he was going full tilt for the line? Would he let loose with a burst if he came round a corner and there was the other bloke confronting him, some person's face determined by a ma and pa? *You're thinking too precisely on the event, Horatio.* He tried to extricate himself from the inconvenient meander of his thought. O but it was the appalling rapidity with which the event would happen that Alec dreaded. That fact, and the radical switchover, from being one kind of person in this moment, then irrevocably altered in the next.

Of course he saw how this was the common plight of every uniformed sod across the whole embattled globe. But that consideration did not allow his own small knot of dread to sit more easily with the view he had of himself. Was this switchover the cause behind that reticence of Mr Dakin and those ex-digger shearers from his boyhood? Well then, how did it get to this pass, a fellow being put in the way of extinguishing other fellows? The Dakota's engine howl, the slipstream audible through the open door provided a suitably tense background music for thinking these vital matters through.

If a bit last minute.

Compounding his meditation was Alec's dread of letting down any of these fellows packed beside him. He glanced at Pte Hoyland. Alec had penned the odd letter for Hoyland whose writing skills were not the best; tortuous had been the process of getting those few sentences of declared emotion out of this otherwise entirely reliable member of his stick and onto paper. *If I persist in this line of bayonet thinking I might easily let that fellow down.*

He might almost have uttered this thought aloud, so forcibly did it occur to him. Yes, he dreaded being the cause of harm to these congenial blokes. And yet he recoiled from doing harm to any living thing. Conundrum. Doing harm was what he had been most conscientiously prepared for, and he had been acquiescent in that. *There's your inner workings of warfare,* reasoned the Cambridge graduate who was not yet tried by war, and who, maybe, like like the majority of humankind, believed you could mostly rely on others to be well-disposed.

Sidelong he glanced at his fellows, crammed together down each side of the fuselage aisle. How to account for the fierce impulse of present affection he felt, not to any particular person, but toward the corporate presence of them all? Was it an affection more real than he had felt for Ma, Nance or Bell? Hard to say when it came to rude plain thinking. Whatever the truth, the emotion aroused in him at that moment, from whisky or otherwise, was warm, a little heartbreaking. And recognisable from odd moments in their more recent training, there was his very palpable liking for them, and sense of obligation toward them.

Clearly he had succumbed to the army's design on his outlook. Well, so be it. He would have quite liked a second swig from the bottle, but took his cue from how modestly his fellows had availed themselves of the liquor. He turned his attention to the exchange of ribald commonplaces shouted between one soldier and his neighbour up and down the reverberant fuselage. Jones had farted loudly, it seemed. It was usually the deadpan Jones.

Deeply impressive was the immobility with which some of the fellows reposed in apparent serenity, eyes closed in a doze, or pretend-doze. Were some of them in prayer? What an extraordinary place for prayer, this metal ribcage high above where people did their living. Should he try a prayer of some sort? How? He looked at his watch. It was some twenty-five minutes after midnight on this particular June 6.

'Won't be long now, sir,' from Hoyland.

Alec was still not entirely at home with a Pom saying 'sir' to him. And yet, of all the various human loves (he pursued his wordless enquiry), was this affection between fellows pitched into the military business the most entrenched of the human affections? If Hoyland's number was up, he, Alec, may well be committed to watch the fellow die. If his own number was up, it was probable someone within this cave would be nearby to account for it. Palpable, spontaneous the emotion of that proximity. Yet how cheerfully it subverted itself at every turn in order that it might preserve its distinct delicacy and ruggedness. The military business. So coarsely, so finely worked.

'Is this the right bus for Australia, sir?'

'That's what my ticket says, Corporal.' Alec turned to Shaftoe who sat on his right. Outlandish, the grin on a face smeared with black war paint!

Once they had cleared the cloud cover around Fairford and gained altitude, it was evident from the open doorway there was a fair old moon. Over the English Channel Alec leaned across Ferris and Shaftoe to regard the spectacle visible through the open door. Exhaust fumes from the aircraft engine blurred the view, but even within that small rectangle of sky and sea it was possible to gain some idea of how momentous was the armed strength of the forthcoming battle. Around, above, below were the blunt silhouettes of the other transports. Here and there the pinprick blue lights on a tailplane. Visible, too, the three white 'invasion' stripes on the nearer planes, Dakotas, some Stirlings. Otherwise there were no colours. Receding from his gaze in their V-formations like cut-outs from black paper, the aircraft he could actually see and the multitude he could surmise, appeared to him as though animated by the one inexorable impulse.

Here was another claim on his feelings that needed to be watched, the thrill aroused by the sheer magnitude of that war-bringing purpose. How did that thrill go with plain moral thinking on the issue? Sentimental? If he strained forward he could glimpse the sea and spy some of the thousands of ships of the Invasion. They were like black scrape marks on the Channel's night glint. He resumed his upright position.

'We appear to be many,' he offered to Sgt Ferris. Awkward, the manner you need to adopt toward sergeants. You put on seniority where plain thinking tells you it doesn't properly exist. Maybe Ferris would think his comment ingenuous? Then Alec became aware the Dakota was gaining altitude and the view from the doorway had become a grey blank. Cloudbanks? If so they weren't getting the break in the weather the meteorology blokes had hoped for. It would disperse the formations, muck up the jump altitude.

'As long as our driver don't take a wrong turning, sir,' said Shaftoe.

'My oath, corporal.'

Now the red light above the door had come on and Jumpmaster Ferris was shouting his orders down the plane. Everyone stood, hooked their static lines to the overhead wire, checked that of the man in front, and then waited, one behind the other in the aero noise. In the queue before Alec were Hoyland and Shaftoe, and Ferris on one side to count them each out.

'A bit on the high side, still, sir?' bawled Shaftoe from the door opening.

'He's taking us down.'

Alec saw the blank grey of the cloud go streaky and then, not quite to be believed from the darkness, their Dakota appeared to be attracting fire from the ground. A hose of tracers materialised and vanished. The pomm! of some heavy stuff close enough to rock the aeroplane and cause the fellows behind him to stagger, steady themselves, as the pilot bucked his craft in evasive turns.

You stand one moment in your own body, invulnerable. Then, without being aware you have even blinked, the world you thought you knew has become something entirely other.

He did not know how he had got into the predicament. Yet Alec found he was trying to extricate himself from under an incomprehensible crush. It was like a collapsed football scrum except without the expanse of a sports field around you. There was an air-rush whistling through the plane from some unfamiliar aperture, not the door, and the whine of the engines was rising in pitch. Blink an eye. There was Ferris, bundling Hoyland and Shaftoe through the door. How did Ferris get a bleeding hand? Why was the little light still red and not green for go? Hah, the leg with the weapons bag strapped to it was now clear, though the bag was askew. The leg seemed asleep. Now yank his static line clear of the tangle. Blink an eye and there was the jumpmaster right, as it were, in his own face.

'Get fuckin' clear of this, sir,' Ferris had said to him. Impressive how in the emergency the bloke could remember the protocol of 'sir'. And Alec's sergeant seemed already to have grasped the nature of an event that had not yet successfully sorted itself out in his own head.

I should have jumped on that, Alec would blame himself in the coming days. But clutching at the stupid weapons bag, he had paused to glimpse across his shoulder.

Ah, piteous.

Fellows were writhing in an imbroglio of limbs, static lines, equipment tumbled from the racks. Who was it? The fellow who had stood immediately behind him in the aisle? O'Loghlan? Lance Corp Brown? Whoever it was, Alec glimpsed how the man was still fighting to be clear of the ruck in order to be ready for the jump. Only he had lost his face. Blown off? Burnt off? There had been some catastrophic change, and that change effected in the blink of an eye. *Yes, it had been Brownie,* Alec would conclude one early morning exactly forty years later. Atrocious to meditate how, where eyes, nose, mouth conform in such a confident arrangement one moment, you see havoc in their place. If he had been less self-preoccupied, more attentive to the life in his vicinity, in his care, would he have remembered the identity of the wretched fellow at the time? Ah, atrocious, that somehow the hideous disfigurement immediately behind him had already suggested itself as having always belonged on that particular face by right.

Blink an eye. How can an instant in time bear the weight of so much thinking? Manipulate the weapons bag back to its adjacency on the leg. Where is the grip? Focus on the drill. The engine whine continued to rise in pitch and the fuselage floor was slanted at an improbable angle, meaning their stricken transport was tilting into a dive. Blink an eye. Whatever happened to the green light? Glance at Ferris again for confirmation. The veins of the sergeant's wall-eye were momentarily illuminated by the small red light.

'Go, fuckya!'

So he had leapt, making that half turn away from the slipstream. And may have heard a punctilious 'sir' pursue him into the dark.

During the practice jumps his whim had been that a parachute jump was like casting off one self in favour of another. Here, instantaneously he was divorced from the fuselage chaos, plucked away by the ferocious slipstream, jerked backwards and swung downward as the chute opened. Mercifully the thing had flared, as it should. The Normandy wind was gusting more than was comfortable, he realised. Following the drill, he lowered the weapons bag to hang below him on its cord, briefly glimpsing the parachutes of the two fellows who preceded him through the door. Blown to buggery across the black landscape like seeds from a dandelion. Poor Shaftoe who had a missus and kid, Hoyland who had his girl to whom Alec had penned the letter. Why had no one at the briefings mentioned strong winds? At least there were no pinpricks of gunfire from the pitch-black below.

Too frightful for words the idea you can have been in company one moment, then in such lonesome descent the next. Hoyland and Shaftoe, patient companions through all the mad rehearsals of the last months, now heading for perdition. Most like. 'Is this the bus for Australia, sir?' *Precious Alec going the same way, again most like.* The abruptness of it. More abrupt than brutal. He tried to get a sense of the terrain below as he approached. Black. The abruptness with which a fate took hold of you may be a supreme mercy, the thought occurred to him. As a result of his weapon bag's weight he had grown aware his left knee hurt. Quite acutely in fact.

The weapon bag splashed and a quarter second later Lt Alec Dearborn went into the water. The cold infiltrated his jump smock and the carefully meditated under-garments, the needs-of-campaign placed in handy pockets. Immediately he sank, swallowed water, the parachute settling around his helmeted head as though to efficiently smother him. He managed to release one of the Capewells at his left shoulder but could not get his hand to that on his right. He should go for his knife and cut through the webbing straps. Top left hand pocket of his smock. On its lanyard.

Now I will be swallowed by the black earth, he thought as he groped for the clasp-knife, as the water in his air pipes and the eighty pounds buckled or roped to his person for the liberation of Europe conspired to pull him down into the morass.

Ma? Bell? Nance? Here's to tell you that at this moment I am being cancelled. And he saw himself with a shy, disappointed grin on his face as he informed them of the fact. Where was that stupid knife? His mills bombs, phosphorus grenades, beacons, Sten gun tucked through his front webbing, ammunition, Verey pistol, trenching tool, mess-tin, first-aid kit, iron rations etcetera, now turned against him in order to ensure he drowned effectively. Even as he struggled, this thought of his imminent extinction, taking place in such a solitude, filled Alec with an engulfing sadness. He had heard how, *in extremis,* your life flashed before your eyes, and as he fought, some corner of his consciousness waited for this. But the flashback did not screen itself. Instead, he felt how, against his scrabbling feet, the bottom mud possessed the consistency of engine grease. About his head the parachute had absorbed the weight of the swamp water and clung to him like an embryo's caul. He tore at the thirty-two lines and endless silk folds, flung free of them, surfaced. Then, as though from a voice inside his own head, he heard her call out to him.

'Mister, you will be safe.'

This extraordinary assurance came from directly behind him and, no doubt about it, what he heard was in the English language!

He tried to swivel his head in order to get a look. But impeded by his ridiculous kit and the tangle of parachute, the effort served to sink him further in the awful mire. He was tethered to the weapons bag that dragged him down, and he swallowed mouthfuls of the muck.

Not a good lookout, his plain thinking voice thought it timely to remark.

'You must believe for yourself you will be safe,' he heard from the same voice, which, indeed, was distinct from himself, behind him somewhere.

Again, with desperation, he tried to swivel, thrashed the water, gave up groping for the knife's lanyard. Ah, there she was, if he could trust his eyes, a youngish woman, distinct in her unbecoming nightgown against a jagged black background of the vegetation. Evidently there were patches of safe ground available in this quagmire and the *Mamzelle* knew one of them.

'Difficult!' he managed to splutter before his head went under again.

Unaccountably unable to lay his hands on the carefully pocketed knife, he tried to undo the cord connecting him to the weapons bag with his fingers. But the knot had become wet and awkward while the bag anchored him to whatever gluey substance constituted the swamp. He gave up with the knot, thrashed and flailed some more, managed to get his mouth above water again, jerked a glance toward where she stood on her tussock of *terra firma*, holding high the hem of her nightgown with an odd daintiness. For some seconds he scrabbled to keep his mouth above water but knew his strength was unequal to the weight of the equipment about his person. It was evident he would drown now, and in the presence of a young woman. How peculiar. He had assumed the Invasion was to be, at the least, an affair of men. She was rather winsome in her concern and Alec's impulse at this extremity was again to shout out that he was sorry.

The young woman appeared to make up her mind that he should not drown, so sloshed into the ooze until she was a few yards from him. For a moment she hesitated, then she launched forward and was a-swim. It appeared she had snatched up the parachute lines, sloshed back to her high ground, where she wrapped swathes of the silk around a handy sapling.

'You will haul yourself, Mister. For I have not the good strength.'

Lt Alec Dearborn, BA, obeyed this direction with some promptness. Gathering the several lines, he dragged himself to the safer ground, hauled his stupid weapons bag after him. There, half in the water, his drenched clothing and kit clinging around his foolish body like a reptilian skin, he retched the mud he had swallowed, tried to regain breath, retched again. The great darkness above them was saturated with aircraft drone and from somewhere in the middle distance had come an incidental pop-pop of gunfire. Alec, graduate and soldier, was glad his extinction was, for the moment, not so necessary.

He was also struck by the ordinariness of his thought. He had been delivered. Yet here he was, regathering himself like an animal which, having fought free of a trap, will pause, nervous, immobile beside the danger for some moments, as though not yet believing it is free. At home once, on Smoko Hill, he had leaned silent against a tree, and watched a dingo do just that.

It was for this almost feral reason that he did not marvel especially as to why there should have been a person, (better to say, angel) so immediately on hand to lift him clear of Earth's disgusting maw. His marvelling, like all wonderment, needed the quiet of ensuing years in which to recognise what an occasion has meant.

For the interim, he accepted her presence as the dreamer accepts the bizarre conveniences of a dream. She had materialised, she possessed a good nerve and a practical turn of mind, and she spoke very passable English. Once on the safe ground and having expelled the river mud from his guts, he freed himself from his harness, detached the weapon bag, tried to stand, whereupon his left knee gave way and he found he was on his bottom again in the shallow water. How had the knee injury happened? He could not recall a cause. He clutched at the sapling and used it to get once more to his feet, then detached his Sten gun from the webbing straps and used it as a foreshortened crutch.

Only when he stood, did he discover how his foolish body, as though possessed by some deep new conviction about itself, must tremble. Must!

'You are the invasion?' she asked.

'M-m-m-modest part of it,' he managed to reply, leaning at a ridiculous angle on the makeshift crutch of his Mk IV Sten gun.

4

WHEN THE FOOLISH BODY
MUST TREMBLE

He saw how she rubbed her arms for warmth while watching the antics of his distress with great attention.

'C-can't s-s-seem to b-b-behave for you with any d-d-decorum.' His consonants aflutter. 'H-hate b-b-being hu-helpless,' he managed. As when The Dad used to blaze at him, standing against the sunlight. As when that time he watched the rugby trials, his leg in plaster. Now his teeth must chatter. The *Mamzelle* was gathering up the sodden parachute, huge in its bulk.

'You will give me your soldier's knife,' she instructed.

He tried looking for the elusive instrument again and found it on its lanyard exactly where it should have been. Handing it over to her, he watched as she cut away the harness and rigging lines until she had isolated the silk, which she began to tuck away under her equally sodden nightgown, then hugging the great bulge to herself.

If we are stopped by the Boche, you will hide, I will be with *bébé.*'

'M-may you be safely d-d-delivered.' He tried to pull off some gentle impertinence in this absurd situation. His quivering must make her think he was a complete ninny.

'All this silk! If the war will end, I will find the usefulness.' She stood with the knife and cord.

'M-m-my word!' he managed gallantly, impressed at her eye for opportunity. Your old-time peasantry would strip the battlefield dead down to their last rag in an hour or two, he remembered from his history. 'G-g-good to p-plan ahead,' he jittered, baring his teeth in the effort to speak with credible charm. At Pembroke and among his army colleagues Alec had some reputation for his 'colonial' suavity. *Can I help it if I adore the company of women,* he would say, this airiness not entirely disguising his natural shyness, flicking his cigarette, giving them his sunny, sidelong smile.

But his effort to demonstrate a credible charm appeared grotesque to him in these circumstances where he could not prevent his trembling nor rid himself of the image of that fellow behind him in the Dakota with his vanished face. An instant, less! And there was this abominable mangle to supplant the exquisite order of a human countenance. How?

He looked at the woman, but could not prevent the tracks down which his mental activity must hurtle. So he did not, as it were, see her. How can you lose a face?

'C-c-can't im-m-m-magine what's g-got into me.' He tried to hurry the syllables out in the hope he could outpace his jitters. He chose to believe this bodily reaction was the effect of his dunking.

'You are terrified,' she stated.

That was a bit rich, he thought, though not implausible. He could summon occasions on the sports field, or on a route march, when he had been soaked, cold, bruised. Yet these times had not caused his torso to quiver like that of an over-excited mongrel.

'N-n-not used to mmm-making a ssss-spectacle.'

'You will follow me please.'

Alec pointed out there was the problem of his knee. It had copped a savage knock. His consonants rattled like dice in a beaker.

'We will make a walking stick.'

She wandered here and there, eyeing the stunted trees and hedgerows, then with one hand holding the bulge of her stomach, and the other using the soldier's knife to slice inward and inward, she weakened a length of sapling sufficiently to attack it fiercely, bending it, twisting it, splashing about in the water for some minutes until a useable, if crooked stick was wrenched clear and presented to him, along with his knife.

'Now you will follow.'

It was good to get clear instructions. He restored the knife to its pocket, tucked his Sten gun back through the straps of his ammo pouches and assured her he would d-d-do his best.

'Of course you will.'

He added how sorry he was that his words came out in such a hellish flap. There was no end to the courtesy he felt he owed her.

'I will find for you your calm.'

'Should link with my fellows,' he felt he should insist.

'Of course,' he heard her fling back, as she led him away from the black place of his coming to earth.

Because the track was narrow she preferred to walk ahead rather than lend her shoulder to assist his doubtful knee. He followed at an ungainly hobble, relying on the crutch, which was greasy with the river mud. Sometimes he was in a panic that he would not keep up with her brisk pace. Her nightgown wavered before his eyes as she brushed past foliage or occasionally vanished at a turn in the path. He lurched toward the darkness ahead, and then would find her waiting, watching for him without any notable anxiety in her manner. As he staggered, he also tried to arrange his sense of what was occurring. His rescue had a queer providence about it, as in dreams, where events come out of the blue at the same time they present themselves as destined. Maybe all the *Mamzelle*s of Normandy spent their nights out in the swamps watching for descending soldiers.

At intervals during their progress there seemed to be high hedges on either side of them. In other places they waded in water to the mid-thigh, the spiky trees on either side suggesting orchards. Twice she held up her hand indicating they should stop to watch for a Boche presence, and he could see the profile of her head tilted to one side in an attitude of alertness. She wore her hair in a loose ribbon, he noted, and he found this attractive.

Boche as a word for the other bloke; he could go along with that. Someone else's language with its purse of associations attached. Boche, bosh, it allowed the difference, and the right tilt.

The drone of the aeroplanes had, for the moment, receded. The gunfire was also further away. When they re-entered a stretch of water she told him to move through it as though he were on a dance floor.

'You glide. *Pas de bruit!*' He saw her put her finger to her lips.

'I'll w-waltz it,' he whispered, close to what he hoped was her ear. It would be a comical old waltz with the knee sending a spasm of pain each time he bent it.

'You waltz. It is good for our safety.'

Before long they came among solid outhouses looming from the water like steep islands. This brought them to the rear of a taller building, which they entered by a small scullery. He brushed past some heavy coats that hung from pegs on a wall, and assumed the robust outdoor wear of a farming household.

'F-fff-family?' he stammered, indicating the coats.

'I live alone,' she answered, then added, 'for the present.'

Like the outhouses, this anteroom was also underwater to his knees. She instructed him to wait and be silent, then she vanished for some minutes.

He dumped the absurd weapons bag into the water at his feet. For all his lurching pursuit of her along the paths, he had not warmed his body sufficiently to stop the shuddering. Could he now venture a conversation with her and not stammer like an idiot? Could he find out where he was, how far away were the river bridges, and the DZ's where he was supposed to have supervised his fellows in the placement of landing flares? What, at a basic level, was the stupid time? He put out his hand to support himself, clutching at a coat, standing alone in the small dark with the miserable tremble of his body and the plip-plip of water dripping from himself and his kit. Slowly it dawned on him that the coat he grasped was a military greatcoat, insignia on its buttons, flashes on the lapels. The 1940 French army?

Or Boche?

In the dark he handled the several other coats and found the same arrangement of buttons and lapels. Too dark to see the details on the insignia. Fine, but what was going on? Surely she wouldn't have taken this trouble for him simply to bring him back and turn him over to the other team.

Now here she was again, delivered from his parachute. She had spied him in the act of fingering the military buttons and for some moments Alec was aware she was regarding him appraisingly. Vainly he tried to make out her face in the dark.

'You will be safe, mister. Now you will follow.'

And led him, wading with his kit and the sodden weapons bag through the water into her house.

Its main room was wide, with a low ceiling, and the floodwater glinted in the scant light, creating an impression that the floor was ormolu. The water transformed distances and scale strangely, foreshortening the dressers, table, chairs that furnished the space. Dimly against one wall, Alec could discern the cabinet of a grandfather clock, and began to wade toward it.

'M-m-much d-d-depends, you see, on my kn-n-nowing the t-t-time' he managed as the excuse for his sloshing about her home. The ridiculous shuddering of his person had grown worse. How could he believe he was himself?

'This grandpa does not work.'

He asked if she could find him one that did.

'Once are many clocks in my house,' she said. 'Now there are none. I have learned to do without telling a time. You will follow me.'

He tried to impress upon her how vital the matter was that he should know the simple exact hour of day, but she was heedless to his interest in this.

Holding the hem of her nightgown above the water, she waded through the rooms with delicate steps. He was compelled to watch where she went, of course, but he found he was charmed by her movements, too. Just a little. They reminded him of how he once saw Bell picking her way across a rock pool at Ulladulla, each step watchful, heron-like, the ocean behind her, remote, sapphire in the evening light, some clouds grey and bright fawn gathering on the horizon. He had been seventeen and growing into that youthful awareness of how one both watches a thing and watches the self in its watching. The eye follows and ignites a delicacy in the mind. Even here, in war's agenda.

How could he not follow her example, wading with the grotesque lurch his injury imposed upon his dignity? They came to a stairway that ascended from a vestibule to a landing, and with their different gaits mounted this. At the top she turned to him.

'Mister, I will tell you things you must obey because it is for the best. You understand?'

'C-c-completely.'

For a moment she seemed to be assessing whether his acquiescence was sincere. Her own wet nightgown clung approximately to her figure, the whiteness of the garment creating a dolphin-like profile against the dark of the upstairs interior. Then she directed,' Please, you will remove all these,' and indicated his sopping clobber.

'Well! L-l-look here.' His objection was to the idea of separating himself from his military identity.

So this was his acquiescence.

'You are wet, you are …' she paused to find the English word, '… distraught, and have a hurt. Now you will be made dry and calm, and your knee will have my inspection. I can do this.'

He tried to get a sense of that dolphin shape in the gloom. She had summed up the situation with admirable concision. Was this a sample of what his Pembroke tutor had called the lucidity of French thought? Undoubtedly, together with her charming unconcern for the military situation.

'Ah, *Mmm-ma'am*, N-n-not d-d-d …' He had followed her example and kept his voice in a murmur but still could not get out the thing he wished to say, which was his sense of how indecent of him it would be to go along with the simple direction to shed his clothes. Of course her plan for him was nonsense. Marvellous that she was a young woman doing her level best to help out. And strewth, she was practical as anything. Warmed, calmed, attended to, howsoever she wished to contrive it, of course he could see the advantages this offered to his getting on with the military business. But the indecency of it.

'N-n-not decent,' he managed at last.

'Not *decent*?' Her murmur came, incredulous, from her indistinct face. Could she read his thought? For Alec was not entirely certain he had actually voiced it.

'To the other f-f-fellows,' he stuttered what he could sense were to her his inscrutable moral objections. Not decent with respect to those of the battalion who were descending like seeds upon the treacherous countryside, tumbling hither and thither in the dark, as they got on, unaided, with the military job, the inescapable job.

'Will your comrades not wish you to be effective?'

A fair proposition, the Cambridge graduate recognised. What could be more useful than to be spirited out of war for an interval of necessary respite? Could he do it? Could he simply step away from warlike considerations, from the rigours, rehearsals, and *ésprit* of the preceding year for this agreeable option? Was it not for the good?

And yet.

At this moment I'm supposed to be out in that dark extinguishing the Boche, the bosh, he might have explained for her.

'B-best ...' he in fact whisper-stammered, '... if I d-decline your k-kindness.'

'Pfui.'

So again he insisted he needed to discover the exact time. For there was The Invasion Plan, at least that small portion of it entrusted to him. *By 0120 hrs RV at ... by 0217 hrs be in positions surrounding ...*

Packed around with helmet and kit like the Michelin man from the tyre cartoon, Alec had stood with the battalion officers on the airfield under the propellers of their transports, synchronising watches, drinking a bumper of tea from the mobile canteen. What an aeon back in time that now seemed. And yet the Plan, if he could keep himself convinced of its urgency, its centrality, it would be his true North.

'N-n-need t' know m-m-more or less where I s-s-stand.'

'You will be enjoying your discomfort while you rest with me?'

There was a power of forthrightness in this woman, he observed, and she rapped out her *Anglais* so it sounded like an assessment of his intelligence. It was more eloquent than his own *Anglais* at that moment.

'Mmmust thinkabout c-c-catching up with my f-f-fellows,' he explained, listening to himself dripping onto her floorboards. 'Owe it to 'em,' he added. He meant, of course, not his own planeload of fellows, the entire platoon of intricate, yearlong relations, man and man, who were now presumably incinerated somewhere in this black countryside, but the other multitudinous planeloads scheduled to come over, presumably taking their chances with the unforseen cloud and winds.

'You have no knees for the catching up.'

He objected that one knee was still serviceable.

'Mister, I think you shake too much to hide even from a child.'

A trained fellow must press on with the business, no matter what, was the idea he needed to communicate. But he acknowledged how she put herself so formidably in charge of their situation. She had opened a cupboard, taken from it a towel and a pale garment similar to the one she was wearing. In a moment she discarded her sopping nightgown and began towelling herself with some vigour. Dimly, momentarily, he glimpsed the contours of a large, shapely female form before it was plunged into the fresh garment that crackled with the stiffness of its laundering.

'Decent,' she said, then took another nightgown from the cupboard, shook it out and offered it to him. This garment was voluminous.

'Like you my papa has been a big man. You will wear this for one hour or maybe two. I put you into a bed. You will be warm, you will be dry.'

'M-m-must get c-c-cracking.' For if he did not remind himself sternly to keep the military business in mind, how could he know he was not being taken over by plain funk? And yet.

And yet it was easy to see how he might succumb to this peremptory direction of his affairs. Did he not have an excuse to sort himself out a bit?

No! Take your eye off the ball for an instant and who could tell how far he might go down the cushy road. Imagine his Airborne fellows turning up here in the course of a house-to-house, bursting in upon him tucked up safe in a French bed? Not just ridiculous. They would smirk in the same instant they would wonder about the entire fabric of their trust in him. O the army had made him wise along trails of human bonding his schoolboy and undergraduate self could not have guessed at.

He stood regarding her on the dark landing, his recourse to the Dearborn charm made useless by the dark and his abject stammering. How could a proposal that he be restored to the warm dry life be so blessed awkward? O, take on trust that she meant well. But Alec felt impelled somehow to communicate to her the urgent, intricate business of his loyalty. That, and the anxiety as to how he would measure up?

Because she had pulled him up on dry land, saved his life, so to speak, he felt an overwhelming urge to deal with her candidly.' I f-f-f ...' he began, but the substance of his allegiances only made the fluffing of his speech more pronounced. Unless he got the better of his jitters, Alec saw, he was in a sorry condition to argue anything, let alone traipse cross-country on a crook knee in order to effectively join battle.

I am ridiculous, he managed for himself. 'Y-y-your offer n-n-not well c-covered in training,' he managed for her.

Then she clinched the matter for him. 'Mister, I show you a nice sight. Here, you will be interested.'

She took his elbow, led him to a small casement window. There was something heartrending to note how she approached a window with the same sidelong wariness they had been taught as soldiers. Was she conscious, on this night of alarms, how her white garment might make her a sniper's gift? During his training Alec had occasionally wondered about which parts of war would move the strong emotions in him. This one took him by surprise. Here was a person living among a population who could not take the innocent standing at a window for granted. Carefully she lifted the curtain with one finger.

'You will like to look.'

At first all he could see was the profile of roofs interspersed by the dark of tree canopies. Here were the dwellings of a smallish hamlet; did it even have a name on the map? There were patches of flooding before her own house, then steps to a causeway that divided these lower houses from a bank of further habitations. The causeway may have been a recently constructed thoroughfare. Here and there, in the grey luminescence he could see a track leading off between buildings and at one of these was parked a motorcycle and sidecar. He recognised the outline of a Spandau machine gun mounted on the sidecar, and the two crewmembers standing beside it, helmeted, smoking.

He told his hostess he could slip p-p-past one measly sentry post.

'You will like to look!' she repeated, murmuring, but with ferocity.

Again he peeped, and again it was not immediately apparent to him what he should be looking for. Then he saw what he had missed.

Tucked into the dark of the houses and trees opposite was a column of serious weaponry. Among the nearer vehicles he recognised the Boche Mk IV Panzers, and at least one half-track vehicle, suggesting units of motorised infantry. The immobile column stretched right and left on the darker side of the causeway and similarly up the darker side of the adjacent track. With the exception of the two motorcyclists there was not a human in sight. But the vehicles had evidently been parked with painstaking care. Not a turret reflected light, not an aerial showed its profile.

'They keep their machines below the houses to avoid the Allied bombing,' she explained for him, pronouncing both b's of 'bombing' impressively.

He could see that, he told her.

'They swarm here.'

'W-w-well believe it.'

So here, after all the make-believe of his training, was the other bloke. Alec pondered the spectacle. There was something monstrous in how inert the lethal power of it was. The massed vehicles, perhaps thirty or more, could have been so many huge stones laid out in a Neolithic site. She held the curtain that he might fully consider his predicament.

Here was *Mamzelle* living cheek-by-jowl with the other bloke's best strength. What then should he make of those coats downstairs? He shuddered beside her and wanted to explain his shudder was not funk. It shamed him that she might think he had gone to pieces. He could experience fear like anyone, but this …

In the paddock at Portobello once he had been confronted by a brown snake that had reared on him suddenly. His impulse had been, not to flee, but to mentally fold himself away, make himself smaller. The big snake had swayed and watched him, then subsided into the grass, but Alec, perhaps twelve at the time, had remarked in himself that distinct effect, how fear made you want to lessen your presence. From then he had noticed around the sheds and homestead how a cat would do the same thing when cornered by a dog. Faced with all that firepower, it might have been a good idea to shed a bit of presence now, he surmised, for evidently he was in the midst of peril. Yet it presented itself as so ordinary.

'But you will have your English *sang froid*, Mister, ' she intruded on his thought.

Australian, he managed to get the word out, glancing quickly at her. Then he continued to assess the stony vehicles on the causeway.

Ordinary, yes! One might stroll out, knock on a hatch and ask a fellow for a cigarette. As though here were not so many cannon, small arms, coils of ammunition. As though his charming Australian self was bound to attract a sympathetic hearing from them, bosh or no bosh.

The overlay of his training reasserted itself. He had dropped into a war. With this impressive hardware poised to be unleashed on his f-f-fellows there was all the more reason to go looking for them promptly. He made to take the curtain from her as a gesture to resume control of the situation. But the trembles of his body resulted in this simple action causing the material to shiver too conspicuously. Gently she removed his fingers and placed his hand at his side.

'Mister, I do not like to argue. In your front you can see you have this army. Perhaps they look like your good friends but they are not so good for your safety, I think'

'N-n-not wrong,' he had to agree.

'And at the back you have our pleasant French *marais*.'

Compared to his garbling her propositions were so crisp. It was only now she explained how the Boche had flooded the rivers as a defensive measure against possible invasion on this stretch of coastline.

'If you wish, you can choose to swim to your comrades.' Here was another of those enquiries like a spot intelligence test.

It might come down to that, his disarrayed self was tempted to tell her, if only to regain his sense of being in control of matters.

Instead, since her English seemed up to it, he was moved to say how, with that lot out there on the p-p-prowl, it had been p-p-plucky of her to take that risk j-j-just to fish a poor beggar from an unwelcome c-c-consequence.

She was holding out the great nightgown again. 'For everyone it is a different dread.'

Still he baulked at accepting the apparel, for to do so seemed like crossing some line. But he was serious about his gratitude to her and wanted to make his point, if only to deflect the nightgown.

'P-p-plucky of you.'

In turn *La Française* had a point she wished to make about the nature of danger. 'Four years, *tu comprends,* we live with The Dread. And yet you cannot understand. You come with your friends to battle. Here, we live, where everything you trust will turn to powder. One's self will become powder too! There is nothing cannot be powder. *Rien!*' For all that they were murmuring, the French word *Rien* ripped the air. 'How do we live with this? Some are brave. Some have no complications in the life. For myself, I have the complication and I am not brave.'

'So how do you cope?'

'I make around myself the enchantment.'

'What enchantment?'

There were some moments before she responded. Then she answered with her own question. 'You wish to know? So it is possible you can forget your need to know exact time for some little?'

It was his turn to ignore her enquiry. Yet it was true, she had distracted his attention from the military business for a moment. Instead of awaiting his response, she led him away from the window and shook out her papa's copious garment in front of him. 'We will find again your calm,' she repeated the earlier avowal. She made it sound like the best possible short-term objective. 'And when the Boche outside come through my house, you will be …' she was unsure of the English word, '… *déguisé*.'

'C-c-camouflaged.' Despite his jitters, he could laugh.

'You decide yes to *la robe*, Mister. Quick.'

His parachute training had not covered this contingency, he managed to stammer out for her, and relented toward the change. She was hurrying him along a bit faster than he might wish, but there was good sense in allowing her to direct him for the interim, he supposed, not knowing it would affect his circumstances lifelong.

5

YOU DECIDE YES, MISTER, QUICK

He hobbled after her down the corridor. This turned at an angle and at length confronted them with a door to a room at the back of the house where, accustoming his eyes to the gloom, Alec could distinguish a high bed with decorated boards at either end. The window lay open, as though to air the space in preparation for their coming here, and from the night outside came the churring of a fresh wave of the Airborne transports. Visible against the charcoal sky, an occasional ribbon of anti-aircraft tracers rose in beautiful slow-motion, pink, green and for some moments he watched this display of lights, fascinated by the illusory slowness of tracer-fire; like sparks more afloat than propelled, the destructive power not quite to be believed.

She drew his attention to the bed. 'Since *La Révolution*,' she explained, 'some person in my ancestors sleeps on this bed. Here some have been born, some have died, all on this.' She pushed into the mattress with the palm of her hand. 'Now, if I sleep, I prefer it is here.'

He took note of that 'if I sleep …' Why should she not sleep? But it was better he stammer a conventional enquiry. He got out a question as to whether sleeping with all those births and deaths spooked her at all.

Not in the least, she told him.

'M-m-maybe it m-makes you v-v-venerable.'

Again he was trying gallantry, because it was awkward to stand before her without some pleasant guise of chat while he allowed her evidently tough fingers to unfasten his awkward army buckles. If the coats downstairs pointed anywhere, was she perhaps practised in dealing with the unloosing of military straps? The military business would require that, before he left these premises, he ask her about those coats downstairs.

Now his pouches, haversack, water bottle, holster with its 9mm pistol, bayonet, all his webbing like so much scaffolding fell away from his person. She un-notched the chinstrap and removed his helmet to one side.

'Ch-ch-chipping me out of my mould.'

The equipment discarded, she next pulled the layers of sopping clothing from him and kicked them into a pile. His knee twinged painfully as he shifted to allow the trousers to come free of his ankles. And then, for a moment he stood before her, naked, strange to himself, shuddering like an imbecile, feeling humiliated. His torso and legs were being briskly rubbed down with the same towel she had used for herself. Finally, not pausing for breath, the *Mamzelle* threw the great nightgown over his person and manipulated his arms through the sleeves.

When she had finished she stood back as though to appreciate her handiwork. He attempted to comment that he must appear 'w-w-wonderfully ru-ru-ridiculous to her in this f-f-f-finery.' It was a gasp each time he came to a simple English syllable. Had the removal of his kit increased the violence of his shakes? Yes, he thought it had.

'You are not so ridiculous,' she assured him, 'but perhaps you are a little disarmed.' He could see her in profile against the window, how she appraised him with her head on one side. He liked that.

Now she folded back an eiderdown and sheet, then directed him to climb in and lie on his back. Again his knee caused him a spasm of sharp pain when he bent it. Something busted for sure. As soon as he lay there, she calmly bestraddled him, created a tent of the eiderdown above them both, then probing along his nightgown to the place of his genitals, she cupped them firmly in her two hands.

'Here is where the heat begins,' was the matter-of-fact explanation she gave for the immodest procedure.

Nor did she manipulate his parts in any way. It was her intention they be enclosed in the simple envelope of her hands, and she seemed not in the least self-conscious of the liberty she took.

'N-no- n-not wrong,' he managed.

For Alec was a sceptic when it came to quackery and yet it was evident to him that a remarkable warmth radiated from those cupped hands through the coarse fabric, into the region of his groin, and spread outward from there.

Now she was saying in a tone of complete reasonableness, 'Mister, you have been nearly drowned in our *marais*. But we are already one thousand years since then, you understand? It can be quiet in your mind now, I think.'

He stared up at the indistinct face in the dark. Quackery? Or can a form of words put a recollection to rest? Hard to say, for he was aware she had taken her hands inside the robe and placed them directly around his parts, the warmth from her now more concentrated.

'You have seen the ruin of your fellows, perhaps,' she said after a minute had elapsed, taking her hands from his bollocks, flattening them against his inside thighs and moving the heel of her palm like a person handling dough. 'This also can be an old thing in your mind, having its place, but quiet now through long acquaintance.' And again she asked him if he understood.

As well as the laundered smell of their nightgowns, there was the distinct scent of her body in such enclosed space with him. And there was the smell of the room itself. What was it? Something mildewy? Something suggesting generations of use, the clothes put on and taken off, the perfumes dabbed, the contents of pockets scattered onto tabletops, belch and fart. Maybe here was essence of Old Europe, he daydreamed under her attention. As he felt her hands coping with his shivers he began to wonder if he could indeed practice on himself the kind of mental trickery she was suggesting. Push the horrid into a pretended remote past and look how it becomes docile in the mind. The room's elusive aroma, the artful distraction of her hands at work on his inner thighs and midriff (as though they were shovelling back the chill mud from his bloodstream); these influences did indeed tend toward a dilation of time that allowed the ghastly scene inside the fuselage to find its place in his mind like a fossil in a geological stratum.

Besides, this person seemed to connect with some wizardry. Had she not used the word enchantment? How else does a person turn up in the middle of nowhere waiting for Alec Dearborn to come floating down? She was formidably self-assured when it came to the restoration of his foolish body, her face hovering in the dark above with one tress of her hair straying from the ribbon to hang downward.

And as she worked on him he tumbled to how devious the effect on him she was hoping to bring off.

Perhaps you are a little disarmed.

A disarming of the fright he had been given? Well, her handling of him could work, if he allowed himself to believe in the treatment. But …

'I'm not very good at leaps of faith,' he spoke to the dark presence above him, and realised he had not stammered in making this declaration.

Leaps of faith; she appeared to find that phrase comical. 'But you are *parachutiste*, Mister?'

And at that he could laugh with her a little.

She returned her hands to the envelopment of his bollocks, business-like as a vet might handle an animal. The sensation for him was firstly of warmth, but yes, also one of safety. Now he thought what bad manners it had been of him even to think this person would resort to quackery.

There was a quickness and fineness in her intelligence that moved Alec. Her attention to his precious self was altogether too innocent, too intent to qualify as mumbo-jumbo.

For the moment she had nothing she wished to say to him, so he too waited to see what would happen next. After a time she released her hold on his genitals, placed her body lengthwise along his own and, careful not to jolt his damaged knee, clasped her arms and legs around him in two tight cinches, like twine around a hay bale. Then she drew her embrace tight and he experienced the strength in her arms.

Once or twice in London, out on a 24-hour pass with two or three fellows from training, Alec had paid some money and been with a woman. These contracts, begun in a spirit of escapade, had ended by making him feel melancholy about the physical congress that had seemed so delicious in prospect. The exactness of the money changing hands followed by the phoney good cheer aroused in him a suspicion that there might be something paltry in his nature to have sought out such fleeting gratification.

By contrast to those unsatisfactory occasions he marvelled here at the strangeness of the physical contact. *Mamzelle's* manipulation of his sexual parts displayed no sexual intent whatever. She was altogether too practical, too unconscious, yet spontaneous. No, not a trace of fakery in it.

Mister, here is where the heat begins.

Nor did her proximity arouse an immediate sexual longing in him. He had no impulse to bind with her, to clasp her in the urgency of sexual arousal. She adjusted herself so that her length and his came into the most effective adherence for the thing she had in mind. Did she give any heed to the dignity of her posture? Apparently not. Her breasts were, he supposed, squashed against his front, further down he could feel her belly as a source of warmth through the fabric. His arms were bound by her embrace though he could have placed his hands on her hips had it been the likeliest place for them. Should he? Better not. Couldn't be sure it was the courteous move. He was under treatment and it occurred to him a nurse might adjust an eiderdown over him in the same manner this person efficiently adjusted her body's coverage of his own.

As he lay there it was a mystery to him how she could have recovered her own bodily heat, for had she not herself floundered in the *marais* up to her neck? Immobile, self-conscious, he lay with her like this for some minutes. Was he shuddering less now? Yes, considerably less, he thought.

But he would not trust himself to believe the enormity of his recent experience could find a docile, remote place in mind, as she wanted for him. He stared upward at what he supposed was the ceiling of her ancestors, aware of that prodigious strength in her binding arms. So persons had died while lying upon this bed, and had been born on it. Conceived too, no doubt, he thought with detachment. Her face came across his gaze and she had placed her hands on his temples with some tenderness.

'I think it is better with you,' she gave her progress report.

'N-not wrong,' he looked back at the indistinct features above him.

Why, even now when she was this close to him, he realised he had not yet gained a clear idea of these features. Eyes, mouth, nose, the profile of cheekbone and chin. What age was she? He had assumed a *Mademoiselle*, but she may well have been in her late thirties. Married? That did not quite bear thinking about in the circumstances. A simple candle might have helped him scrutinise her were it not that any light would risk drawing sniper fire. Was there a tinge of apple on her breath when she spoke? He could feel the curves of her body, the nub of bone at her lower ribs, that potency of her body heat. And yet an entire dimension of intimacy was denied here because he could not read the fine clues of her facial features in the gloom.

'We've g-got to know each other entirely in the d-dark,' he observed.

She chose not to answer.

'I wonder if this w-w-war might allow us to exchange names,' he persisted.

Still she declined to respond.

'As a m-matter of fact I thought I was on my way to a war,' he tried next. Yes, he could trust his voice now, which was a step in the right direction.

For the third time she offered no answer but sustained the tight clasp around his torso. It was as though the task of transferring her body heat was one thing, and conversation would have been another, a distraction, a risk of false understanding. After some further minutes he felt he should show her that he might be competent to take charge of himself.

'You know, I reckon I might t-talk a little now without muffing it.'

Still she was uncommunicative, conveying to his mind the sense of a person wanting to proceed methodically.

All right, he concluded, so I've landed in a peculiar situation. I'll go with it for the while. Better this than under that river mud. He felt her stir and next moment she had slipped down from the bed.

'You will wait for me.'

She stood before his clobber and commenced to separate the clothing from the equipment. 'These I will wring out,' she said, rolling shirt, socks, trousers into the jump smock and holding them away from herself. She left the room and was absent for a period. When she returned she was without them. Now she gathered up his equipment, boots, and weapons.

'Whoa.' He saw the Sten gun being taken from him. There was a need to regain control of his situation. 'I can't allow you …'

'I hide these. If you will trust, you will be safe.'

'I'll hang on to my pistol, ma'am.' He adopted what he hoped was the tone of an Allied officer of the liberating army giving a direction to a French civilian, but she ignored him, was gone through the door, her feet thudding on the corridor floorboards. Should he follow and insist? With the knee?

He lay back and considered. Maybe the removal of his two firearms made him safer if any of those Boche outside the window decided for some reason on a house-to-house search for stray Airborne types. How would the French he learnt at Hume stand up to interrogation from a determined fellow of the other team? Really, did he have any option other than to put complete trust in her? Did she not keep insisting he was going to be safe, as though he were some warrior from a romance made immune from hurt so long as he wore the shirt his girl had stitched for him?

Hah! Was being safe his first business at this moment? If he considered matters in the large, if he calculated what was expected of him? There was no doubt some good luck had come his way, his foolish body more manageable. Sobering to learn how fearfully he could blubber and quake.

You are distraught, she had informed him.

A criss-cross of tracer fire momentarily lit the rectangle of the open window, too far away to hear the cannon-stutter of it. Overhead the transports droned. You could doze to that drone. Now he was warm, calmer, he'd need to take care he didn't doze …

… *but must wonder instead about her word 'distraught'. Bit shocked by that performance earlier. Could not say to this point he'd seen how a distraught person behaves. Body going one way when the mind says stoppit. Were Ma, Bell and Nance distraught when The Dad's chewed-at body was brought back on the dray after two days in the paddock? Bell was The Dad's favourite rather, you'd expect an upset, though when she came up to town to give him the news she had the look of someone maybe given a bit of a scare. Not riven, not all over the place. 'You'll see we've laid him out in the front room, Goose,' she told him, matter-of-fact. 'We dressed over whatever it was had a go at him.' 'Whatever?' he asked. 'Pigs, dingos, whatever,' said Bell. On the return train to Queanbeyan, trees ghostly in the mist, he had to wonder how he would react when looking at his first corpse. 'Will I go to water, Bell?' 'No fear, Goose, not us.' Dread more than fright was the thing in him then, that shrillness along the bones, warning you off, advising you to become small like with the brownsnake that time. He had not gone to water, but was relieved when The Dad, yellowing, blotchy, was in the ground. But acting distraught? Body taking its merry course while the mind tries to hold the line, otherwise no appreciable sensation, that was altogether more strange. Yes, Bell could make The Dad's eye twinkle. Not Nance, not him who could only rub the old man the wrong way, rivals. Bell who liked to say, 'Time to take things in hand, Goose,' who came up to town a couple of times in a term to watch the game then would wait till he came, spruced from the shower block and say, 'Let's go on the razzle, Goose,' and off they would go in the tram, rattling down to The Metropole, tucking into the roast and three veg, lemonades and Sydney's hoi polloi, catching the ferry to … Bell who took on the farm …*

He woke. Invasion day. How much time had elapsed? Had he slept? Why had the *Mamzelle* not turned up again? He strained to hear her footsteps on the wooden floor. Would the procession of aeroplanes overhead never stop? He could hear the odd stuttering of gunfire, sometimes from a middle distance, sometimes from further afield, nothing visible through the window now, which had been shut. So she had come and gone. The gunfire could have been the Airborne Brens and suchlike from the river bridges. Or the battery emplacements at Merville. If he could rely on it being the latter he could work out …

But Alec's attempt to estimate his whereabouts was interrupted by shouting from the Causeway at the front of the house. What can you tell about shouting when you can't get access to the lingo? Was there a move on? Too remote to tell.

A bit remote for care altogether. There ensued an interval of quiet when aeroplanes and gunfire receded. Allowing the damaged knee to lie straight, Alec had curled the rest of his body into a foetal position in the big bed in order to concentrate the renewed warmth in his person. He also wanted to concentrate his hearing on detecting from the sounds of the house where *Mamzelle* might be. Did he hear legs sloshing in those level waters below stairs? Hard to be sure. Sometimes a gust of the wind, O that deadly June 6 wind, rattled the closed windowpane.

He had done the right thing in allowing himself to be warmed up. But now he really should get on with the business, hobble off in the direction of that gunfire. Unworthy of him to lie around when other Airborne fellows had got down, set up their beacons around the DZ's, moved off to accomplish their tasks, when there were those tens of thousands now closing with the beaches. Unworthiness! If he survived, he would have to live lifelong with that sensation.

Maybe the crook knee would hold up. He could bind it with something and scrounge a better walking stick from *Mamzelle,* then manage some kind of effective waddle. At least he would be on the job. Doing that would keep at bay the ghastly events inside his Dakota and in the flood. Had to prove he was not unnerved by it. This was a war, what did he expect? Best to think of the job, the drill. Alec's mind ticked through these considerations, and yet …

There was the Boche out front, a huge quagmire at the back. What if he was more useful here, affording this rather extraordinary person some protection? And having fished him out of that sinkhole did she not now have a right to see him safe from his own foolhardiness? Why had she been out there in the dark if it were not for some longer purpose?

Tick tick tick. He should at least find out what was happening to his clothes. Getting a fix on the exact time would also be a help. Somehow.

6

YOU WILL DOODLE A SOMETHING

He eased himself down from the bed, then wrapped the eiderdown around himself to preserve that splendid warmth she had got into him. His knee felt ponderous like a fire log, the pain dull now, so he used the walls and any handy furniture for support as he limped off in search of his rescuer. Trying each of the upstairs rooms in turn, he saw some had coat stands and bunk beds without mattresses, as though they had been converted for use as dormitories and were now abandoned. In one room his fingers ran along a sideboard and felt the texture of the cloth. Lace! Normandy lace. Mention of this medieval industry had cropped up in the context of one of his undergraduate Middle English essays, he recalled. This piece would be from Lisieux or Alençon maybe. Women at their close-work, eyes ruined by it. So easy for his mind to drift off war.

When he came once more to the small corridor window that gave upon the causeway, he peeped out at the parked armour. There was no apparent life around those immobile vehicles, not even the pinpoint of a lit cigarette. And yet overhead the aeroplanes continued to pass, their formations rolling in cushions of sound, as though from horizon to horizon. An outbreak of shooting commenced beyond the roofs opposite, perhaps a mile or two off.

He could tell by his bare feet the floorboards were antique, the gaps worn by centuries of minute adjustments between summer and winter temperatures, wet and dry, the abrading of human feet. He entered the last room on the corridor, smaller than the rest, a sewing retreat evidently, for there was a sewing table with machine and treadle set at the window. On one wall hung a long mirror set in a gilt frame. New? Antique? How long does a mirror last? Alec looked into its darkness and allowed his fancy to wonder what kind of humanity might have stood in his place, turning this way and that, trying on a garment as the sempstress fussed. A *Madame* from Napoleonic times in her lace bonnet from Alençon maybe? A daughter trying wedding clothes in the year of the 1918 Armistice? That was the year he was born. The mirror faced the room's window, which yielded just enough light for Alec to distinguish his own reflection. He appeared obscure to himself, robed like a ghost.

And then, to his ears the queerest thing! Behind the long glass, but somehow at a height above it, Alec believed he could hear *Mamzelle* singing.

Or rather, she seemed to be taken up by a wordless croon. This was quite low in pitch, blended with the overhead aeroplane drone, but interspersed by moments when she (if indeed it were *Mamzelle* and not an un-met occupant from this labyrinthine farmhouse) took her trancelike hum to an intricate, keening melody. The singing was intense, a bit unearthly, he thought. Was she in there with someone else? He went lurching in search of a door into this chamber but could find none, so returned to the mirror and listened, fingered the gilt edge. He could just push his fingernails behind the frame whereupon the mirror sprung open on a simple spring mechanism and he found himself confronted by a hatch opening on a narrow wooden stairway into the roof cavity. Putting his good leg first and feeling his way by the panelling, he ascended until he found himself in an attic room with three small skylights along one of its slant walls. But for these rectangles, a tone or two lighter than the dark of the loft, there was no further lighting.

'Look,' he spoke into the dark quarter from which the singing came, 'I don't want to press you, but …'

The dark quarter ceased its humming. 'You will trust yourself to speak now, I see.'

'You've done a good job on me, I reckon.'

Yes, she said, she was glad she had been of some use. Then she requested he pull the mirror door shut behind him; it would give a gentle click when properly closed. He shuffled back down the confined stairway, did her bidding, then approached the place from which her voice came.

'You have been asleep maybe?' she asked, not turning to him.

Not sure, he replied, shifting the eiderdown on his shoulders, may have dozed, felt he had been here for an age already, should really get a fix on the exact time.

In the gloom she sat at a piano with her back to him. And it was a remarkably straight back, he could see. *Mamzelle* was a big-boned girl. Her hair, now unloosed, fell a little below her shoulders, dark on the pale cardigan she had put on over her nightgown. It was the absence of a shapely hairstyle that suggested to him now she might have been more maiden than matron.

Though she had the lid of the piano closed, he perceived she had recommenced singing to herself, unabashed by his presence. The long loft, with its v-shaped ceiling, appeared to be her music studio, and faced the rear of the establishment, so that he could see through the skylights, between the crude black profiles of outbuildings and orchard, the steely sheen of the flood under the cloudy sky. He returned his attention to the contents of the studio and could make out several music stands, some wooden chairs arranged in a circle, while on the gable wall hung a guitar. Piled beneath this instrument, much to Lt. Dearborn's relief, was the neat total of his kit, boots and two firearms, the floorboards around them wet. His clothes appeared to be absent from the heap.

'I'd better get back into my clobber, I reckon,' he tried again to intrude upon her singing trance, 'if it's not too much trouble.'

She ceased humming, but did not immediately turn to face him.

'You are no longer in the trembles?'

'For now. Thank you. Time to get cracking.'

She stood and took one of the wooden chairs, placed it near her piano stool and indicated he might sit himself down if he wished. He had the sense she was smiling in the darkness. He reiterated his desire to get cracking.

'Do you know perhaps a little about music?'

This time the ruse to deflect his attention from the pressing military job was altogether too provocative.

'*Look here!*' And yet immediately his good nature regretted this outburst of impatience. 'I know you've been bonzer. It's just ...' He trailed off, helpless.

'Bonzer?' she enquired brightly. He had the sense she was gazing at him steadily, coquettishly perhaps. What was she up to? Had the whole night's escapade been some trick? Was he the victim of some clever tease? Given his obligation to her he still had no bloody right to think it. Yet one moment she appeared to be so intent on his behalf, the next so offhand. Perhaps he had landed himself with a loony who was quite heedless of how momentous were the events already on the go in her portion of Normandy.

'Bonzer's when a person has done handsomely by another,' he supplied.

'Mister, you will trust me.'

'How can I not?'

'I ask if you know a little about the music,' she repeated her question.

What should he trust? If he could have seen the exact expression of her eyes ... but it was just too dark to tell what tilt was there. He had resisted her offer to sit down beside her, but now (obediently he surmised), he indeed sat down, arranging his injured leg stiffly to one side, spreading the folds of the eiderdown and voluminous, idiotic nightgown so they were decent.

'I make you feel desperate?'

'Ma'am, like it or not, I'm a commissioned bloke. Officer, you know.' He felt the antique Australian need to deprecate his authority without extinguishing it. 'I've been landed with a job to do. Tonight, or what's left of it.'

'Are you only a soldier?'

'I used to be one thing, now I've been dressed up for that.'

He did so want to remain patient. But it was true; her nonchalant attitude to his soldierly self provoked him to desperation.

'Dressed up,' she could not help repeating.

So he gazed back at her, baffled, wanting to keep their interchange light. 'I suppose one might say you are my present military problem.'

'How so, mister.'

'Well, I have to get myself back into the schedule with as little discourtesy to the *Mamzelle* as possible.' He glanced to see if his lightness registered with her. She deserved his patience, having, after all, pulled him from a morass then transferred a good portion of her body heat into his own deficient flesh.

'Music,' she reminded, her interest in the military difficulties she imposed on him lapsing abruptly.

'Hah.'

For there was nothing for it but to play along with her ruse to distract him. If ruse it was.

'We had a piano as part of the furniture. Ma played. My younger sister Nance could play a treat.' (But not Bell, he remembered, who had resisted attempts to make her musical.) 'We had a sheep farm which was up-country, so people made their own entertainment.'

'You can play piano?' she pounced.

'I was given the odd lesson but remained a dreamy pupil.'

'Yet you can like what the music might do to you?'

Her interest prompted in him an impulse to deal with her question truthfully, so he recounted what he could remember of the effect of Nance or Ma playing in the room with the French doors.

'I felt as though music was a kind of daze.'

'How so?' She asked questions like a schoolteacher.

'You could be on the inside of it. Or outside it altogether. So I used to sit on the carpet pretending to read a book when Nance or Ma were at the tingaling, feeling I should be on the inside of something, but not convinced I was. Then they'd play "Moreton Bay" or "The Last Rose Of Summer" and there I was.'

'On the inside,' she clinched it for him.

'On the inside,' he said, vaguely aware that consideration of the war was contracting away from him like some weather front moving eastward back home. 'I've just reasoned that out, and you're the first to hear it.'

'*Merci m'sieur!* Did you slip into the inside very often?'

'Not when it came to the lessons,' he recalled, and noted how attentively she watched him now. 'At school it was the Sundays I liked. I would slog away in the classroom all week; Saturdays were crazy with football, or the athletics. But Sundays, maybe a bit muscle-weary from the sports, I went looking for … well, whatever you'd call it …'

'The inside of your daze,' she supplied promptly.

'If you like,' he gave her an appreciative glance. 'I used to sidle around to the Music Block and doodle on one of the pianos in the practice rooms. On hot days I could hear the fellows at tennis on the nearby courts. Kepoc, kepoc! That's the balls pinging on the rackets. So I would doodle around those kepocs.'

'Doodle?' She had taken the hem of his nightgown and lifted it so that his tender left knee was exposed.

'Making up tunes as I went along,' he explained. 'Idle palaver, you'd call it.' He felt her fingers around the injured knee, pressing here and there gingerly. 'But really I was looking to slip inside that privileged daze. I could sit for hours; doodle my way into quite a trance. Kepoc tingaling! Lucky that no one ever rumbled to me. I wouldn't have been able to account for myself.'

'So you improvise?'

'You could dignify it like that,' and in the dark he gave her a sidelong smile.

'I do,' she said in the same dark, his sidelong smile clearly disabled from having the disarming effect he had usually been able to count on.

'It was the appeal of getting myself at a remove from all the dailiness of that school life,' Alec pressed on.' I liked meandering into a tune that existed for that moment and was irrecoverable when you thought about it an hour later.'

'You improvise,' she explained his Sunday dazing to him.

'If that's the label that fits.' He resisted the stark relegation of it. 'It was still an exquisite sensation. God knows what soup of emotions I was stirring. I could tinkle my way into such a glen of happy sadness my eyes would go prickly on me.' He found he rather enjoyed taking her into his confidence in this manner. It was …

'Youch!' He was brought up sharply when she touched a place on the kneecap that made him wince.

'It is very swollen up, Mister. Perhaps you have a crack in this part,' and lightly she fingered the patella again.

He asked her if her wonderful practical sense about human bodies came from her having been in the nursing business to which she replied with a strenuous '*Pas du tout!*' For her livelihood she gave the music lessons, earned some extra francs from selling the jams she used to make from her orchards and her canes before the ruinous flooding. Bodies! You live among farmers, you help with the cows, the sheep. 'And the occasional goose,' she added, archly, for her idiomatic English was uncannily good.

'Back home I'm a Goose,' he disclosed.

'Then there you have it.'

What he had exactly he wasn't sure. In any case she had abruptly risen and left the room, her bare feet on the small stair, the mirror door clicking behind her. Had he said anything out of turn?

He limped to the window and in the manner of his training, looked out on the flooded orchards and low ground while careful not to be visible. It would be handy to know what *Mamzelle* was up to, his kit all here, his clothes somewhere else.

She reappeared from the stairwell and had several pairs of thick-woven socks under her arm and a pair of scissors.

'You will be in your seat again. I will fix.'

Alec hobbled over and bared his injured knee. He found he had started to rather like a certain charm in her peremptory management of his welfare. She took a sock, crudely cut off its end and repeated the procedure with the other from its pair. Then tenderly she took his foot, eased one sock into position around the damaged joint before manoeuvring the second so that it thickened the sheathe made by the first.

'Big socks,' she said as she manipulated them, and began preparing a third and fourth layer.

'They belong to that dad of yours too?' he asked her.

Yes, the socks have belonged to her father.

'How will he feel about having his thick socks cut to pieces?'

He is not minding that at all, she replied.

'Is he somewhere here in the house?'

'No,' she stated flatly.

'You live alone?'

'I have told you this,' she reminded him. 'All houses here are empty since the Boche make the flooding,' she explained, manipulating two further layers of sock around the crook knee, thus creating a makeshift poultice from the man's mid-thigh to mid-calf.

'Do the Boches leave you alone?' He wanted to angle toward the greatcoats hanging downstairs.

'They have lived here once,' she answered, preferring not to treat his question directly.

'Billeted?'

'Just so.'

Hitherto the sounds of the invasion had been the relentless boom from the skies interspersed by sporadic gunfire erupting here and there in the middle and further countryside. Once or twice it seemed to move nearer. Alec observed it was the harsh, arbitrary clatter of the closer machine-gun fire that the lady seemed to dislike in particular, and she put her hands over her ears.

If she was musical, no doubt she had a sensitive ear. Himself, he should have been inured to it, but now, hearing the racket from this new viewpoint of a night-gowned guest in her sanctuary, it struck Alec that the clatter was indeed a brutal one; altogether too automatic. Then a series of three large detonations went off somewhere to the right of them, reverberant bangs like someone flexing a metal sheet, and Alec saw her shoulders jump at each.

Suddenly these further sounds of battle were replaced by an uproar very much nearer. From the causeway side of the house it appeared one tank engine after another was starting up. Steadily the volume of noise increased as though to appropriate grid by grid the entire scope of their attention. Now she had her hands over her ears again and her face quite close to his so that he could make out her pained smile. It occurred to him he should put his arm around her or some such comforting thing, but did not quite trust himself to this.

'It is not so easy to breathe,' she called across the few inches that separated them. 'They all ... *you* all ...'

'The invasion,' he assured her. 'Soon it will all be over.'

She would have none of that. 'You think it is so simple?' She looked at him from between her hands.

'I say it is.'

'And I say that when you come hunting for each other among us you leave no space for the good that has happened of its own accord.' She needed to use a half-shout.

He had to think about this. 'You include me in that?' he half-shouted at length, and she nodded.

For it was clear she meant the entire military job. Unfair of her given all those thousands now riding the English Channel, prepared to stick their necks out in order to free these folk from the Boche tyranny. But she had already looked away from him.

Now, audible above the tank engines, were voices bawling orders along the causeway. Did his duty require him to hobble down to a front window and observe the movements in order to make a later report? As he wondered this, there came the tremendous banging of a flattened hand against a door from somewhere below. *Mamzelle* had risen immediately, and descended the small staircase. At the mirror door she glanced back. 'You will excuse me. You will stay here if you wish to be safe.' Then she clicked the door shut on him and was gone along the corridor. The banging continued from below, accompanied by at least one voice. This was more interrogatory than savage in its calls upon the night.

Alec's instruction was to bide in the room, but if he was to retrieve any useful purpose from his misadventures, he should at least observe what all that hardware on the causeway intended.

It is not so easy to breathe.

He needed also to ponder that accusing complaint of hers. Not good for him to be too detached about the military job at this juncture, he knew. Nonetheless she had won her point against his soldier's outlook. With that huge racket in the street, where was the room to have a thought of your own?

When she had been absent for half a minute or so, he discarded his eiderdown shawl and limped down the stair after her, closed the mirror on the attic room and, as inconspicuously as he could, stationed himself at a front window to see what might be occurring. Despite the shut window the dense clouds of diesel exhaust from the vehicles rose to infiltrate the interior of the house with their smell. His observation point allowed him a view of a smallish staff car parked beside the nearest Mark IV, bearing the unmistakeable insignia of the Other Team and with a driver visible in the front. Immediately below, standing knee-deep in the floodwater there was an actual Boche, tall, an officer if his cap was an indication. Alec saw him slap on the door once more, and then take one step back as it opened for him, remove his cap and tuck it under his arm. He had a long forehead, a man in his forties perhaps.

Here was the first close-up specimen of the Other Fellow that Lt. A. Dearborn had set eyes on. He appeared to have a revolver on his belt, carried a small container under his right arm and dealt with the floodwater as though it were a familiar inconvenience. He remained in parley with *Mamzelle* at the door. Would he be invited inside? He would invite himself more likely.

And then Alec thought of his battledress.

She was drying the garments. If she had strung them somewhere in the house, how could they not be in full view and promptly discovered by this Boche. He saw himself being taken, *Mamzelle* being shot, or put through some sordid interrogation and then shot. Ah, here, distinct from his earlier involuntary trembles, was the dread. That shrill along the bones.

With exaggerated care he limped back up to the music room, rummaged in his various pouches. Think, from training, what were the house-to house procedures, what might he need? Grenades to create some initial confusion, the Sten and his spare mags for the shootout, his pistol. Ah, but then it became apparent his nightgown had no pockets in which to put these lethal items and amiable Alec Dearborn's grimace in the dark was an exquisite mix of anguish and self-mockery. He took only his Sten gun, clicking home a magazine. Notorious contraption, the Sten gun, prone to loose off by itself. That would cook his goose. Alec limped back to the large staircase where he attempted to follow what was occurring below.

He was in time to see *Mamzelle* trooping across the flooded hallway, holding high from the water her second nightgown of the evening. The tall Boche in his boots stepped carefully behind her.

She was taking the man to the drying battledress. What could be more obvious? She was about to give him away. What other choice did she have?

This was his first thought. Then he brought to mind again her last comment in the dark of her music room. *They all ... you all ... when you come hunting for each other among us you leave no space for the good that has happened of its own accord.*

He would later feel remorse for his suspicion, but now Alec's mind ran on this, and on the idea of her doubleness. When one is alone, in the dark and in peril there is only the imagination to consult. He should have had more nerve, he knew, but if the lady made no distinctions in the soldiering trade, if it was convenient one moment to save him, the next to turn him over …

He waited, expecting that Boche downstairs to emerge in a hurry, slosh up to the causeway, summon a search party from those tank crews inside their vehicles. Why, in no time they would be all over the house, barging upstairs, manhandling Lt. Alec D. in his idiotic nightgown and with his (only now he recalled) blacked face. Maybe they'd shoot him out of hand, *Mamzelle* looking on coolly and saving her neck by a narrow squeak. For she was a cool and resourceful *Mamzelle*, no doubting it.

Unpleasant to conclude his precious life had only a few minutes to run.

And what if his imaginings were all wrong? *Stay here and you will be safe*, she had instructed. Perhaps he should have tucked himself into a corner of the attic and trusted her assurance. O no, for what if the assurance was a ruse to have him taken more conveniently? He could see how a person who put her hands over her ears at the bang and rattle of warfare might prefer him to be taken without all hell breaking loose. Sensible girl. As for what he might conclude of their relationship, how do you trust a person who you have only seen in the dark?

Cautiously he peeped over the banister. This was it, then, the war was about to come at him, not quite in the manner he had imagined.

If he was to get a decent bead on his pursuers, the staircase offered a most effective field of fire in the first instance. With his one mag there would only be the first instance. His military problem would begin after that.

In the quick glance he gave the downstairs he was in time to witness *Mamzelle* and the Boche shaking hands formally and the latter, having restored his hat to his head, wading away through the door.

Alec limped to the window and saw him get into the small car, which then drove away. For all the roar of their motors, the column of armoured vehicles remained stationary under the dark of the opposite houses. Here and there a human head muffed with headphones had emerged from a cupola.

He turned to see she had come up the stairs, and taken a momentary glance at the weapon in his hands. Saying nothing, she passed through the mirror door and ascended to the hidden music room. He followed her, closing off their hidey-hole behind them, managed his knee up the staircase and leaned his weapon under the guitar again.

'Am I correct in thinking you are furious?' he asked.

She would make him wait for his answer, he saw, and there was silence between them for some time. At length she informed him, 'My Boche comes for *la confiture*.' She had her face averted from him.

'I saw danger. I saw something under his arm and could not tell what it was in the dark.'

'He carries an ammunition tin. It is empty for where he will put the jars full of my jam. In this way they will ride safely.' She paused, glanced at him quickly. 'He tells me his detachment will leave shortly. So he thinks he will take some jams with him. This man pays me. Properly he pays. If you are the invasion he will be dead tomorrow maybe.'

She allowed several moments to pass then asked, 'What will you be doing with your gun in my house, Mister?'

Alec did his best to stare back at her. This was difficult, for the dark would not allow him to read her features exactly. He concentrated his attention on the darker-than-dark area where her eyes were and had the impression she might have been glaring at him now, but with an appraising hauteur.

'I saw danger. I have my training,' he said.

'You will shoot this Boche?'

'I would have preferred ...' He changed his mind and said, 'In this business one gets into a corner where there's no choice.'

She would not grant him his corners. 'So all his friends from the outside come running here? Then you will flee from them into the swamp? With your white dress flapping around your not very good leg? It is good training you have had!'

'As a matter of fact, that course of events went through my mind.'

'And?'

'I could see it was a little chancy.'

'I tell you in the water that you will be safe.'

'Yes.'

After this they sat in silence for a long while. The commotion of engines from the front of the premises continued without any sign that the vehicles were in fact moving off. Sometimes a spasm of gunfire could be heard above this throb, though the skies were, for the moment, quiet. Alec was thinking that since they appeared to have fallen out, perhaps this was the moment to press her for his clothes, to buckle up and make across country as best he could.

'Now will I ask you for your name, Mister,' she decided.

'I'm Alec,' he supplied, and then to conciliate her, added, 'And as you see, maybe not such a smart Alec.'

'Maybe I know that English expression.' And this time, he was convinced of it, she had a smile on her face.

'A simple Alec.'

'And a goose.' She began to hum her tune, and from the humming she seemed to catch at words—a Normandy folk-song, her guest surmised. Then the song ceased and it became evident she had been putting together a little rhyme for his benefit.

L'Anglais, Alec,
il tombe au lac
mais il reste noir,
noir et sec.'

The rattle of her French was altogether too rapid for his schoolboy competence to follow.

'You've lost me.'

In response, she leaned forward, wiped from his face a sample of the charcoal paste and then held her finger close to where he could see.

'I tell how the English Alec falls in the lake but remains dry and ...' she cleaned her finger by taking his palm and rubbing off the smear upon it, 'still so black in his heart.'

Playful she now seemed to be, though he did not miss the criticism of his murderous contingency plan and his distrust of her. But if her earlier physical contact with him had been entirely practical her finger now on his cheek and palm was intimate, teasing, and, along with the quick recovery of her humour, rather pleasing to him.

'Australian, in fact,' he corrected her for the second time that evening.

'For now it is all one.'

So he changed tack. 'In England just a few hours ago we stood on the grass below the planes,' he told her, 'plastering each other's faces with that devilish ointment.'

Again they fell silent for an interval. Now her small gesture of intimacy and conciliation prompted Alec to want to elaborate on his various names. Like many people of easygoing nature he acquired names and shed them. 'It is my sisters call me Goose ...'

'Sisters must have the brother in his place,' she commented.

'And whenever I went out on the sports field the blokes called me "Teapot" or "Handles".'

She was interested in this.

'They reckoned that, when I stood waiting for the ball to come down after kick-off, my knees made the shape of a teapot handle.' And in the gloom he made the outline with his hands and held them close to her face that she might see his meaning.

'Alec aux jambes arquées,' she pronounced, and added that people who acquired lots of names were usually well liked. She took on her finger a smear of the charcoal paste from the other cheek and wiped it on his other palm. 'Now you look more regular, Mister Handles.'

O yes, it was far preferable to be played with by her than be glared at. Bugger the war, you could find yourself saying. And mustn't.

He saw how her gentle mockery of his ludicrous appearance sought intimacy with him, not his belittlement, and asked her in turn for her own name. But she was not inclined to be distracted from her interest in him.

'You play the football, and then you go secretly to the piano. I believe you do not think you are such a simple Alec.' This conclusion of hers made him shrug, so she probed. 'In this war, I have seen some soldiers who watch themselves very carefully despite the bang-bang.'

'The Other Bloke?'

'The Boche who are here, yes.'

'I'm a common enough article, I reckon,' he parried. 'Like most soldier boys, probably.'

For modesty was his first instinct when folk tried to draw him on his introspective side. Years ago in the school changing rooms after a match, one of the fellows had stopped in the midst of the raillery to look at where Alec was sitting apart in his muddy togs. The look of that otherwise bland scrum player had been oddly piercing on the occasion. Then the bloke had decided to advise both the team and the away side of his piece of insight.

'You know, I reckon Handles is actually a darker horse than he lets on.'

And Alec, quashing the agreeable reverie, which, unguarded, had overtaken him, had been alerted by how the other blokes had paused in their roughhouse to ponder him.

'O come off it, you fellows,' he had replied

His response to this attempt to penetrate his inner being had been to launch himself into the scramble, for what better place than in a free-for-all to conceal that part of yourself which yielded the mental textures of an inner life, so fragile, so opulent, and which he was surprised his person, big as it was thought to be, could contain.

'Perhaps you do not like to be picked out in this manner?' *Mamzelle* pursued. But the element of tease in her interest had lessened.

'Not keen on it,' he admitted.

Then it occurred to him that perhaps *Mamzelle* was someone in whom he might confide this idea of his dual self. Why not? He'd be on his way before daybreak, wouldn't clap eyes on this person again.

Except it was indecent to burden folk with his foggy notions of himself.

'You like swagger a little. You like to be modest. These are your strings maybe.'

He wouldn't give her a response to that guesswork.

So she watched him for some time, and he determined to stare straight back into the darker fold where her eyes were. Outside, the engines of the tanks and half tracks churned without sign of dispersing. His conversation with her had remained at the semi-shout, and now she encouraged him, 'Doodle for me, Mister Alec. Here,' and she lifted the piano lid, then made more room on the piano stool beside her.

'Not sure about the competition,' he called back to her from two feet away, and was sure the circumstances could not permit him to find that reverie he had cultivated on those quiet schoolboy Sundays.

'Come, Mister Alec, you will doodle a something. You will find how to charm away this crescendo.'

7

AND FINGERED 'MORETON BAY' FOR HER

O she was insistent about the music. Not hard to guess at the effect she was after. *Mister I will restore your calm*. Shrewd of her, he admitted.

'You know ...' he had shifted his weight across from his chair to sit beside her on the music stool, and now paused.

'Yes?'

'Well, it crosses my mind ...' he wanted, without detriment to the military job and the loyalty he owed to the fellows, to say how a bloke might be touched by the kind of enchantment he had wandered into. Still he hesitated.

'You are saying?'

'… That if you put me too much at my ease, I could end up camping in this loft forever,' he tried to pass off the suggestion as the airiest nonsense.

'Could you indeed!'

'Then what kind of face could I show to my fellows? Blushing red, I guess.'

'You will doodle a little. In return I will fetch your clothes and your boots from where they dry,' she coaxed. 'Then you can limp to your war with your black face or your red face.'

'A bargain,' he said, placing the injured leg stiffly to one side, 'made between a black knight and a *belle dame sans merci.*' He could feel the warmth of her thigh through the fabric of their nightgowns, and knew his French accent was atrocious.

'I am not so,' she feigned indignation.

'Undoubtedly so,' he assured her. Their raillery, his proximity to her, allowed him the sensation he was flirting outrageously.

'You will play.'

The ivory keys of the instrument were sufficiently luminous for him to locate the notes of the scale. He plunked experimentally here and there, then, playing safe, announced, 'This one's Australian,' and fingered 'Moreton Bay' for her.

'A pretty tune,' she approved, tested some notes at her end of the piano and quite soon had acquired the confidence to play the tune through herself, an octave or two lower than his, then vary its tempo, first this way, then that.

'You've got a quick ear, I reckon.'

'Maybe so.'

From a box on top of the piano she had taken some cigarettes, put two into her mouth, lit them, and passed one to him. In the instant that the match lit up her features he saw that she might be rather lovely, a soft cheek, dark, lively eyes that, ever so slightly, did not balance on the oval of her face. For an interval they sat smoking, saying nothing, ashing their cigarettes in a tin she had placed between them. The thought occurred to Alec that it might be rather agreeable to please her, so, with one hand he ascended and descended an arrangement on the ivory keys. As the tune formed itself he made the variations that used to occasion his satisfaction whenever he took himself to the school practice rooms all those years ago.

Outside the war bumped, coughed, droned invisibly.

And to his surprise, he saw it was possible, despite their peril, to go to that glade in his mind where his innocent musical vagary could occur. He saw that she had begun to play a simple foursome of bass notes, pitching them to rumble and blend with the steady roar out on the causeway. His ear favoured the contrasts within an octave, so he patterned among the higher sharps and flats and the result allowed him the sensation of something watery and sunlit. They were in accord. He had no doubt their music making was an ingenuous affair when seen against the mystery that he conceived properly composed music must be. But if his inner being was pleased and stirred by it, was there not something very ancient in the mind being sounded? He let his fingers stray and cross, ascend and descend, like a child's hopscotch patterns, while listening for her bass.

And here was a new thing for him, this spontaneous liaison of their doodling fingers. He wondered if his companion's proximity exerted some occult influence on their situation. *Belle Dame Sans Merci*. Yes. To lightly apply to her this Keatsian fancy suited his notion of her, for she did place herself so very formidably in charge of him. How long did he doodle? It seemed irrelevant to estimate it in minutes. At length his playing petered out, and they were left with the sound of the tank engines filling the background.

'Can they hear us?' he asked.

'It is war. Soldiers will shoot if they see a light, not if they hear a piano,' she advised him on his own profession.

Alec idled across the keys, meditating. Would a seasoned man like, say, Ferris, gun down a Boche if he burst upon him halfway through a sonata? She had an intriguing point about music and the disarming of war's arbitrary rage.

Then he switched topics to rationalise for her. 'You see, my doing the doodles in secret was always a part of the business. I took some trouble not to be seen when I made my way to the practice rooms on those Sundays.'

'Why is it secret when you want to play music?'

'If you're a big ignorant footballer like me you have to find a way of protecting the bits of you that are, you know,' he eyed her, 'the crystal ware.'

'You are big, yes, I can see. You play the football?'

'No choice, ma'am,' he explained. 'I was not only hefty, but according to my gym-master, fleet of foot.'

'You are both a Goose and a sportsman?'

'Looks like it,' he rejoined. Really, it was most agreeable, this banter of hers, how she could both cut and compliment. 'Actually I got to like the game,' he elaborated, 'was reckoned to be quite good at it.'

'Indeed!'

'Win possession of the ball, do some rather witty dancing, touch the thing down, and suddenly there was everyone along the touchline showing they were rather pleased with me.' He paused, patted the injured knee, then added, 'Up to now I've had the legs for witty dancing.'

But his companion preferred to stick to the point. 'I do not understand why the music is secret.'

'It saved the bother of being chiacked about it.'

'Shy-akked?'

'The coarser fellows in the community bothering me.'

'And you, such a big man.'

'If you think so,' he smiled sidelong at her.

'I think so.'

They sat facing the piano. 'And now you have let me into your crystal ware part,' she stated.

'Must have done.'

After a moment, he decided to flirt more blatantly by declaring how welcome she was amid his crystal ware. She gave a short laugh and proposed they should make another conversation on the piano. 'To keep away the shooting,' and she crooked her finger toward the danger on the causeway. Then she doodled a tune on one of the bass octaves, using perhaps seven notes.

Longer-languor-linger-longer-loom.

'You will answer?'

Still dubious that the music would ward off snipers, he made a variation at a higher octave, in a falling pattern, linger-languor-longer-limn-n-loom, also on seven notes, to which she spontaneously added her musical comment, and then was replied to by his own. Consensual, one-off, they challenged and pleased each other for an interval, which again was not to be measured by minutes, but seemed rather like an island of subtle, exquisite pleasure. As they improvised, their fingers approached each other along the keyboard then, as though in the formal tease of a dance, dispersed according to what the evolving tune required. Outside the Panzer engines rumbled, the scattered opening battles of the invasion erupted and subsided severally at a middle distance. As the piano notes spoke for them, there was no need for any more of their semi-shouted speech, but when she did speak again she asked him if he still wanted to do his shooting inside her house, and he admitted to feeling not quite so tense.

'Maybe,' he felt he should qualify.

'Then see what you have managed with your doodle,' she said.

'Our doodle,' he rejoined, and as an afterthought, 'I suppose you will want to call it an enchantment.'

'I am interested in what you will call it.'

'It must be a spell because I can't see myself as a natural musician.'

'Perhaps you are not. But you too have a good ear, and with your fingers you can find a pattern. If you can find a pattern, you can make a spell.'

'Maybe,' he said again. But he could not suppress the thought that the thorough-going military training of the past three years also had an aspect of the spell about it, mind and body kept at the business night and day, never a pause or faltering in that focus upon meeting the elite standard required by Brigade.

'You've still not told me your name,' he applied to her again, reasonably.

She did not answer immediately. At length she informed him, 'I am Vivianne. When the Boches are living in this house they are calling me Viva.'

Alec looked at her quickly, while she, after this disclosure, kept her eyes resolutely to her front. Suddenly, from a military perspective, it seemed necessary that he should clear up a point.

'Do the Boches still have quarters in the house?'

'I say this already, they move out when the flooding comes.'

'The man who came for your jam?'

'He lives here one year. He is a doctor.'

'Were many here?'

'A big house with many rooms. Of course there are many. Coming and going. Some I liked. Why should I not when I must live beside them?'

Alec paused before asking, 'Will you be in trouble?' He knew the savage stories of civilian reprisals against collaborators from parts of liberated Italy.

Her shoulder touched his and he felt her shrug. 'Perhaps the *Maquisards* will arrive and cut off all my hair so that I may be shamed.

Perhaps they will hang me from the gibbet somewhere. Perhaps they will do both.'

'But you have helped me.'

For a second time he felt her shrug. 'I do what I do. How can I help what people will make of it?'

'It is hellish for you,' he said, feelingly. That she had grown fond of some of the Other Team billeted in her house did not trouble him in the slightest.

But he was also oppressed by the need to clear up a second point. 'Is this why you have fished me up, because you'll need an Allied soldier by you if the Resistance call by?'

'*Perfide!*' she rounded on him. He was going to be glared at from the dark again. It had been a necessary question, why should he quail? Yet quail a little he did.

Ah no! It seemed that this time she would hold her affront in check. She took what was her last cigarette, applied a light to it. Momentarily he registered the injury in her slightly unmatched eyes. She puffed, passed the cigarette to him, allowed him a drag of it, then took it back. When it had gone back and forth a few times she stubbed it out and said, 'You wear my papa's nightgown with your black soldier face and you think you are giving me my protection? Is this your famous training?'

He decided he would try and keep the initiative this time. 'I think you are brave, and practical, and kind.' He couched his reply in this formal tone. 'My question intended no offence, and I do not know how I have outraged you this time.' He turned on the stool to face her because she had aroused in him some obscure impulse of chivalry and so deserved from him at the least his most candid front. Did the formality make him pompous?

She had not finished with him. 'You do not imagine very far, Mister Handles,' she said, facing him. Then she made herself plain. 'I do not wish to keep you by me. For my own dread I can bear responsibility. Do you see?'

'I'm sorry if I ...'

'Do you see?'

'I see.' But he still thought his enquiry had been fair.

'You say so.'

'I see.'

'I think not.'

She was unfair to him. He saw far enough to recognise he had come up against some moral consideration that was very close to her. Her displeasure with him suggested this might be fearfully delicate, perhaps more than anything he had encountered in his life so far. But it was the fair thing to know how he stood.

'I barge into your life with my queries. You must think me brutal,' he conciliated.

'An ass,' she said, brutally enough, relenting a little perhaps.

'Will you light another match? I would like to get a fair look at you.'

'So you will now forget your fellows and your war?'

'I can go after them,' he assured himself. 'When the time comes.'

Some moments passed before she answered. 'We will do each,' she agreed.

She rummaged about in the dark and he saw she was finding a cloth that she could arrange across the nearest window. Then she returned, struck a match, gave it to him and allowed him to hold it so he could appraise her. In the few seconds before the flame reached his fingers he saw the strong throat and small concavities of her collarbones, then the shapely face of a woman who could have been any age between early twenties and mid-thirties. Her thick dark hair fell over her shoulders and fringed on her brow in a small vee. The match flame created highlights on her cheekbones, which had a rounded delicacy. And her eyes, also highlighted by the flame, what was it about them? Their slight difference in shape gave her face both a small irregularity yet also its liveliness. Herein lay the strength of her countenance. And now those eyes danced, he was relieved to see, with some merriment of their own.

'You are amused by something?'

'That we are having only the time it takes for a match to burn to the fingers with which to inspect each other,' she said. 'My turn is now.'

She struck a second match and held it up so that she could take in his long face, the flap of blonde hair he habitually combed or swept aside. 'You have the mouth of a person who is used to getting his way,' she observed, 'And you are watchful, I think.'

'Watchful for whichever way the ball bounces, maybe,' he laughed.

'The sport?' she took his flippancy literally, turning his head this way and that. 'It is also more quiet,' she insisted, adding that the face-blacking did not help his *belle mine*.

She allowed the match to gutter out in the ashtray then told him, 'Because you are big, I am allowed another match.' But first she took up some pieces of the socks she had cut and cleaned away the charcoal from his face before holding a second lighted match to it and peering. He felt her use her finger delicately to wipe away some residual smears of the blacking from the soft skin beneath his eyes. As the flame reached her finger she blew it out, lit a third, and continued her thorough inspection of his phiz. When this match died, they sat looking at each other in the dark, the engines of the Panzer regiment still throbbing steadily from behind the slant of the roof. She took her thumb and forefinger and lightly pinched the muscle in his upper arm, made a sound part appreciative, part impudent.

'Will I fetch a good price at the ram sales, do you think?' he asked when she had completed her inspection.

'I think that now we might say we know each other thoroughly,' was her own view.

He had not needed several matches. He found her features immediately attractive. She was comely and this fact had touched him. How absurd that he should be sent off to war and fall into this ... what? This situation. He wondered what she had made of him, with and without his war paint.

'Do some more doodle. Then we will fetch your clothes.'

'Look, I want to say I think you are brave ...'

'You have said so already. Do some doodle.'

'And seem to have a clear head on many things.'

Impatiently she took his left hand and made it plunk on the piano. Again he worried that he was now too self-conscious to do his keyboard meandering to any effect, but commenced, obediently. At first nothing but a facile dissonance came from his fingers, and she waited for him to find his way, listening, very erect at his side. In her alertness and whiteness it occurred to him that she resembled a white deer.

She commenced to play her half dozen bass notes and gradually Alec found he was able to insinuate himself into a melodic pattern, then follow the variations it suggested for itself. He would rather like to have put his other arm around her shoulders at that moment, perhaps kissed her appreciatively on the nearest of her bonny cheeks. Whatever the mess was that she might have got herself into with the Boches, O strewth, yes, she was rather fine.

Yet the emotion with which he felt this seemed to isolate itself in his thinking, like a star remote in its own part of the sky. This dislocation in his sense of reality was, he could guess, the effect of the night's events, so extreme, so out of the ordinary, so compressed into whatever interval of darkness it was since he had flung himself from the doomed Dakota. One part of his mind accepted he had been in this flooded house for a thousand years, another that he could not have been here for more than three hours.

As he contemplated the uncanny sense of The Faraway into which he seemed to have been cast with *Mamzelle*, his fingers dallied on the notes, finding, discarding their folksy, symmetrical and counter-symmetrical patterns. The tunes he found were inevitable enough, maybe, but the one he elaborated now had a gaiety that pleased him, dancing as it did against the background noise of grim war. As though to emphasise the contrast there came now, above the tank engines, a series of middle-distance explosions, like someone beating a carpet that has been hung on a line. This would be the jokers in Bomber Command probably. The bombardment came to the pair of them, not quite rhythmic, yet suggesting rhythm. If it was the Bomber boys, then the other team's poor buggers were copping it sweet. He played his gay tune with more firmness to appease the increase in the background upheavals, and when he glanced sideways at her he had the impression she may have been crying a little.

It was easy for him to idle the gay, haunting, reiterative tune, half his mind on the white keys, half his mind wondering about her. No, he had better not put his big footballer's paw around her shoulders. It would be too bloody gauche. They doodled, and almost below their notice, the bombardment's concussions ceased and the inexorable grind of the engines appeared to recede. By the time they desisted from the piano the small hours of Tuesday, June 6 1944 had, if only for a small interval, become calm around her house and its flooded orchard. It occurred to him to wonder if any fellow in history had ever asked a girl to marry him on the basis of an hour or two's acquaintance, and was brought up short when she observed the silence that had come for an uncertain duration to this portion of Normandy.

'You see what you have done with your doodling?'

8

YOUR ENGLISH IS FIRST RATE

The next thing she said to him was, 'You will wait,' and her bare heels thudded on the narrow stair.

When she returned she had assessed what was happening on the causeway. 'Now it is deserted,' she hovered in the stair recess and reported. 'There is barbed wire at the crossroad still. They will come back, and then it will be bad, I think.'

'The actual fighting could miss you by miles,' he assured her airily about warfare. 'Armies behave like the weather. You stand up on Smoko

Hill, watching a downpour pelt down on your neighbours' picnic while the spot where you are is sunny as you like.'

He knew he was sounding off in a manner more cocksure than his conscience quite allowed, for he could calculate one brutal fact from brigade training, which he preferred not to disclose to her. It was this. If it came to the ground hereabouts being fought over, then her house with its clear view of the causeway posed a military problem. How could there not be snipers or an observation post in her rooftop? So the allied gunners would lay down their stonk, and this cannon fire would obliterate her house accordingly. Her person, her bedsteads, her lace, her home of ancestors would be transformed into the powder and matchwood of what the history books would eventually call a turbulent epoch. Good old Pembroke plain thinking. Morals didn't come into it.

'Thank you,' she said, her tone indicating she had her own ideas on armies and the weather. She felt like another cigarette, but her supply was no more, and she shrugged.

He had brought over with him some of the American Camel cigarettes, having before take-off had the forethought to transfer them from their packets to a tin.

'Best Virginia! I'll dig them out.'

And he made to lurch over to the pile of kit but found her restraining hand on his arm. No, she should not deplete his store. He would need all his best Virginia if he were going to wander over the countryside with his clobber and his broken knee.

He patted her hand comfortably for he had become determined to show how appreciative he was for all the help she had given him. 'When my mind's made up I can be a mulish sort of a creature,' he told her. 'Grown too big to thrash, as The Dad used to say.' This kind of vernacular line-shooting had made him popular among the Poms. He hobbled to the pile of kit, rummaged among the sodden contents of his haversack until he had located the tin. 'Whacko,' he held the trophy aloft, before passing the tin to her.

She would not touch his Camels, but let them sit on her lap while she regarded him refastening the haversack straps.

When he swung jauntily back to her side on the stool he took them from her lap, unscrewed the lid, and said, triumphantly, 'Magic! Dry as you like. Ha! Well, mostly,' as carefully he separated some soggy specimens and placed them in the ashtray. This cigarette hoard had been calculated to last him through the dire first days of the fighting—for as long as he was spared, at least.

'I've got a theory about Best Virginia,' he expanded his idea on the Yanks for the sake of conversation and because her proximity had stirred an expansive mood in him. 'What America does, I reckon, is take the Platonic idea of a thing—your cigarette, your car, your vacuum cleaner—mass produces it for every poor beggar because, since the onset of democracy, every poor beggar has combined feeling important with feeling hard done by …' He had heard someone adumbrating this idea once in a barrack dormitory.

She waited as he rattled on, and her immobility against the dark conveyed the impression to him that all this cleverness was not very much to her interest. So his theory trailed off and he placed the tin once more on her lap.

'Look, in the absence of flowers, why don't I give the cigarettes to you?'

'You will have need,' she pushed the gift away.

'I can scrounge another ration when I catch up with my fellows.' He placed them back again. 'Take them, please.' Now it was serious for him that she should accept his gift. 'Take them because you fished me out of trouble.' Why would she not take such a simple recompense? 'Not much else I can offer by way of appreciation.' She had been prompt enough when it came to his parachute.

'And this is truly the Invasion?' Her question shot from the penumbra.

'Truly,' he answered, surprised at the line of question. Then, her anxiety dawned on him. 'Hey, there's no secret police going to catch you with these,' he appeased. 'Those types are on the run. Definitely.'

'And if your Invasion fails, Mister Handles?'

This prompted him to tell her how, a few hours ago he had looked through the open door of an aeroplane and spied such a spectacle of ships and aircraft that … well.

'We've got an even chance, I reckon,' he was prepared to avow.

It was not the even chance she saw in her mind's eye. 'You can fail.'

He had to watch he did not stray into loose talk. Loose talk cost lives, harped the noticeboard posters. Yet how could he not be entirely honest with her, now that she had entangled herself so much in his welfare?

'We're well-rehearsed for all this palaver,' he encouraged.

'You can fail,' she insisted again. 'When you do, then the Boches return.'

'But you can hope,' he suggested desperately.

'They *return*,' she insisted. 'They have their clever police. These will come back behind the Boche army to search all the houses where the invaders may have been. You have your English word 'scrupulous'. These men are most scrupulous. They know how to ask questions while they watch Vivianne's face. Whenever Vivianne wishes to keep a thing hidden, these men know how to imagine the hidden thing. Do you see?'

'Thugs are never that clever.'

'*Fou!* It is their job to be clever. They are selected out of millions. They are trained to be clever by the clever. They will find where Vivianne has hidden her American Virginias because they know to look behind the books on a shelf or inside a shoe in her cupboard. They will find the butt squeezed carelessly between two floorboards. They will be waiting to arrest my friend to whom, carelessly, I have given a gift of a few best Virginias. *The best Virginias, Mademoiselle,* they will sniff and inspect. *Not so easy to come by, you agree.*

'So then they must take me, or worse, they take my friend, to their building with many rooms. And among these rooms is one with a bath. And they say, *You will kindly remove all your clothes, Mademoiselle,* for they know how nakedness is helpful in the pursuit of truthfulness. Then they make me, or my friend, go into the bathwater, and they will hold the head under until a person thinks he might die, when they pull up this head by the hair and say, *We are interested in your best Virginia's Mademoiselle,* at which they put this head, you see, Mister Handles, *this* head, under the bathwater again until the body fights and writhes and thinks, *now I will be no more*, which is when they pull the body up to breathe, and the poor body does not even know what it is exactly they wish to know, but they have convinced Vivianne, or her friend, that they know some valuable thing for which the best Virginias are the keyhole. Do you see, Mister Handles?'

'I think, maybe, you could stop.'

'I will not stop for you! When Vivianne, or her friend, have been put under the water many times by these clever people, I confess to them, *An English parachute soldier gives me these after I save his life and restore his being, and I do this because I welcome the Invasion that has now failed.* And they will say, *Thank you Vivianne, teacher of music.* Then they will take me to a cell in the middle of this same building where I can hear everyday the firing squads … And they know it is a horrible music for me because I am a teacher of music.'

'Look …'

'You wonder I put my hands on my ears when I hear your shooting? So it is the dread. But it is my dread. For how can you guess at such big consequences from such a small gift? How can you see such a small moment when you do not imagine far enough.' She paused, then placed the tin back with him. 'No, you will keep your best Virginias. We will smoke one or two, and then I will supervise while we destroy completely the evidence of them. And we will hope we have been more clever than these clever men.'

'But you took my parachute. What if they find that?'

'*Everyone* calculates. I calculate. I calculate how I can find a parachute *en le marais*, but cigarettes they will conclude are a thing that is given.

Your parachute I explain without guilt because this I find. Your cigarettes I cannot explain without guilt because you give. I have no skill to look at a person's eyes and say, I find these cigarettes in the swamp.' She was evidently impatient with how dim he was. How could he not see how impossible it was for her, who could not look a person in the eye when she knew a guilty thing and not assume that the guilt must radiate from her person?

Alec listened to the nicety of her dread. So this was what she had meant when she had told him, *You imagine nothing!* A casual gift of cigarettes unloosed the pent, hideous images of terror. The English Channel, that narrow strait of sea, had kept from his appreciation such a veil on the possibility of a world where a humble bathroom could be a setting for torture and the calculation of anguish. At one level the *Mamzelle* made no sense. Could she not hide the tin of cigarettes wherever she had hidden the parachute she had gathered to herself so opportunely? Could she not be scrupulous in effacing the butt of each cigarette she smoked, or explain it plausibly to the hideous investigators who followed in the wake of armies?

No she couldn't, he realised. And this was simply because she was a bad liar and an exemplary truth teller. The person at his side, the thought struck him powerfully, had a physical and a moral beauty beyond anything he could recall encountering before. Was this wide-eyed colonial credulity? Very well, let it be that.

And with his realisation Alec perceived how he had no right to expect her attitude about the cigarettes, or her reaction to his very presence in her house, to be reasonable. God knows what horrors in her life were behind the talk of bathrooms and firing squads. Had she suffered arrest? Maybe her experience was no more than the power to imagine these ghastly outcomes against the everyday threats of her existence in this farmhouse, where tanks were strung out along her causeway, barbed wire and an MG post occupied her crossroads. She had shown a power of imagining when it came to his own excessive reaction in the aftermath of the morass. *For my own dread I can bear responsibility. Do you see?'* Yes, he began to see just a little of the alertness expected of him when treating with a person who has been living under a devious, cruel occupation, and the recognition put him somewhat in awe of her.

'We'll smoke what we want, dispose of the remains efficiently, then I'll pack the tin away in my haversack again,' he soothed.

This time he took the matches lit two cigarettes and passed her one. For an interval they smoked in silence

'You know, your English is top rate,' he observed in an invitation for her to explain the fact.

Her Papa, she told him, was the second brother when it came to this farm and its orchards. So he had gone away to the university and become a teacher of Modern Languages in an English school near Taunton during the 1920s. French, German, English, for Papa had an ear. Later they had gone to Cambridge where Papa was with the university examination board and she had attended school with the English girls. There was no mention of a mother.

'So, naturally, my English is becoming top rate, and I can pass for an English young lady. But I have little conversation practice in these years until you have dropped from the sky.'

'Is he a musical man, your pa?'

She paused before saying, 'It is his guitar, this one you can see here. Sometimes he is playing, I am singing. We make a good company, the two of us.'

'He's a good ear and a good pal.'

She was not inclined to respond to this, but wet the pads of her thumb and forefinger, snuffed the end of her cigarette and took it to his haversack where she slipped it inside. She then did the same for the end of his own fag. Looking for a congenial topic, he prompted her on Cambridge and for some minutes they compared notes on the university town. She had bicycled with her English friends all over the countryside, collected the blackberries that grew in the lanes and taken them home to make *la confiture.* She had taken the English examinations, then returned to France in 1938 when Papa had inherited this house and its orchards from *le frère aîné.*

He told her he had been an undergraduate at Pembroke and marvelled how they must have been living in the same town for a period.

'And we neglected to arrange an assignation!'

She laughed at this idea and it led them to talk of their respective childhoods.

He told how, on the sheep farm during his Australian boyhood, they had employed an English governess, a Miss Dorothea Sponner.

'Spoon, we called her because her head was round and her body long. Her ambition was to get the three of us to speak the English language with decorum so we would tramp out into the middle of a paddock where she would get us to declaim a poem to any handy sheep that may have been nearby. I remember my poem went,

O the cuckoo she's a pretty bird,
She singeth as she flies,
She bringeth good tidings,
She telleth no lies.'

'You know,' she had turned to him to comment, 'Your English is first rate.'

'Too true,' he said, and they both laughed at her sly impertinence. He was pleased some vein in his being could cause laughter in her, so continued to work the humour afforded by sheep. 'Your average merino, you see, has a very reflective way of chewing its food which made me think the sheep quite liked my poem.'

'Clearly it is a very cultivated place, your station for the sheep,' she commented.

'Very,' he pronounced, deadpan, then added, 'Bell, Nance and I, we thought Spoonsie was a bit cuckoo herself. For her part she thought us rather wild.'

'And yet your poem is very dainty in such a hefty man,' and she nudged him.

'I'm inclined to agree,' he said, and told her how he was sent off to boarding school aged twelve where he learned more about football than decorum.

'When you speak of where you come from, Mister Handles,' she responded to his Australian childhood recollection, 'I think of sunshine like your best Virginia, affordable and abundant.'

'Since coming over the seas I've missed it just a little.'

'You will tell me what you have missed,' she insisted. And if he could please her by picturing his country, then why not let the military business slip from consideration for a space.

'The rosellas,' he began. 'Can you imagine birds as red as strawberries?'

'I cannot imagine,' she said, and clapped her hands at the thought of them.

'But plump as a bourgeois, you see, and matrimonial as you like!'

'I do like,' she affirmed.

He described for her the lifelong pairing of rosellas, how you could watch them chomping the purple wisteria blossom wastefully. 'Then they whip-whirrup away if you clap your hands. Whip-whirrup, whip-whirrup,' and he made a whistling sound as he fluttered his fingers about her head.

'Think of another thing,' she commanded.

He took a moment to consider. 'Can you imagine a tree with bark so white it looks like a skeleton just jumped from its pyjamas?' To be sure, he was flirting with her.

She could not have imagined that thing either until he had said it for her. 'Tell me another.'

This time he told her about the picnic races at Queanbeyan or Bungendore where once a year the families met each other, Cunninghams from Lanyon, Morrisons from Tralee, Kilmartins from Redhill. 'You'll be wearing your whitest moleskins and you'll go up to the prettiest girl in sight and, trying out the decorum learnt from your Pom governess, you take off your hat and say, "Now Betty, why don't you let me put a two-bob on Goodradigbee Whisper for you?" And Betty Morrison lets you place the bet, or she doesn't, depending on Betty's whim.'

'She is fickle, this Betty.'

'We can all be a bit,' he deprecated.

'You will not be fickle with me, Mister Handles,' came his companion's orders from the darkness, and again the imperative charmed him.

'How would I dare?'

He went on to describe the Murrumbidgee River that flowed beside The Dad's place, how it used to run flush after rain, with the brown waters mounting each other like so many panicky sheep in a pen. How it might be a trickle at the end of a summer without rain, like glassy infrequent spillages between rocks. Being with this person somehow brought on his eloquence and he liked the sensation of it and, knowing he was having an effect, he looked at her to see how it expressed itself on her dimly lit features. Attentive, pleased, she gazed ahead rather than toward him.

'When the war finishes and you come on your visit,' he instructed her—for he shared the playful manner of his countrymen to take some new chum's future and make it rich with notional opportunity—'we'll have you in your moleskins, wading into a pen jam-packed with rams. You'll grab the biggest and the ugliest by its horns. You'll throw it over onto its hind legs, then walk it backwards to where the auctioneer is yelling out his jiggery-pokery of numbers.'

'I am not used to the walking backwards.'

No? Well, he had done a bit of it sometimes in the school vacations, when he had gone with The Dad out to Merrivale to buy a stud ram or two.

'I have not had a wrestling match with a big sheep,' she assured him.

'You should try your hand.' He laughed, and told how hands and trousers would be greasy as soft candles with the lanolin after a morning of it.

She knew the feel on her hands of *la graisse de laine* from living hereabout, she said.

'We'd put you on a pony.'

'Once I would like to have a pony, I think.'

'Not too late,' he breezed, 'We'll arrange it.' Though there was the business of victory in this war to attend to first. 'Or we could set you up to go visiting in a sulky.'

'Sulkee?' She picked up on the word, tipping her emphasis onto its second syllable. Charmingly.

'The fancy word for a carriage,' he supplied.

'At your Bidgee River these neighbours visit you in sulkees?'

'My word!'

'It is the word I like.' And she said it over once or twice. 'Sulkee, sulkee.'

Alec realised that, however strange, however improper to his purpose of waging war, he was enjoying himself. He described for her the January fortnight each year when the Dearborns went up to town and stayed with his gran at Coogee, spent all day in the surf. 'Going with it like a blessed dolphin. Or just watching it come in, like liquid mountain ranges.'

'Bidgee, Coogee,' she tasted the funny words with a puckering of her lips. 'This ocean you let me picture,' she allowed.

He told her all he could think to say, recognising dimly his seven-year absence across the seas had made his home into a slightly less homely thing in his mind. Perhaps this small estrangement was what gave the edge to his descriptions that caused *Mamzelle* to laugh with delight, to press her hands together and urge him to continue.

'When you talk about your home you are *joyeux*,' she informed him.

'You could be right,' he said.

Certainly her word *joyeux* touched that fine uplift of spirit he used to experience, when, at the end of a school term he came back on the early train into the tableland country, the mist allowing the grey, two-dimensional profile of trees or a windmill to make an exquisite profile against the white opacity. Equally this elation used to be aroused if he came down on his pony from the top paddock at the hour when the sun had sidled below the canopy so that the air between the tree trunks was as though saturated with gold dust. The surge in his sense of wellbeing on such occasions had been quite beyond his schoolboy power of words to express, and the sensation of uplift both pleased and mystified him. *Joyeux*. The emotion had been absent in his life since he went off to Cambridge in '37, as though, obscurely, he had permitted himself to be distracted.

He sat in the dark beside her, narrating these things and wondering at himself for doing so. And yet, O it did him good to see that she had recovered her morale from the terrifying bathrooms and firing squads. Another wave of aircraft were droning overhead, not intrusive enough to prevent him noting how her reversal of mood made his own mood sunnier, how in the space of a mere few hours her happiness had connected itself with the sense he had of his own wellbeing.

9

IF I GO ALL RIGHT

The overhead aero-din became more relentless, oceanic, as more transports brought in the successive Airborne waves. From the modulations in engine-pitch Alec could tell how the planes were shedding altitude, the pilots aligning their craft with whatever pathfinder flares were visible from up there. Fellows would be streaming backward in their hundreds from hatch or door like eggs from some shoal of monstrous fish, crack crack crack, as the chutes opened. All this he could sequence before his mind's eye, *blind Harry as I am, in this attic with a woman and piano for company,* he placed his absurd self in the scene. From afar came the responsive crackle of ack-ack.

Mamzelle hummed her open-ended tune, rocking back and forth ever so slightly as Alec's wonderment about her continued.

It is a kind of sorcery, this, her simple singing.

Yes, she conjured in the mind such a trance of sensations as would interpose itself between her preferred place and the brutal clatter of battle with which the world—land, waters, sky—were presently convulsed. She was a music teacher. How else other than by humming herself into elsewhere could she defend the place in the mind she wished to keep intact?

O, she is marvellous in this.

For some moments the outbreaks of small arms shooting became fiercer, and there were two or three whomps from some larger consideration, gammon bombs going off maybe. Alec estimated this nearest ground fighting was at least four miles to the right and front of their attic room. Could he judge where he might be from the nature of the gunfire? In the neighbourhood of Merville, where there was going to be a fight for the gun-emplacements? Close by the Orne bridge, or those over the Dives? Odd how this battle-clatter did not persist, as you would expect from a real stoush. Instead it erupted and petered out, as though these skirmishes were not the main event.

What if the whole airdrop had been a gigantic cock-up, and the clatter and boom came from the first pathfinder fellows still trying to secure the DZ's? What if the various battalions had shared the same weather and luck of his own planeload and were scattered halfway to Paris? Being a mere lieutenant, Alec knew only a fraction of the schedule. *If you are captured, my old china, hold out in interrogation for twenty-four hours. Manage that, and all you know will be old hat,* was how the instructor had answered a question at the last briefing.

He reminded himself of the spectacle he had glimpsed through the doorway of his own Dakota. *No! What I saw was too inexorable,* he assured himself, and immediately his mind's eye was confronted with the ripped away face, the charred helmet strap of the man behind him in the aisle, whereupon again every probability on earth became uncertain for Alec Dearborn, BA.

Rid the mind of that, subaltern, the voice of his parachute training stipulated now. *Focus on something gainful like, for instance, how long you have been here.*

Place and time. Yet in the instant he tried to think practically, his mind wandered to how curiously unquantifiable had been the interval of his biding at this waterlogged place, the time sense dulled by the successive waves of aeroplane drone from above, and below this rambling house on its floors of onyx-still water.

If he did not move, his bung knee felt at peace, tightly enclosed within the layers of sock. He idled, as she did, with undeliberated successions of notes at each end of the piano and the quick horrors that had come to his mind's eye subsided for the time being.

What if it really is for the best that I stay put?

This thought cropped up in his mind quite suddenly and he was surprised at how free of self it was. For suddenly he found he was looking into the idea of a larger good. Here he was, beside this providential *Normande.* Was she not more strange, more marvellous than anyone he could count among his acquaintance hitherto? So where, if he put it plainly to himself, did life find more hope for, not just survival, but enhancement? Surely his part in pursuing the good lay in taking this opportunity to fathom the mystery of her? Could it be that he should put the war out of mind because the peace that must ensue was making a larger claim on him?

Tingletangle tingletangle their doodling talked on the piano.

To his way of thinking she had such a power of presence here beside him. It lay in the scent of her, the odour of the laundered garments they both wore, the astringency of the cigarettes they had smoked. It lay in how their temporary lapse of conversation resonated still with what they had already said and done, how it was potent with the things he rather wanted to impart to her, and hear from her.

Could he accept that this was the outlandish way in which war worked? Hellish in one place, it rips away the face from a fellow, blows two blokes to buggery across the countryside. Benign in another, it lands Alec Dearborn, graduate and lieutenant on a piano stool beside a person who awakens in him his power to be fascinated?

Ah, if these were the fortunes of war, how could you square that with the fair thing? Thus did his decent Australian instincts recoil against the temptation to stay put. The fair cop, in this instance, should have landed him in the battle to dash about, loose off with his weapon, do the business he had allowed himself to be rehearsed for. Had this occurred, by now he probably would have done for a few Boches. Or been done for. Who gets pleasure from extinguishing some mother's son? No one with any power to see. But being the common plight, it would have been fairer, simpler, had he been dropped in the deep end with the fellows. To cope. Maybe he should have been a conchy. One or two fellows at Cambridge had gone down that road. Somehow this was never quite expected from Alec Dearborn who had won praise on the football field for his aggressive spirit.

But that is a game!

Not quite, he recognised. There was also the pressure to acquit himself before a witness; The Dad, his sister Bell maybe, the touchline crowd, and so on through Cambridge and latterly the military business. This need to be witnessed was a part of his character he shied from, sometimes tried to disguise with suavity or plain bluff, and he grew impatient with himself whenever it reasserted its pressure.

I fear doing harm more than being harmed.

He allowed himself this recognition. But the thought was followed by his recollection how at school, or with The Dad, he preferred to get the worst over promptly if a caning was in prospect. So now he rationalised brutally. *Having put myself in the way of doing for some poor bastards out there in the woods, then I should get on with it.* For he would not accept that exceptions could be made for him.

At which *Mamzelle* announced, 'Now we will make you prepared,' as though she had followed his inward conversation.

She picked up the items of his kit, indicating that he should himself carry his Sten gun and the pistol, which, fastidiously, she removed from its holster so that he should have responsibility for the weapon. Then she lugged her burden down the small staircase, her guest following, with the pain in his left knee reawakened each time the narrow confine compelled him to bend the limb. Along the corridor he limped after her until she stopped at the cupboard. He saw her remove various items from a higher shelf, then take these with his packs and webbing into the room where they had lain together and place them on the high, dishevelled bed. When he fingered them he saw she was offering him her pa's underwear.

'Now I fetch the rest of your uniform.'

Unable to resist it, he made the request that, if she were going for a prowl around her house, he would rather enjoy hobbling quietly behind. Stickybeaking, if it wasn't too impertinent of him.

To this proposal, she shrugged and led him down the main stair. When they arrived at the flooded ground floor he followed her example, picked up the hem of his nightgown daintily with his free hand, tried as he limped between chair and sideboard not to create any turbulence in the floodwater. Two or three dark rectangles on the paler walls suggested ancient paintings, the tables and sideboards were bare of objects. They waded along a corridor, *Mamzelle* waiting patiently for him each time his curiosity led him to peep into the gloomy interiors behind the several doors they passed.

'Now you will lift your dress higher, Mister Handles,' she warned.

He saw her descend two steps until the water had come to her mid-thigh. Her movements through the deeper flood, with the nightgown lifted to just below her bottom, were slow, a balletic swivel of the torso, and rather lovely. She made no discernible swish as she parted the water, while he could not help but slosh as he followed. How ridiculous if someone were in turn following him and able to view him in this 'dress' up around his bum. She enjoyed chiacking him about his 'dress', he could see.

They passed into what was evidently the old kitchen where he could see on the walls the profile of pots, knives, ladles, and the arch of a brick hearth protruding above the level of the flood. From the kitchen she took him through one scullery, then up half a dozen steps to a further scullery where the floodwater had not reached. Here, on a rack attached by pulleys to the ceiling beams, his various military garments had been arranged to dry and in the small light afforded by a window he could see the crude silhouettes of his jump smock, and battledress. The air in this room was distinctly humid, and he could feel the radiation from a boiler.

'You will not touch this,' she indicated in the direction of the heat.

Alec was briefed as to how, while he slept, she had rinsed the garments to rid them of the mud and put them through the mangle. He could discern this contraption on top of her washtub. She lowered the rack, fingered the garments. 'Still they are damp.' Nonetheless she handed him the pile.

He told her how good it was of her to have drudged for him like this and was struck by her reply.

'There are women who will wash the clothes with a good joy. For a sweetheart, for their child or a beloved papa. One hears this.' Then she told him they would now return upstairs where he might take off his dress.

'I'd love a look at your jams,' he requested on a sudden whim.

Once more, against the darkness, he saw her white shoulders shrug. 'This can be.' Most jams, she explained, had been stored in the sunken kitchen and were now spoiled by the floodwater. 'You may see where I keep the sample jars,' and led him back down into the kitchen then up the small step to a room off the corridor. This interior was pitch-black, but if he felt gingerly with his fingers he could identify rows of vacuum jars. She had preceded him into the close confine so now he could not even make out the slight paleness of her form, while her voice came to him, disembodied.

'The apple, the apricot, the blackberry, *la gelée de grosailles*, which we make from the redcurrants.' She could not possibly see these jars in the blackness, yet enumerated them confidently enough. Then she asked whether he had a favourite jam.

'My word,' he replied, conscious that his voice must be as disembodied to her as hers had been for him, and narrated how his sisters and he could do justice to a moderate tin of raspberry in the course of one high tea. 'That sweetness,' he remembered, 'the lovely barbarity of it.' And he hugged his battledress to his person, could feel the damp through his nightgown.

'*La confiture de framboises.*' Then he could hear the clink of jar on jar as she felt her way along the shelf with her fingers. At length she triumphed, '*Le voilà.* Now Mister Handles you will permit that we go upstairs again where you will dress and taste this barbarity, perhaps.'

They retraced their steps to the bedroom where, item-by-item, she handed him her pa's undergarments: vest, long johns, socks.

'These will be next to you, so you will be dry.' A little nervous as to what her answer might be, he asked whether her papa minded the appropriation of his clothes, to which she disclosed, 'My papa is elsewhere.'

'Safe, I hope,' he wished for her, but she shrugged and would not pursue the topic.

He pulled on the dry under-garments, found them to be a good fit, then commenced with the damp battledress. She watched, passing each garment as he needed it. They were still warm from the boiler. 'Your mangle has put creases into this clobber that makes it fit for parade,' he complimented her. Next he tried to lace his boots and buckle the gaiters without bending his bung knee, but could not. She bent to grapple with the laces and buckles.

'Tight would be good.'

When she had done this for him he saw her pick up the jar of preserve, release the metal spring, then stand before him with her spoon. 'You will make open,' she commanded, touching his lips with a finger, and when he opened his mouth, she fed him with her sample. The jam was pleasant, more astringent than sweet perhaps.

'Barbarity?' she asked.

'A fellow could place a regular order,' he complimented, not sure he was being sincere, though he opened his mouth again. Her face was close enough to his own to register that it amused her to feed him these spoonfuls.

'My jam pleases you, Mister Handles?'

'Thank you, my word.'

'If that is so then perhaps you are not so different from the Boche who came here earlier.'

'If that is so then perhaps I am not,' he allowed this consideration, on his guard that this was a ploy of hers. If it was, if the jam-tasting and her reference to her Boche visitor were designed to disconcert him from the military business, then she might, after all, be rather sly.

'One more,' and slipped the spoon into his mouth again before pressing down the metal spring on her jar.

Now he buckled on his harness of belt and cross-belts, ammunition pouches, water bottle, bayonet and revolver, then slung the haversack onto his back. The various extras in the weapons bag, wire cutters, some PIAT anti-tank ammo and gammon bombs, were a burden it would be expedient to dump, he decided, as soon as he was well clear of her house. Meanwhile she had been busy at the small fireplace in the room. He could hear a knife scraping at the hearth. She went out, and when she returned the charcoal she had collected on a plate had been turned into a paste.

'You will be still while I paint you,' she said, and began applying the muck to his forehead and cheeks with three fingers of her right hand.

'You amaze me,' he said.

'Why so?'

'You have the same attention to detail my sergeant has.' He let himself be painted, gazing straight ahead as her eyes moved back and forth across his line of sight. She was very intent on her handiwork and it was pleasant, having those fingers working this way and that around the contours of his face.

'You think I make a good sergeant?' she pretended to be scandalised.

Suavity would have prompted him to say, 'Of course,' but instead, in a blurt, he found he had weakened. 'Do you know how very inclined I am to stay here for the next day or two. So my mind can be easy that you will come through all right?'

Of course he could not kiss her now that his face was covered again with blacking, but never in his life had he experienced the desire to kiss a person with as much naturalness as he did at that moment.

She brought his helmet, tufted with camouflage, placed it over his head. He felt her piano fingers grappling with the chinstrap. Then she was gone for a minute or so and returned with a proper walking stick, which she gave to him.

'Now it is done. You may go and hobble after your war.' And she led the exit from her bedroom, and along the corridor. He wished his boots did not clunk so on the wooden floor. With the stick, and an ungainly swing of his bad leg, he descended the staircase, waded quietly to the door where earlier the German had knocked. His gaiters kept the socks she had given him dry for the most part. She was at her door first and opened it for him, stood with her bare, delightful Norman knees visible to him where she held high her nightdress.

'You know, I worry that, with all your goodness to Mister Handles, you might have disarmed me just a little. For the business ahead, I mean.'

And yes, if, at that moment she had requested he bide with her, then Alec Dearborn, graduate and soldier, would have considered this obligation the most vital job-of-war he could have been entrusted with. Get her safe through the brutal, clattering, lethal business his fellows had set loose once more in her neighbourhood. For warfare was going to intensify in the coming hours until it was the utmost that nerves and eardrums could endure. A simple request from her would have legitimised his own inclination to stick it out here, mediate when the tanks and riding infantry came rumbling along the causeway, aerials flexing, pennons fluttering. He would be doing the fair thing.

And yet he would be aware, forever after, that he had somehow made the unworthy choice.

'If you will think about me, then, when you are gone, I will be arming you still, I think,' she assured him, mysteriously.

'Decent of you,' he laughed, and lingered, watching her. 'If I go all right and send you a postcard, do you think you might invite me back here after the war?' He waited, then added as an afterthought, 'Only if you think I might be welcome.'

'Why will you not be welcome?' she answered, and closed the door on him rather sooner than he might have wished. For it had occurred to him that the name and direction of the nearest town or village might have been helpful. He slapped on the door to bring her back, and waited. She did not come, and after three attempts at this he surmised that this was deliberate.

Had she finished with him? He had not properly thanked her, he realised. Or even discovered a sufficient name and address to which a postcard might be directed. Depending on what happened, he would contrive to retrace his steps in a week or so after the armies had been through, check that she had come through OK and sample one of the other preserves, the redcurrant maybe.

10

WITH HALF A SELF TO
LOOK FOR THE FELLOWS

He managed to scramble up to the causeway, then limped until he had cleared the few houses, whereupon he scrutinised the horizon all around, attentive for the flash and clatter of battle. The barbed wire barrier at the crossroad behind him appeared unmanned, the houses and street of this seemingly unnamed Normandy *hameau* were deserted in both directions. There were bouts of gunfire erupting mildly to his right though no luminescence from tracer or phosphor bombs rose into the night sky. On either side of him the flood was a dull sheen snared by the black, half-submerged vegetation. To his front the skyline appeared as a silhouette of trees, perhaps a mile distant.

Alec became self-conscious that his profile on the causeway would invite a nervy Boche sentry or sniper to kill him, so he slid on his bottom to the foot of the embankment, regained his feet, then set out in the direction of the most recent shooting. On this uneven lower ground his progress was clumsy. Sometimes he found a stretch of dry path; sometimes he waded through shallow water where the flood lapped at the rise.

And as he limped, it was discomfiting to reflect what an idiot he was. His knee pinched the nerve at each step and he could not bend his leg at all, causing his gait to be an exaggerated sway from side to side. Furthermore, it was almost impossible to move silently. So his approach would be heard from half a mile away, and he had precious little facility to skip nimbly for cover if a bullet or two was fired off in his vicinity. *Dearborn's keen mind and superb athleticism assures him a most promising future. Good Luck!* He remembered Old Truff's farewell comment on his last school report in '37.

That keen mind, pondering its makeup as he pursued his way, found it dealt with his immediate predicament in an oddly detached manner. He should have been keyed up, at the edge of himself. But he found his interest in what might happen was reflective. For instance, if he ran into trouble, would he try and kill one or two of their lot before they nailed him? That was the job, technically speaking, and he hoped he might have the nerve for it. Of course the matter would have presented itself as more urgent were he alongside his fellows, guarding the perimeter around their strategic bridge. You tore about, loosed off before there was time to think much, lived at the edge of yourself, shot some poor bastard or were shot. Listening to MG fire, you heard an almost routine automatism, but what was the sensation as a bullet slammed home?

And as to the matter of his being quite alone, here in the dark, this made Alec perceive it would be a peculiarly forlorn idea, dispatching anyone who came at him from the night, and then being casually dispatched in turn by some inevitable other.

Yet you have recovered your calm, Mister Handles?

For it seemed he was not quite alone after all, and the vividness with which she had established her voice in his head was almost enough to make him turn around to check she was not actually following him.

'Yes, thank you,' he said out loud.

And then, directing his unspoken thoughts toward her, as one might direct a prayer, he summarised for her his inner state. 'I have settled that vile swamp in its place. I cannot yet do this for my fellows inside the plane. It is too easy to believe they will turn up. I imagine them when morning comes, cheerful, grimed, in the doorways of the wrecked buildings I will come upon.'

And?

He needed to think about why she had placed that interrogatory *And* before his mind. He tramped, his boots and stick in their eccentric rhythm on the path and through the encroaching sludge. 'I feel distress at having relinquished you,' he supplied on consideration. For it was distress, he recognised, to be walking away from this sudden new claim on his life. 'It is this that has disarmed me, I reckon,' he explained for her.

I will be arming you, she reminded.

His conscience on her behalf was fastidious, would not let him ditch the foolish kitbag of bombs and ammo until he was well clear of her establishment. Nor would his crook knee tolerate the extra weight of cutters, anti-tank and other hardware. So he dragged the burden behind him on its cord, where it bumped, perhaps dangerously.

'Do I look like a ninny?' Alec asked her, and imagined her gaze on him, the playfulness he had glimpsed in her eyes during the brief flame of the matches.

Yes, she confirmed for him. *Nigaud aux jambes arquées.*

There was no sign yet of the dawn which, when it came, would at least give him an idea of the east, and therefore the north where lay *La Baie de la Seine*, now potent with the multitude of invasion ships. The dawn would also allow him to learn what hour of the day it was by the clock. Useless to try and assess in hours the interval he had been with *Mamzelle*. An era or so by internal sensation.

By the time he reached the line of trees his own efforts, and the undergarments of *Mamzelle's* papa had warmed him more than he would wish. Alec eased himself down at the foot of a beech tree, drank some tin-flavoured water from his canteen, took a bar of chocolate from his haversack, munched …

… and conjured her image to his mind again. Did the generous oval of her face and her rounded physical frame suggest an ancestry more Scandinavian than Gallic? A lineage back to those tenth century 'Normanni'? Wherever she came from, her picture in his mind caused him to be *joyeux*. *Joyeux* and anguished, both.

The sky was quiet, the small-arms fire rattled away from at least a couple of distinct locations. Still there were no visible flashes and the distance was too great to hear the accompanying bellow of orders, or the screams of wounded men. Would a wound cause him to scream? He could not recall having screamed in his life. The two or three casualties he had seen during training had lain on the ground and exhibited a kind of exhausted patience. It had been the same in the paddock when he had come across a half-dead lamb after a fox had been through, the mild bleat, the feeble attempt to lift its head in order to get the world back to a right way up. What would it be like for him, or the fellow sharing his foxhole?

He decided he should change his line of thought. Gunfire, when listened to in the abstract, suggested rhythm, played with rhythm but then resisted a rhythm, as if perversely. Dit-dit-dit-dit-dah, pommff, dit-dit-dah, went the triggered musical phrases. He hoped his own fellows were coping.

He sorted through his kit for the items he could afford to abandon. Retain one spare mag for the Sten, ditto for the pistol. Discard the grenades and phosphorus bombs. Should he hang on to the trenching tool or *The Oxford Book Of English Verse*? He had brought the book in case there were respites from the fighting. Retain the book, he decided, but keep the tool handy for now in order to scrape a cache for the discarded equipment. In going to the trouble of hiding his evidence in a hole he was being far too scrupulous on her behalf, he knew that. Why, already this entire countryside would be littered with the evidence of the airdrops. But when she had delivered her thoughts on the secret police he had glimpsed some essence of her predicament, so digging a hole for her was the thing he felt he could offer. Keeping faith. Not much else she had wanted from him, not even his best Virginias.

Have you formed a plan Mister Handles? She was present again.

'I plan to join up with my fellows.'

Why so?

'So that I might feel valid,' he was ready to admit immediately. Yet in his mind's eye it seemed his honest self-assessment made her look away from him, unsatisfied with the answer. So he protested. 'Look, like everyone else I was roped into this military business. You sometimes talk to me as though I could just step out of the world.'

Am I talking to you?

'Yes and no,' he smiled ruefully. Beneath his beech tree he could smell the humus of rotting leaves and hear frogs from a nearby ditch. 'Does your Normandy frog have a viewpoint on the military business?' he put the whimsical question to her. 'Its puddles and ditches trampled through by one lot then another?'

But she had vanished. So he removed from his wrist the useless watch and tossed it with the rest into the weapons bag. Then without moving the bung knee, he plied his trenching tool and excavated a scrape under the tree, placed within it all the treacherous items for which he was responsible, then covered the whole with soil and dead leaves.

'One for the historians when I'm just a stain in the earth,' he patted it down, leaned back against the tree, and tried to adjust his position to ease the ache across his kneecap. Ridiculous wound! Even if he found his own fellows, the injury would make him a liability to them.

They would get him to a casualty clearing post from where he would probably be shipped back to England and nursed until the limb grew strong again. He could see them. Battle-weary under their helmets, some familiar faces missing, they would wish him luck cheerfully, while envying his actual good fortune. And all this, he knew, would make him feel unworthy. But for the interim he would press on, so that he might establish his validity.

Valid for what good? Here she was again.

'Don't,' he said out loud. 'Don't divide me.'

Above his head in the overcast there was a single aeroplane, small, he surmised. He mustn't allow her to overween like that, for all that she was a dear girl.

'Had I stayed with you,' he conceded to her, 'maybe I might have afforded some useful company. We'd get through whatever terrors are imminent for this part of the world together.' Then he reminded her. 'After all, it was you sent me packing.'

For my own dread I can bear responsibility, she reminded him in turn, as the small plane droned in the cloud above.

'Me too,' he replied. 'But maybe my better self should have offered that we keep each other company through the various dreads. So that we might know them better.'

To this she did not respond, though she was present to him still.

'Why should you have the right to face terror on your own?' He asked her, and she was reticent on this question also.

He got to his feet, resuming his way, came after a mile or so to terrain that was unaffected by the flooding. Here the hedgerows and interspersing wire fences of pastoral country replaced the embankment. His progress became difficult, so he decided to risk walking along the road itself. If there were roadblocks, snipers, whatever, then too bad. His boots and his stick clunked on the gravel surface. With luck, his own fellows or the other lot would call out a challenge before loosing off at him.

Now, he scrutinised the sky to his left. Was the horizon starting to brighten slightly? He thought so, limped some more, clunked some more, and monitored that portion of sky on his left hand. Yes, the pallor was definite, the relief of the skyline trees showing more starkly against the background. So now he could locate east and therefore north. That host of ships must be close inshore by now. Dawn, he knew, was scheduled for around 0530am, at which hour the Navy was going to lay down its contribution, an impressive percussion piece, as the intelligence officer had promised during the last pre-invasion briefing.

Alec walked, rested, walked, and after an interval came to a crossroad. Here he turned right down a track that led west, away from the daybreak. The voice of *Mamzelle* in his head had not spoken for sometime. As he lurched along he remained unchallenged, which was a mercy, but the outbreaks of small-arms fire were starting to bewilder him for he was not sure his progress was bringing him closer to battle. The lane's direction seemed neutral. No civilians passed him. If the name of a village should appear, he could start using his map. If there were birds in the hedgerows he neither saw nor heard them. Unnerving, just a little, the clop of his boots and stick, and the bouts of gunfire that appeared to drift around his location.

Maybe he should abandon these lanes and strike out across the countryside. With this in mind he managed to scale a rise and peer through the hedge. He could distinguish a smallish pasture, then a further hedge, a spinney or two of woodland to one side, no apparent dwellings. This was the Normandy *bocage,* as the briefings had described some of the terrain they could expect to encounter. If he struck out across those paddocks in the hope of following a shortcut to the shooting, he foresaw he would have to make interminable detours to penetrate the hedgerows. His crook knee would not tolerate the roughness of ground he could expect. Maybe a signpost or civilian would materialise. What an idiot he was to have left that attic room.

'Would you have thought well of me had I stayed with you?' he asked *Mamzelle,* who provided no response to this. 'I'm trying to locate what the word "honour" requires from me,' he explained for her, and her attentive face seemed interested in the question, but had no ready response for him.

He limp-tramped. At his back the daybreak was the one sure sign of alteration in the world as light suffused along the undersides of cloud, like the white in a fleece's under-wool, pale without particular brilliance.

Then, like some monstrous underswell to the sporadic small-arms fire, Alec heard the naval bombardment commence. For a few seconds there came a series of concussions separated by small intervals, but very soon these had crackled into a continuous thunder, oceanic, unusual, claiming his attention for all that it was remote. Indeed, he deduced, every sentient creature in the region must have been held by this profound bass note, the livestock in the fields, rodents, birds, frogs in their hedgerows and ditches. Momentarily in his mind's eye he saw *Mamzelle* taking refuge in her basement kitchen, her hands over her ears and her nightdress trailing in the floodwater.

'I should have stuck it out with you.'

Her answer to this was peremptory. *The invasion fails, we are discovered, you they take to a prison, I am taken quickly to a ditch and shot.*

It was fearful, the detail with which she could imagine her fate. He was still moved to argue back across the miles, 'But that would be the worst case? We can hope for better fortune.'

She would not comment on the matter of hope.

So he insisted, all but voiced his conviction as he stumped along. 'We can hope for that.'

For some minutes Alec could assume the barrage was raining down on the beach defences to his north somewhere. He could feel the earth tremble but was unable to perceive from his lane any smoke from the explosions. Then he became aware of projectiles passing overhead. He looked up. There was nothing visible. It was more he could sense a violation against the overcast of the sky, and a rumbling perhaps at the edge of being visual. He wondered what network of observers was guiding those shells, which appeared to be falling in the swamped countryside out of which he had limped. Was some fellow tapping the current coordinates of the Boche armoured regiment he had seen from *Mamzelle's* window in the small hours? He wondered if the Boche officer who had waded through the flooded house to buy *la confiture* was under this bombardment somewhere.

Alec continued in his progress along the lane, whatever havoc the shellfire might be causing either falling upon the beaches ten miles away, or passing over him.

His complacency about the barrage ended abruptly when he registered that several tons of earth had been heaved into the air in the paddock immediately behind his hedgerow. There had been an appalling crack-crack-crack, so rapid he could not say for sure he had actually heard it, but the concussions had rendered his ears suddenly ill-tuned to the ordinary sounds of the planet. His strenuous training had never placed him at the receiving end of a remote naval cannonade and it occurred to him that maybe he should find a safe place. Those gunners out to sea appeared to know all about this arbitrary patch of Normandy earth. Why was he not terrified like a rabbit in an automobile headlight? Yes, maybe a safe place.

Set among trees beside the road ahead was a small shed, and to this he hobble-skipped, aware another high explosive round had lifted a picnic-sized patch of countryside into the air behind him. What was going on, from the military point of view? Ranging shots? If the gunners knew something he didn't and he had wandered into the middle of a Boche concentration, surely they would have done for him already.

The shed was locked but he found a smashed window, used the strength of his arms to hoist up and tumble inside. The interior smelled of creosote and hessian bags, contained some farm machinery, with a trough and a quantity of loose straw piled against a further wall. In one corner the roof had collapsed but otherwise the interior was dark. Absurd, he recognised. One H.E. shell will blow this to smithereens. Yet as a third salvo came down nearby, deafening in its force, Alec crawled under a seed drill, hoping its rusty iron would offer some protection if the shelling came closer.

No sooner had he done so than he found himself attacked by some awakened fury.

In the confined space under the machinery, the Australian young man reacted with responsive terror. But in his extremity his mind also allowed him the curious detachment, perhaps also quite animal in its nature, that observed what was happening to him as though at a remove. Here is a hand at my throat, and this has short, strong fingers, apparently intent upon strangling me. The fingers are greasy with some substance. Where is his other hand? Groping for a weapon? I must prevent that hand while getting my own left hand on my bayonet. I have banged my crook knee on a flange somehow and the spasm of pain is excruciating. Or should I try for my service revolver and shoot him through the neck? Well! It seems this is it, the moment I kill a fellow. Or he kills me. So what is his story that we should have met in this way?

He is a Boche presumably. Then where are his mates? Also this fellow seems to be separated from his firearm.

Which means he will produce his knife or his bayonet, Alec deduced as the confined, wheezing, life-and-death combat continued. He has not the strength of arm I have, the Cambridge rugby blue assessed his opponent, dislodging the greasy hand at his throat. I can smell the mud on his uniform, and on his breath the signs of his most recent tucker. Familiar, that smell. Where from? And the hands, greasy from what?

The two men grappled, counter-grappled, the German's head banging on the underside of the machinery. My pistol is impossible, Alec assessed his capacity for manoeuvre. I will have to stick him with my bayonet. If my left hand can be freed in order to get to it. Ah, he appears to have his own bayonet out, a shortish, but sufficient thing.

Now my throat will be skewered and I will go out of existence. This man's face is scarcely twelve inches from my own but he will not look me in the eye. There is a fine bone structure in that face, a blood vessel pulsing on his forehead.

And as Alec waited for the blade to force its entry through the tendons and pipes of his neck, he noted the way a mind relaxes from its furious scrabbling panic toward that inevitability at the last, as though surrendering this life for another, again, of course, an animal reaction, he reflected like a person with all of time before him.

'Genau so gut könnten wir doch leben, wir beiden.'

He found he had put this German proposition to the Boche. How the hell had he contrived it? He had never learnt a word of German in his life. Yet crystalline in his understanding, he knew the gist of what he had said. 'We could also both live, the two of us.' How the ...

And his assailant had become abruptly still, would not look Alec in the eye, but had mysteriously decided he should wriggle backwards, get to his feet as though thoughtfully, jump up into the light of the window and vanish through it. During their dire struggle the shelling appeared to have moved on.

Alec lay back in the straw, unable to quite take in what had occurred. He had averted his death. Somewhere in his reading he had come across the idea that the human mind can call upon extraordinary resources when it finds itself in extremity. But surely those resources have to be within the archive of a person's experience. He knew for a fact he had never learnt anything of the German language. Not a verb, not an iota of Germanic grammar. Why, he had scarcely set eyes on a page of German text. What had occurred in this straw?

I will be arming you still, I think. She had decided to re-open their conversation.

'You have,' he accepted. Recognising her assurance was so simple, such a fragile piece of enchanted stuff, he feared its spell might shatter if he put to her any question at all from the rational side of things. But if the rational side of things was where your natural self felt at home, how had those German words got into his brain?

He fingered the soreness of his throat, and whatever greasy substance had been on the Boche's fingers left its aroma on his own. Yes, the smell was familiar, apple or pear-like.

La confiture! The fellow had been feeding himself jam!

Alec's immediate conclusion was that the crude meal further suggested his assailant was a deserter. Probably he hoped to hide in this shed until the Allies came through, sustained by a tin or two of *Wehrmacht* jam.

The immediate pain from Alec's knocked knee subsided a little as he lay back, regaining breath and composure, nonetheless wondering. From the start it was all too peculiar. Of course he knew that by jumping into war he invited the circumstances of haphazard and danger. The military business was of its nature peculiar. But he had expected the experience, however unimaginable to peaceable folk, would at least be common to …

Well Mister Handles? Common to what? It appeared some aspect of her was on hand to put this enquiry to him.

'To combatants,' he answered her. 'The scrapes I get myself into would be common to those of my lot and the other lot.'

I take you from the common experience to that which is for you alone, she enlightened him.

'You take me, or I take myself?' he asked reasonably.

It is the same thing.

He wriggled from under the seed drill and crawled to where the straw was piled thickly. As he did so, he saw in the straw the fellow's watch which appeared to have come off in the struggle. Busted strap. He put it to his ear and it ticked. The thing would come in useful after what had happened to his own timepiece. Then Alec crawled out further and managed to kick the Boche fellow's abandoned jam jar. A jar, not a tin, here was something! Not unlike those he had been shown at *Mamzelle's*. Hardly surprising in a jam-growing region maybe. He sniffed it; apple, he thought.

11

HAD YOU DOWN AS DEAD

As he sat in the straw gazing idly at the jar, Alec pondered his choices. He couldn't be more than ten miles from the beaches where the landings were imminent if not already under way. Should he sit tight until the invasion troops overtook him? If the assault went to plan, he could expect the forward patrols to find him within twenty-four hours or so. Or should he persist in trying to join up with his Airborne fellows?

'Am I so much of a team player that being on my lonesome unnerves me?' he felt he should interrogate *Mamzelle*. In his predicament, he knew that when it came to making a decision, the presence of just one of his fellows would allow him to squash his foolish inner self.

What self?

Why just that part of Alec Dearborn who could listen to the best advice—*it is better that you are found alive, Mister Handles*—and then ask himself whether, if he sat tight, his life would ever be free from the suspicion he had skulked in his straw bed through funk.

'I have to acquit myself,' he reiterated for her.

And I say, I take you from the common experience to your own particular, she shot back at him.

'I'm becoming aware of that.'

He turned his thought to his Boche assailant. What was he? He seemed to have left precious little jam in the jar. It occurred to Alec to scoop out the residue. But it had been, after all, the fingers of the enemy busy within the interior of that jar, so he placed the thing, unsampled, on the seed drill. Could it have been one of *Mamzelle's* own? Unlikely, in this region of orchards.

And as for the Boche himself? If he were a deserter, he would have wanted to get clear of his own side's concentrations. Logically therefore, if he had sought refuge in this shed, then Alec could assume the lane and surroundings were not teeming with Boche soldiery. On the other hand, if the man was not a deserter, but had crawled in here to snatch some kip, then very soon indeed he would bring back his pals and there would be bayonets probing the straw. If that happened, would his keen intellect oblige with more Jerry phrases to assist him?

He favoured the deserter hypothesis. 'Maybe I'll press on,' he referred his decision to *Mamzelle*, then went to the window, made the best surveillance of the visible countryside he could, hoisted his sound leg through the aperture, and followed more gingerly with his injured limb. Shouldering his Sten gun, taking his walking stick, and with no confidence at all he was pursuing the wisest course, he began limping down the lane.

The bombardment, for all it had passed over, had transformed the world roundabout. In the pasture to his left, where there had been cows grazing, he could now see through gaps in the hedgerow where the black and white beasts were scattered about the place, legs sticking grotesquely upright in the air. The sour cordite smell of the explosions lingered still. On his right hand he saw he was passing woodland, but this had an unusual airiness where the terrific shelling had taken away the canopies of trees. The lane began to wind, such that it was not possible to get a view ahead for more than eighty yards or so. The daybreak was now complete, though the overcast made the light dull like zinc-plated cutlery, the vestigial smoke from the explosions laying a milkiness at ground level and among the stripped trees. Once more the sky was reverberant with aeroplanes, higher, more contrariwise than the lumbering Airborne transports had been. With the aero-whine and the continuum of the bombardment he assumed he would not hear any challenges bellowed at him from the hedgerow. So whatever lay ahead with intent to do him harm would dispatch him without preamble. Just as well, he shrugged, march-limping, step, stick, steppity, stick.

When a vehicle swayed around the curve in the lane behind him he did not hear its approach until it was upon him. Too late to determine which side it might be on. He registered the tufts of camouflage on helmets, a bristle of weapons, and a stretcher case strapped over the bonnet with a mess of blood where an incomplete foot might be. These details were glimpsed in the instant of its passing, for the vehicle, it was a jeep, had travelled fifty yards beyond him before it crackled to a halt.

And here was Ferris no less. He had been sitting up on the spare tyre and now jumped off the back, strode toward Alec, short, fierce, evidently unscathed but for a bandage around one hand, Sergeant Ferris all grins, gorblimeys, and his disconcerting wall-eye.

'Mister Dearborn, sir! I swear I saw you dead.'

The two men shook hands with some vehemence. Alec reminded the jumpmaster how he had bellowed him through the door of the aeroplane. That lifetime ago.

'Dead as mutton, sir,' Sgt Ferris marvelled, standing back. 'You'd bought yours for sure. Last thing I was looking at before I left the Dakota.' He was as certain of the fact as anything in his twenty years of service. 'Made up a list of those who copped one for the medical johnnies, and had you down as dead sir.' He tapped a pocket of his battledress wherein presumably was his list.

'But I'm here, Sergeant.'

'You are, sir. And you shouldn't be.'

'I left the aeroplane before you.' It seemed important to Alec to insist he was alive and could account for the fact. In case he wasn't.

'Dead as mutton.'

'You got out all right yourself, I see.'

'Did indeed! Came down in a tree. Cut meself loose, spent the night walking westward trying to stay on dry land in all that mire. Along come these glider fellows in their jeep. Just before the bombardment started. Got themselves lost from 6th Airlanding. Now we're all looking for the Canadians. Them that was dropped near Varaville. Airborne fellows wandering lost all over the shop. Right cock-up. At least until proved otherwise.'

Ferris was a disconcerting fellow, the way he stood rather more close to a body than one quite relished, scrutinising a person while appearing to be looking beyond. Even so, useful attributes in a sergeant, Alec supposed, needing to think the fair thing.

He was aware of five Allied faces in the jeep, still blackened for the night-fighting, watching him from under their helmets as he approached with Ferris. Fierce bunch, as he supposed he must look to them. He could not make out the man on the stretcher but heard his short, rhythmic moans, like someone pacing himself against his own patience to endure.

Alec explained about his knee and the bare details of his rescue from the flood. Ferris assessed the space in the jeep, made the obligatory offer to squeeze the lieutenant on top of them all. Had to move quick, mind, Jerry, swarming everywhere, poor bleeder on the stretcher copped a bad one, a battalion of Canadians were scheduled to be hereabouts.

You will not go in this jeep. Here was *Mamzelle* again, clear as a bell.

The driver revved. Dicey to hang about.

But here, undeniably, was the company of his fellows. Here he could reconnect with the business he had been rehearsed for. As soon as he had resumed his place among them, he would know how to make up his mind on things, whatever might come up. The military business. He could also use his rank to arrange priorities. Indeed, he could use his rank here to override. If he chose.

You will not go in this jeep, the voice of *Mamzelle* instructed again. So adamant!

And her insistence had brought into his mind the sensation of a perplexing displacement of his being. The jeep of fellows, Ferris, the hedgerow, the overarching cannonade, these were all present, but it was as though he observed them from a remote edge of his existence.

'You fellows get along,' he could hear himself assuring them, excusing himself with the foolish knee. 'Can't fold myself away sufficiently to be an asset to you.'

Ferris seemed relieved. Alec saw the sergeant clamber onto his tyre again, heard him promise they would come back for him as soon as they linked with the Canucks or their own battalions. O that wonderful military manner by which you could promise to arrange convenient pickups when you had a terrain crawling with vehicles and a bit of personal rank. A quick fellow was Ferris, Alec noted, when it came to the prospects for survival. Owe my life to that, he noted dully, remembering the aeroplane.

Yes, Alec could register these observations and yet it was as if the jeep and its occupants were prevented from having full presence in his awareness of self, as if their status was the fugitive substance in a dream. Here was the driver revving his jeep again.

'Sarge?'

The rumble of the bombardment, the growling of aeroplanes continued, while this palpable sensation of foreboding had Alec Dearborn, graduate and soldier, standing in the lane with his military accoutrements, trying to fathom why at that moment he had power to witness, but no power to intervene.

'At the least I had better scrub you from my list I reckon, sir.' Here was Ferris patting his battledress pocket.

'I reckon you had better,' Alec said from his far-off self, watched the vehicle sway down the lane and around a bend, Ferris giving him an uncertain wave.

'Why did you do that?' Alec demanded from *Mamzelle* when the jeep had gone.

She was disinclined to attend to his questions. Was she busying herself at her washtub in the waterlogged scullery? Or was she singing away the brute thunder of bombardment in her attic behind the mirror door?

'If this is premonition, and those fellows are heading for trouble, then their trouble is properly my business too,' he informed her with a force of conviction not to be contradicted. For he knew she would be busy at something. She may have been up all night in his company, but he had learned enough of her person to know she would not sleep through the earth-shudder of this gunnery, supplemented now by the aerial bombing which he could detect as a variant eruptive note to the west.

'If you must intrude upon my thoughts, I think it unfair you should slip away whenever it is convenient to you,' he protested. He was not accustomed to coping with a disembodied voice, and the sheer particularity of *Mamzelle's* presence in his mental process had startled him from the first.

She came back at him in a rush, saying *he is having too much the imagination, she is in attendance, why should she answer each stupid enquiry?*

So he countered her with his notion that, at bottom, he was a dim footballer, that the truly brave were those who could imagine what would come, and were therefore prepared to be foolhardy because they had rehearsed risk in the imagination.

There are no rules for the brave, Mister Handles, she dealt with his notion.

When the foreshadowed event came, it was Alec's training that made his body react rather more swiftly than his foolish knee would allow, made him go for cover in the hedgerow. His sudden leap caused a sear of pain to erupt from his kneecap. He landed in a culvert below the hedge, noted the scurrying of a beetle through the grass stalks, a ladybird open its miniature cupola and fly off before his eyes. I am in pain and ridiculous, his self-appraisal shrieked.

The automatic banging ahead was the nearest small-arms fire Alec had encountered outside training. It was no more than quarter of a mile away. It was a clamour brutal, yet somehow small, like a man rattling a steel poker against the sides of a galvo bucket. The brutality lay in the spasms of it, for by that one knew it was directed with such close calculation, unlike the impression one took from the ambient barrage.

Ah, was he listening to the military business through her ears or his own? A single cr-crack identified someone flinging a grenade or one of those Boche stick-bombs. A resolute thump suggested one of their lot's anti-tank devices. There were no human sounds, no shouts, no screams, just this abrupt clatter. Some event had occurred ahead. Ferris's jeep? Presumably.

He snuggled himself more closely into the hedgerow. The shooting diminished to some random shots and then ceased. Eerie, the silence that hangs in the air when you know an event of consequence has occurred.

'So what's going on?' he asked her reasonably to explain the power of his recent premonition.

No answer.

His thought moved on. If that gunfire was so close, it must mean that these pastures and scraps of woodland were swarming with Boche. If that is the case, why have I not encountered trouble myself? Am I invisible? Can presence simply be suspended? This is idle, he observed how his fancy could both take him and pull him short. As though a person could walk through a battle at that exact moment when the eyes of all who were bent upon seeing him extinct happened to be attracted to some event other than his passing through their midst.

No, he decided. I cannot be special.

Mister, you will be safe. Mamzelle was in attendance, it seemed. He should think of her more specially. Vivianne? Viva? Viva.

'Well, you see, I feel a little unsafe,' he said, wanting her company, trying out whether the syllables Viva worked as a useable invocation for her presence.

And cautiously he looked up through the twisted stems of hedge. If he could ignore the bombardment, the stretch of road seemed quiet. But he judged it best not to try his luck further on the lane. Despite the jam, the slab of chocolate, he was hungry for a meal, for the social semblance of a meal that training had made customary. Fellows around a brew. A hot brew from the cubes with which they had been issued would have been welcome. Fat chance of that.

Where was the larger world? The assault on the beaches may have begun by now though there appeared no let-up in the cannonade and the aerial bombing. There was woodland opposite, those strangely altered trees. If he struck out across that, found a safe hole to eat another bar of chocolate for his breakfast, maybe …

Sleep had a certain appeal too. Was it his job to creep nearer and try to determine what had happened to the jeep? If the Boche had moved on, maybe he could decently collect the dog tags of the poor fellows? Was this his duty? Or was it idiocy? It was idiocy. Starkly his job was to stay alive unless he could be more effective by getting killed. Ignore the fate of the jeep. He would see what prospect the woodland offered for linking up.

Nervously, Alec got to his feet and hobble-hurried across the lane. The understorey of foliage whipped against his jump smock and across the exposed part of his face, and then he had entered the more open, eerily pale wood. Almost immediately he passed a dead fox on the track, its pelt and long tail intact, blood oozing from the corner of its eye.

La bombardement a fait mourir le renard. Why should that not be expected, Viva asked him, reasonably, and because this was her whim, and couched in her own language.

And now, not thirty yards further down the little path, he came upon one of his own fellows suspended by his parachute from the branches of a tree. There was a casual black rose of blood near the man's temple.

Man? The noun seemed unsuitable for such a spectacle of finality. And yet it was the nonchalance in the expression of the eyes of the young bloke that was so ghastly, as though the moment after you have lost your life nothing could matter less. Alec wondered if he should make the effort to climb up to him, cut the corpse down and retrieve this bloke's dog tag? Of course the busted kneecap prohibited such a scramble up the tree, but this did not assuage his sense of what he should at least attempt. He tried to hook his walking stick around the man's boot. It swayed, hopeless, ghastly.

He limped on through the pale wood, came to a wheat field and waded into it. There were craters here and there. He felt very tired and his knee hurt like billy-o. He supposed his presence must be plain to any sniper around the perimeter of the field, but he limped on, now half-persuaded by his fatigue that he moved within some spell of safe passage. He thought he might rest for a little, even kip for ten minutes perhaps, the rhythm of sleep and wakefulness having been entirely disarranged within his person. He lay down with the green stalks of wheat engulfing him, was asleep in seconds, woke to find himself being scrutinised by a dozen or so Boche soldiers in camouflage smocks. One was removing his Sten gun from where it was slung on his shoulder, manipulating the awkward weapon quite tenderly.

'Sixth Airborne?' one of them asked.

They had several rifles pointed in his direction, though he could not say their attitude was menacing. One was snaked about with the belts of machine gun ammunition, glinting coils in the light of the overcast day. Alec sat up slowly, heard himself declare he was bound to give name, rank and number, and did so.

The limit of their English seemed to be '6th Airborne', so he listened to the German they exchanged between each other to see if he actually did have some buried sense of the language that had allowed his earlier phrases to start from his head when he had waited for the deserter's knife to enter him. He could make nothing out. The Boche who seemed to be in charge was gesturing for him to stand up.

'Bitte, bitte.'

Alec obliged, using the walking stick to assist him. They took from him his pistol and bayonet, then began filing toward the further edge of the wheat, their captive hobbling in their midst. His immediate guards adapted their pace to his, and at intervals their comrades stopped to allow them to catch up. At one point in their progress an aircraft came over, quite low and fast, a two-engine job. As a man, the dozen Boche soldiers sank into the wheat, leaving him standing in their midst with his unbendable knee, and when the thing vanished below the tree line they rose, again as a single movement.

'Amerikaner.'

Under their distinctive Boche helmets Alec could see these were evidently seasoned fellows, their faces tanned, their equipment of good quality, their procedures showing a natural discipline. This then, was the other team, his second and more effective sight of them. For two years he had been trained to fight them, and now he was their prisoner, having loosed off not one bullet in the great battle. As he limped along, amiable Alec Dearborn could not remember having ever felt so downcast, so unworthy.

'As though I were neuter,' he made his dull protest to Viva.

Not once has your courage failed you, she felt she should remind him.

'As if I were ashes,' he said, as he push-limped through the wheat.

You will be safe, she said.

'While others are unsafe I do not want that!' He found he was quite angry with her. With himself. Anger, he looked at this rise in him, unusual, misdirected.

There will arrive a reason for it, she assured him.

'I cannot see it.' No never, he reflected, never so unworthy as this.

12

AS THOUGH I WERE NEUTER

They treated him well. When his captors came to the edge of the wheat field Alec found there was probably a battalion-strength of Boche in positions under the hedgerows on each side of another lane. A radio was crackling sporadic messages, the troops lay or sat along the verge below the foliage in that peculiar state of transience with which soldiers can appear at their ease, cooking up a breakfast, while poised to move off at a moment's signal. He was brought before an officer who shook his hand with a curt formality, asked several incomprehensible questions, then indicated Alec should remove the remainder of his webbing including his helmet. The German detailed a soldier to search Alec's packs, where, quickly the man found the cache of American cigarettes and gave them to his officer.

'*Dürfen wir?*'

Their captive marvelled that his permission was being asked, and nodded his acquiescence that they might help themselves. The tin was passed among the dozen or so fellows who had brought him in. Each took one cigarette, then the tin was returned to their officer who indicated Alec should also take a cigarette. In this manner they stood together, lit each other's cigarettes, made various expressions of appreciation at the quality of the American tobacco. With a slightly stagy correctness the officer then put the tin with the remaining cigarettes into Alec's tunic pocket, made various hand gestures, perhaps ironic, to indicate how this restoration demonstrated the integrity of the German army.

As he watched them smoke, take their quick glances at him, make comments among themselves, Alec's sense was less of the presence of enemies as fellows who would have liked a chat had the language difficulty not been there. Outlandish, almost, the way that his war did not conform to an expectation. When two more American aircraft flew over at low altitude, their white invasion stripes visible, Alec observed the entire Boche battalion merge into the hedgerow cover with a single, almost reflexive motion. He was directed to set himself down among them, was brought coffee and a portion of the food they were preparing for themselves. The officer summoned one of his medical orderlies who peeled back the trouser leg in order to examine Alec's knee, and when the poultice of socks was discovered there was some guffawing among the group of soldiers around him.

'*Sixth Airborne! Sehr findig! Ha!*'

He was made to understand how resourceful he had been to steal the socks from the laundry line of some *arme Französin*. The orderly pressed here and there around the knee, then took a leaf from the overhanging hedge, tore part way through this, then showed it to Alec so he might understand his kneecap was *kaput*. With some care the fellow rolled the paratrooper's trouser leg back and re-buckled the gaiter.

The officer made several more attempts to interrogate Alec but it was evident he had no conviction that his questions were being understood. When a vehicle approached down the lane, it was flagged down, and the officer exchanged some words with the driver and two escorts, then handed Alec into their charge. He was permitted to keep the walking stick, and sat on a bench in the back, his new guards having an altogether sourer attitude to him.

Throughout the ensuing journey there was a machine pistol levelled at his abdomen. Several times the vehicle drove to the side of the road to take advantage of such tree cover as existed whenever Allied aircraft made low level passes across the countryside looking for targets. During one stop the larger of his two guards pointed a finger at him, then drew it across his throat, patted his weapon, and nodded purposefully. Alec stared the bully down, conscious how futile such a small display of nerve was. Yes, he supposed they could take him routinely behind a bush and finish him. Bang. They drove on.

'I have been kept from realising my idea of myself,' he told Viva. Where was she now in that rambling house? Asleep, he hoped. No. In a successful enchantment.

His captors delivered him to a temporary cage on the edge of a small town where he was searched again and his cigarettes taken from him, though the deserter's watch in his trouser pocket was again, inexplicably overlooked. A few unlucky Airborne fellows had been brought in already, and during the three days he remained behind this wire, a motley of Allied prisoners arrived, some aircrew, some infantry from the beach landings. They were given little to eat or drink. On the third day of his captivity he was tapped on the shoulder and turned to find himself facing Ferris.

'Took you off the dead list, Mister Dearborn, sir!' the sergeant greeted him, patting that tunic pocket where the list of 'confirmed' was supposed to reside. Ferris, chirpy, unscathed.

'But I heard the ambush.'

'Close as a whisker!'

Do you congratulate a man on life when the several fellows in his immediate neighbourhood have ceased to possess it?

The knack, Ferris expounded, lay in the need to act the moment before, not the moment after you see trouble. He had seen trouble. 'Back flipped from the jeep, sir—parachute roll—equipment cushioning the fall. Other fellows, not so quick off the mark! Now history, the beggars.' As Alec listened to Ferris's shorthand style of accounting for himself, he was struck by the way the sergeant could detach himself so efficiently from the fate of his fellows. 'Scrambled for the nearest cover—woods swarming with Hun—prospects not rosy—figured I should give Jerry the old *Hände Hoch*—landed here— but watching for opportunity, Mister Dearborn, sir!'

Aeroplanes flew over, but they were now beyond earshot of the battle. When the cage was full, the prisoners were taken by a coach to Paris and put in a larger cage where their humiliation could be displayed to Parisians. Small groups gathered to look at them, one woman advanced to the wire, threw over a loaf of bread, and was quickly taken by a guard and led away. Another waited until she was unnoticed and threw in a flower that Alec picked up. He glimpsed a smile before she retreated into the crowd.

The outcome of the great battles in Normandy were not yet decided, but you could see it existed already at a level more profound than expectation in the minds of these people who came to gaze at the Allied prisoners. Alec pondered the confidence in the faces he saw. It was as if an entire population could slip into a dream and skip from the abrupt necessity of the everyday to a take on a slower evolution of processes, a more deliberate serial of events. Some nights it rained on them. The food from their captors was very scarce indeed.

Over the days the number of prisoners swelled, Americans, British, Canadians. In his dejection, Alec preferred to be left to his own thoughts, and he found Ferris's energetic, staccato talk intruded upon the substance toward which his mind was drawn. The sergeant's eyes, *looking at you at the same time as they looked past you.*

The prisoners were taken to a railway siding and loaded into wagons, whereupon they commenced a slow progress into Germany, impeded wherever the lines had been destroyed by Allied bombing. There were days when they languished in the straw on the wagon floor, hearing the shrill and clunk of the wagons as they stop-started. A tin in a corner was used by all in which to pee and crap, and soon the smell was vile. They received occasional food at the stops when the sliding door was suddenly pulled back, allowing the milky light of the Artois to flood the wagon's crude interior.

Ferris had been allotted a wagon further back in the train. Days later Alec heard a whisper that the Airborne sergeant and another man had sawed away with a knife hidden in the NCO's sock and succeeded in making a hole in the wagon's floorboard, then slipped away one night when the train was at a standstill. And a week after this the prisoners arrived at their camp on the North German Plain where Alec spent the next nine months.

Here his knee mended, but not effectively, and he walked with a limp around the perimeter of wires that enclosed them. He took his part in such POW routines as were designed to keep up morale, shouting jocular advice from a touchline at games his inadequately healed injury would not permit him to join. But his brother officers noted his manner was that of one whose centre of being was distracted elsewhere. Attempts to rag him or draw him out brought an amiable smile.

'Get along, you fellows.'

For they could not dislike him, or entirely count on him.

He tried to continue his parleying with her across the distance, but her answers would not come to him as he made his circuits of the compound. In the August sun he watched his face and arms grow brown, in the January cold he watched his breath steam off in the frigid Niedersachsen air. The ease with which, on that first morning, he had been able to imagine her person in any situation diminished to the memory of her white figure leading him through the swamp, hugging his parachute to herself, spectral in her white nightgown. He was anguished by this, her slipping away from his inner eye. Why, if their acquaintance in reality endured only a few hours, was she so dear to him?

Smitten, I suppose, he declared to the featureless horizon.

He meditated upon what had happened to him. His rescue, the restoring of his equanimity, the sudden German words that had deflected the poised bayonet in the tumbledown shed, the extraordinary stridency of his foreboding with regard to the jeep. He could see how, once or twice, one might find in the self some unexpected resource of premonition, or stumble on sheer good luck. But it was the association of *Mamzelle* with his luck that seemed to him a kind of sorcery, and about that he could come to no conclusions.

In early April the guards at the camp vanished eastward. By the afternoon a column of British armoured cars were jolting through the potholes along the sandy road into the camp, mud-splashed, aerials flicking, pennons flying. It seemed to Alec the faces of the crews were significantly younger than his fellow POW's, for all that a mere ten months had elapsed since he had sat with his platoon of blokes, then turned to see the man who had lost his face, and leapt into the night.

13

DEAR GIRL, HE ADDED

Upon his return to England there began in Alec's life an interval of ill health, which put into his mind the idea of his foolish body having recoiled against him as a consequence of his having missed the fighting. For many who returned from the war, a recollection of moments when they had been fighting-mad would give them a lifelong reticence about their experience. They had been valiant only to discover valour can be a paltry or shaming thing in the more generous context of peace. But for Alec, in expectation that battle's experience would allow him to know himself better, he had instead been perplexed by what had happened. So there was letdown. Yet the strangeness of it.

Stepping down from the converted bomber that brought him from Germany, leaning against the rainsqualls that swept the airfield, he found himself being greeted by uniformed folk more sympathetic to him than he thought he deserved. In the ensuing days he collected a new uniform, a ration card and sat at a small table in a great hall where an intelligence officer took down the plainer facts of his experience. He was quartered on a vast camp amid a throng of RAF, army and returned POWs like himself, where everyone seemed fated to stand for long periods in queues, awaiting medical checkups, meals, the cigarette ration. At the canteen tables he smoked, listened to the chat but was disinclined to contribute much to it, not even when the European war ended and he shared a bottle of someone's flat champagne, his legs dangling from a bunk in the Nissen hut dormitory.

'Should we be dancing?'

Dancing, whooping, shaking strangers by the hand and congratulating them for being alive, it was all a possibility as the single bottle passed from hand to hand. Then the moment had passed and the half-dozen men and the couple of WRAF ladies had glanced at each other and exchanged smiles of ironic self-consciousness. Alec thought how some of his rugby victories had been more spontaneously uproarious than this VE day seemed to permit.

Given a week's leave, he took the train to visit Ma's people in Bedford; from carriage windows slashed with rain he gazed at the catkins and buds forming on the English trees. Here was the springtime of the year. His relations fussed him, put tinned ham, pickles, a pear and ginger pudding on the table. As they asked him careful questions about his war, he could see how they watched him for the signs of that 'down-under' nonchalance he had managed for his pre-war visits to them.

'You have your future now, my dear.'

'You're not wrong there, aunt.'

At the end of the week he returned to duty and found he was required to attend a further medical board. In cubicle after cubicle he was tapped, probed, peered at by medical staff desiring his welfare. They had his papers before them with their mention of his rugby, his athletics.

'You're not a married man, Alec.'

'To the best of my knowledge.'

'We want to see you dancing again.'

'Good show.'

The quietly spoken RAMC major purred more than spoke his words, thumbed and pressed Alec's knee-bones, communicated by his modest smile the idea that to be in his care was to be safe.

'This means we must be prepared to take a little trouble over you.'

'I'm game, doc.'

He was transferred to a hospital where a distinguished surgeon broke and reset the patella along its fracture, then immobilised the limb in plaster. There were to be six weeks encased in this white mould.

The surgeon looked down upon his patient. The man had thickly tufted eyebrows, a face that seemed positively muscled with energetic intellect. It occurred to Alec he had been sent halfway around the world to acquire just that kind of energised mind and mien.

'Do you know what I would do if I had six weeks of leisure before me, young man?'

'I can't say I do.'

'I would prepare myself for the brave new world by teaching myself the Russian language.'

'I had hoped for a respite in which to daydream just a little.'

'Hah!' the eyebrows converged. In describing for Alec the imminent world order, this Harley Street gentleman relished the idea of folk being 'up to the minute'. 'In every new phase of civilisation,' the eyebrows explained for Alec's benefit, winding the bandage, smearing the plaster, flecks of it whitening those eyebrows, 'the key is to have access to the lingo of the strange power. *Russki*, in this instance, is the strange power. Learn *Russki*, you'll be a help to the new world, have an assured livelihood, and imbue your life with strangeness.'

'I'll bear your advice in mind.'

If he examined his thoughts, Alec found he rather resented the world's requirement that he be 'up to the minute'. Was he still a young man? He was twenty-seven, but it was as though the substance of his youth had been somehow squandered. Of course Eyebrows was right, if he came to consider the problem of his well-being. As day followed day Alec recognised he really should make up his mind to some mental rigour. For here he was in the convalescent ward where an afternoon could slip by without event beyond the changing angle of light in the window opposite his bed. Occasionally there was a cough from other men in the ward. The suspension of purpose, the enforced inactivity, seemed a continuation of the prison camp. If the food was more regular, it was still fairly austere. Most subversive, however, was this sense of having been put beyond sufficient occupation.

And he was aware how he was troubled by a bit of a cough himself, had brought the thing back from the north German plain. Here it was, growing more persistent as he lay with a book on his lap. He tried to muffle the sound of it through the long night hours so the other blokes on the ward could sleep. Cheerfully the nurses told him he would need to gain weight if he was going to pull a rugby jersey over his head again. When he swayed to the washroom on his crutches he was surprised to discover how short of breath the small exertion made him. At length the Chief Medical Officer decided to send a sample of Lt Dearborn's sputum for analysis and when the result came back Alec was told he had contracted tuberculosis.

'That's a bit careless of me,' he said, passing the diagnosis off flippantly.

'Pure bad luck,' they assured him.

But he looked for pattern in the way the world acted on him and he could not believe this.

Now his cough had acquired a name it was as though the symptoms of the illness became more active inside him. He felt his chest burdened with pleural congestion while his lassitude inevitably made him link his prospects with the doomed consumptives of nineteenth-century literature.

The medical staff dosed him with streptomycin, fussed around him, and on sunny mornings they assisted him to a couch in a carpeted room with bay windows.

'You could just nod off for a spell if you felt like it,' the nurses licensed him.

'I could.'

But it was reverie that took him rather than sleep, sprawled on the old settee that may well have accommodated invalids from the First War. Sometimes in his languor he felt he was a cloud. But then would rise a panic that his active mind might lose all power to summon back *Mamzelle*, or indeed any hold on that part of a life where one existed at the edge of being, say ball in hand and a rampant pack of the other team to fox with a bit of dancing. He looked up from his book to where the staff marched back and forth on the mirrored floors of the ward that lay beyond this bay window suntrap. Watching them clip along with their brisk purposes, he saw clearly that hell was a kind of quiet anguish in a not-quite foreign land. Life for Alec Dearborn would peter out in days, then months of staleness. He knew his treatment was well in hand, and yet how, after the POW camp, the weeks in the ward, could he renew himself?

The news came that his promotion to captain had been gazetted. Yet he had done nothing to justify rising in the world.

'Bear up, Captain Dearborn, sir,' called the day-matron as she passed. These bright-as-buttons English nurses!

'With your irresistible will as my staff, matron,' he replied, trying on the old flirtatious manner. Easy to live two lives, he reflected, the one you believe and the mirage others want from you.

Sometimes, he woke in the small hours of the morning, manipulated his crutches and swayed off between the beds to the washroom. Here he leaned against the mirror, partly filled the basin with water, spat a ball of his saliva to float there while he inspected it for traces of blood. Then he glanced up to stare back at the face in the mirror. It seemed to have grown longer, the eyes not so much tired as dull.

'Mister Handles, you've become a gaunt poor beggar,' he informed himself, hoping the person with whom he had once parleyed with complete candour might hear him across the soft curve of earth.

'Am I talking to you when I cannot imagine you?' he asked next, trying to direct his enquiry toward that exact spot in France where she had popped up from the black waters in her pale nightgown.

'I'm getting good care here. This snaky illness won't kill me,' he offered next, but the face in the mirror remained resolutely his own.

'Ha, Mister you will be safe,' he tried, reminding her of her words.

He took time to frame the next part of his thought, then said to her, 'What kind of an enchantment is it that keeps me safe but removes my power ever to feel carefree again?'

And then he concluded for her, 'The military business would probably have been horrible. But it was my business at the time. I did nothing worthy of the person I thought I was.'

'Pure bad luck,' said the voice in his head, not hers.

So he decided he should stop at this point in his reasoning. He stared into the washroom mirror to see if some figment of her might be found from which he could elicit a response, but he could find nothing in his head for her to say.

O he knew his logic and self-communing was as ill as his body was. On invasion night he had done what he could, surely? How, after the plane took the direct hit, could the course of events in his life have fallen out differently?

Easy-going egalitarian as he believed himself to be, Alec had always been watchful enough to see the deference that came his way from others because he possessed a large and athletic physique. He saw how he was at his most social among the strong and athletic. From the time they had sent him away from Portobello to the school, he had revelled in the triumphs of physique, dashed hither and thither with his foolish body to scoop up a ball, to dodge, fend off, outpace, dummy, kick for touch, score. Wit and limbs in lovely concert. Then later, at Cambridge, he would shuffle various good-lookers around a dance floor, too cocksure of himself to worry about the competence of his waltz or his boogie. As for the parachute training, had he not hurled himself at grappling nets, jumped from a barrage balloon or aeroplane where other strong-seeming fellows had faltered?

Now, as he suffered the military doctors to examine him, or sat dressing-gowned in the July sun, feeling its tentative warmth on his chest, he could not help but associate the comedown in his physical well-being with some personal failure. And the superstition that came naturally to his mind was his peculiarly ineffectual contribution to the battle he had been so carefully prepared for in Normandy. Alec Dearborn, graduate and soldier.

'Bear up! Bear up!'

And they told him he was getting better.

He re-read the Renaissance poets he had studied at Cambridge but could not quite bring his mind to that delectable intensity with which he had first encountered them in his rooms at Pembroke. He sat at an old piano in the sunroom, doodled, tried to think about what he should do with his life. Along with his promotion to captain he had accrued a good deal of back pay. The war in Europe had ended, but there was talk that the 6th Airborne would be sent to the Pacific war. All this medical rigmarole was, after all, designed to make him fit for active service again. Then the Pacific conflict ended with those catastrophes, remote, awesome, at Hiroshima and Nagasaki. Each day the newspapers printed statistics, both from the two atomic events and from the still emerging figures of the death camps of Europe. At the newsreel he had seen the stacked and interleaved bodies of Belsen. The experience left him with a kind of dread, that never again would time allow the carefree interval with this enormity in its keeping.

How can you believe your own life has been preserved within an enchantment when these appalling numbers were the tokens for how casual the difference was between being alive or being extinct?

What right has anyone to be picked out among the millions?

He brooded on these considerations as he stared at the blocks of poetry in the hospital library copy of Quiller-Couch. He tried to bring a clear image of *Mamzelle* to his mind.

When her lose gowne from her shoulders did fall
And she me caught in her armes long and small,
Therewithall sweetly did me kysse,
And softely saide 'dere herte, howe like you this?'
It was no dreme: I lay brode waking.

Indeed, it had been no dream, yet his own daydream was well matched with Wyatt's erotic melancholy. In the room of bay windows there was a battered piano. If he was alone in the room, he took himself to the piano stool and fingered the out-of-tune keys. Tungue. Tung-tungue. The effect was not unpleasing, and he doodled as he tried to talk to her across the fourteen months of their separation.

'If I had been at risk with my fellows, compelled to sudden decisions of shoot or not, I might have done things that made me hate myself. But I would have been acquitted, and my anguish have its place along with the experiences of the other fellows. If I had been at risk with you in your flooded house, that too would have been an experience in common ...' He listened for any response from her that might arise in him. Tung-tungue. 'I wanted to be witnessed.' He waited. 'I could not have foreseen how much I wanted that.' Again he gazed at the keyboard. Tung-tungue. 'Dear girl,' he added.

He examined his experience. It was true that whenever he had trotted onto the field with his first XV, or jumped backwards from a moving army truck, the fact of his physical presence among others had seemed a source of confidence compared to the cruel subversion of self which arose from the outlandish separation he had felt in the countryside after he left Viva.

'Whom will I tell?' he said aloud, then smiled ruefully at how ridiculous he was to allow his ill self-communing to escape him.

You do not need to be witnessed, she replied at last. If he could trust it was her voice. Tungue, tung-tungue.

An airmail letter from Australia was forwarded to him from his regimental barracks.

Dearest Goose, (Bell wrote)

By the time you read this I will be en route to Southampton on RMS *Antonia*, Ma and Nance taking on Portobello while I'm away.

What's in the wind, you ask. Goose, my instinct tells me you are in need of good management. Are you well enough to arrange a bed & breakfast for me near your sanatorium? Get your batman to do it if you have such a person. To get near you will I have to deal with lots of military types?

Pots of love, Bell.

For all its brevity, his sister's message sprawled across most of the airmail's flimsy page. He expected it would take her a month to arrive and had an orderly arrange the B&B. But somehow she had materialised in a week, coming at a clip down his greenish ward, a little more leathery since Alec had last seen her at Circular Quay on the night he had sailed to England in '37. Now he found he had been kissed efficiently and her various parcels in brown paper strewn about his bed. Apparently she had already talked to the Medical Officer and arranged to take her invalid brother to convalesce beside the sea on the Norfolk coast. All this was rattled off brightly in the first five minutes of her being at his bedside.

'So there, Goose! Now we have a grasp on what's going to happen.'

'You haven't changed, Bell.' He gave her his old sidelong look. But she had, he could twig immediately. That leathery, tough minded front; she was placing herself beyond reach of tender regard, as though deliberately, as though impatiently. 'You're wasted on me; you should be running the whole Post-war Reconstruction show!'

It had given him joy whenever she turned up at Hume on a Saturday to watch the game, or on a non-season Saturday, to take him out to a lunch party in Hunters Hill where he might be introduced to her several admirers. His immediate reaction to Bell now, he observed in himself, was one of shyness. That she should see him on his back. That she should see him feeble.

'Incidentally,' he would tilt at her headlong way with him, 'it's also first-rate to see you, Bell,' and tried to twinkle at her. 'That's for sure.' And it was. He could not doubt his allegiance to Bell.

She considered him with amused reproach. 'From what we heard back home, baby brother, we thought we might lose you.' She stated their fears on his behalf matter of factly. Reading her letters at Cambridge and during the war, Alec had sometimes wondered whether that manner of hers was the thing that made blokes shy of her. Was that unfair of him? No. But it was impertinent, he recognised.

'A fortune-teller I met in France promised me I was going to be safe,' he tried to assure his sister.

But Bell ignored his bravado. TB was TB. 'You dress. I'll pack your bag,' she instructed.

Getting dressed in his flannels and sports jacket was like putting the clothes on a person not himself. Compared to Bell's tan, his arms and face were very pale. They took a train and a second train, sat opposite each other smiling, the ice not yet quite broken after all this time. Their hotel had a bowling green at the back, and then the tufty dunes of Hunstanton sands across which almost as remote as Holland, they could discern the sidling tide of the North Sea. On these they walked out, Alec keeping *Mamzelle's* stick by him, more now from sentiment than need, listening to Bell's plans for him, coughing his small suppressed coughs.

'We'll marry you off to one of the Morrison girls, Goose,' she briefed him on her schedule for his repatriation.

'I had hopes of marrying each of them in turn.'

She nudged her elbow into his midriff. Dear, bossy Bell. For the first twelve years of his life, in the relative isolation of Portobello, he had grown up relying on his elder to provide him with a direction for those parts of the day that were not spent in the schoolroom or on duties around the station. And on those occasions when he was not in a complaisant mood, she provided the pretexts for his indulging his stroppiness. He owed what others referred to as his charm to the wiles he must invent to get himself back in her good books after their occasional fights. Bell had a will unyielding as an old anvil. How come at twenty-nine she had not married herself off already? She was a good looker. Yet something in her manner suggested marriage was an unlikely part of her future. Nance was twenty-three and already impatient with her pilot husband, so Bell had told him on the train. Four years younger than him, Nance was the baby and used to arouse in the boy Alec an impulse by turns protective and teasing.

But Bell, forever the elder, required a more thoughtful allegiance. The two of them had shared a nursery before Nance came along, then the nursery had become a schoolroom. When, after lessons, they went out on their ponies, Twitcher and Brume, they could roam an expanse of homestead and pasture they knew intimately, Smoko Hill, The Fiveacre, Turnbull's Hut, Top End. So now, as their shoes sank slightly into the wet English sand, the brittle exchanges of their initial shyness with each other grew from a self-consciousness that they had once been able, fluidly and as a matter of course, to see into each other's mind on all the important matters.

'We've been keeping the place up for you all this while, Goose, but we could start out new if you wanted. Dissolve Dearborn Pastoral, ' Bell continued briskly, 'Go into some specialised line. Yarrawa, Fairy Dell, Rocky Plains, they're all up for sale after the drought. Any one of them you could make a go of.'

The things she wanted to say to him, he recognised, were mostly to do with morale.

'Did I hear drought?'

The brother cavilled with good humour. In contrast to his own fair looks, Isobel Dearborn was dark, with quick eyes and a tensile body inherited from gran's side of the family.

'Or we'll start a ski resort.

'It snows but it doesn't rain?'

'Nina the middle Morrison is your best prospect.'

'And the drought?

'Every day brings a drought nearer to breaking,' she reasoned then said, 'Look, seriously ...' and told him how, after this war the world would want to be warm and well fed again. (Undeniable, if you thought of that ghastly Belsen newsreel). Buy up stock, Bell continued the plan, bank on the rains, make a killing and then erect the marquee for grand champagne occasions. 'Think positively Goose, do.'

As she came out with this patter, he could see where the finer intelligence of her effort to win him lay, how closely she watched him, how she saw without being able to name it the other thing that preoccupied him.

Was his allegiance to Bell one of the reasons the Viva-person had set up such a resonance in his being? Both women seemed able to observe a person at a frequency just below where he watched himself, where the morale flowed and ebbed. Grandiose to call this feminine mystery, he knew, yet he sensed the acuity that lay in both women. How did they do it with their mix of a peremptory manner and the care to see clearly what was still scarcely intelligible to his own self?

He had heard Bell ask, 'Was the war ghastly?'

'For me in particular?'

'Yes,'

'It was the opposite, sis.'

'You enjoyed the fighting?' Her question was suddenly wary of a moral quicksand.

'I was given very thorough training then flicked to the side of the fighting before I could see very much of it.'

'What then, Goose?' she asked, exasperated. 'I'm trying to make sense of your ... well, your absence.'

He gave her an apologetic look. He could see she already knew he did not feel one hundred percent about himself. Yet he wanted to explain it so he could show he had some grasp of his sense of depletion.

'It's as if for the time being I have been located elsewhere.'

'I don't follow you.'

The sister's attitude to her younger brother was that he had always needed more management than care, lumbering and occasionally dreamy fellow that he was. But she had not seen him for eight years and his letters had skated on the comedy of undergraduate or army life. Now his apologetic look, his gaunt features distressed her.

'You might need to warn the Morrison girls off a bit.' He tried to keep the tone flippant.

'Why?

'I think of myself as, well, a bit pledged.' He stopped walking, poked the sand with *Mamzelle*'s stick. Bell turned and faced him.

'Pledged? Have you lost your head to one of the nurses?' For she remembered the way the girls from the properties roundabout had liked him. It was one of the reasons Goose needed managing. The wind from Holland fluttered at their clothing, prevented the sun from quite warming them.

'No. It's the "someone" who said I would be safe. My French fortune-teller.'

'The someone?' Bell waited.

'If she wasn't someone she was a figment.'

'Now you've really lost me.' The sister's protest arrested them in their walk again.

'Bell, I'm trying to avoid, well …' He couldn't see how he could use the word 'enchantment' plausibly. Not with Bell.

'Goosy, you are not an oaf! You went to Cambridge! So explain! I really don't follow.'

All right, he would try.

In the course of the next hour, as they went out to the tide line, then made their way back through the dunes and greens, Alec told Bell about *Mamzelle,* about the hours in her house and his meandering toward battle, about the months that had ensued after his capture. Goose had always had his dark side, but never before had the elder sibling heard him explain a thing so near to his sense of well-being, so unresolved within his person.

When he had finished, Bell stood in contemplation for some moments. 'I find it creepy,' she decided at length to focus on the detail. 'A person can't just begin speaking German if ...' She stopped, and thought some more. Then she decided, 'I don't believe you are hearing voices, Goose. That would mean you were cracked. You have to be making that up yourself.'

'Probably,' he said. And then must instantly correct his moment of bad faith. 'No, Bell, it happened. Take it or leave it.'

'I'll believe you.'

'Look,' and he poked his stick in and out of the sand. 'I have to put my mind at rest about this ... this person.'

'You can call her by her name.'

'Yes. Insofar as I can be confident I know it. You see, Viva spoke to me of her dread. She was not one to overstate her case. She was bold as they come when it came to saving my neck. Didn't like the gunfire much. There's some vile thing bound up in it.'

'You will have to go over there,' Bell told him.

'Too right.' He brooded on his stick and the sand, and said, 'She brings out the anguish in me, I guess.'

'Then we'll do it. I'll come with you.'

There was the army. The 6th Airborne had been sent to the Far East to do civil administration in The Dutch East Indies. At the end of his convalescent leave he may well be required to join them if his demob did not come through.

'Perhaps I could go AWOL,' he smiled at her sheepishly. 'Buy a bicycle and go looking at the spot I last saw her.'

'I can quite see we must settle on something,' declared Bell, unimpressed by the suggestion of AWOL. Their walk out on the sands had returned them to the hotel, and Bell looked down from the tall front-room window to where a group of airmen were playing lawn bowls. She heard her brother emit some shallow coughs in the armchair behind her. After quite a long pause she offered, 'Goose, I'll go to France myself. I'll track down your figment. Or at least find out the worst for you.'

And she would do it. She could bring a project like that off, though the thought of her involvement raised some obscure alarm in him.

'I came down in the dark, sis, and only ever saw the Viva-figment in the dark.' Why must he be nervous at Bell's imposing herself on this?

'You will obtain for me a good map and write down anything that will be helpful.'

'Bell,' he protested.

But as in their childhood, her proposal was already her plan.

She jotted down her schedule. Now it was mid-September. She had an appointment or two in London to deal with. So she would set off for France in early October. Dear, unstoppable Bell, taking charge, yet somehow putting herself in violation of a delicacy, a tact that was required. It was not difficult for Alec to find her the good maps and write down as many helpful directions as he could.

A week later, back in uniform, he escorted her onto the Channel ferry at Dover, then caught the train that would return him to the military business.

14

LIKE A TWIST OF OLD SHRAPNEL

He stayed a night in London and arrived at the regiment's Wiltshire depot on an October day of ragged cloud and downpours. The parade ground gleamed with shallow pools, shivering as the squalls gusted across them, and the four obsolete cannon, one at each corner, pointed their muzzles toward a centre where Alec perceived the compact figure of Sergeant Ferris was conducting a drill for the new intake.

Ferris again, like a twist of old shrapnel. Why, from thousands, should it be Ferris who kept bobbing up in his life? Why were his reappearances … well, troubling?

Alec saw at once the man had noted his presence across the distance. That quickness of eye in the man, like bird, horse, cat, instantly alive to every movement in a vicinity. He watched the drillmaster halt his squad of rookies, swivel them, march them, halt them, double-march, halt, slow-march, those forty-eight boots in spondaic momentum on the tarmac.

'Keep yower eye-ees …'

And the sound corresponding to the syllable '*trained*!' came out as a prolonged diphthong, gusted to where Alec had paused. Not hard to fathom the reasoning for why those eyes should fix themselves to the front. Trust to fate your foolish body. Do not be distracted by whether the foot is placed safely, do not look aside to where horrible injury might zero in on you at speed. Yes, trust to fate your foolish body, in this lay the profound reasonableness of the inane drill. You will be in step, you will be hit or not. The vowels from the centre of the parade ground came like yelps from a Cameroon forest; Ferris, jumpmaster, drillmaster, canny in this most human mystique of preparing raw folk for war. Drill was the staple of barrack life, but Alec found himself watching the behaviour as though with new eyes, compelled by it, fascinated.

'Lay-eff wheel!'

He recognised there was an antecedent for his interest in this. Once in boyhood he had watched a horse-breaker at the Queanbeyan picnic races, mesmerised by the tension between animal and breaker. Round, round, round, back and forth, back and forth, the horse had been impelled by the breaker's twitch of the long lunging rein, the almost offhand click-click warnings of his tongue, or a restrained gesture with the stock whip's heel. It was the energy of that man's attention, the restraint and concision of it! Whenever the horse showed a mind to bolt left or right, the impulse seemed to have been anticipated in the breaker's mind. Alec had stood rapt by the spectacle.

Now here was Ferris with that same quality of attention. Crunch, crunch came those boots toward where Alec watched, the sergeant's bellow almost anticipating the smallest fault in the step, crunch, crunch, and now another yelp, 'Owelt! And they had been brought up, one or two of them still swaying slightly from the momentum of the march.

You measure how far you have wandered into daydream from this, and its like, the newly created captain reflected. But it seemed the sergeant had already arrived before him, pacing stick tucked under his left arm.

'I have you picked, Captain Dearborn, sir!'

An exchange of salutes had quivered, now Alec's hand was being shaken.

'As what, Sergeant Ferris?'

'Well you may ask, sir.'

'I do.'

'As a man with a habit of popping up!'

Alec's hand had been released and the sergeant had stepped back to appraise him. Here was the one eye looking at you, the other looking beyond you. Unsettling. The brass fixtures on the pacing stick gleamed in the louring weather.

'That could be said of both of us.'

Stonily the block of new men stood to one side, the wind at their bare necks. Quick off the mark came Ferris's request. Perhaps Captain

Dearborn sir could address a few words to this shower. Of the inspirational kind.

'From the point of view of a seasoned man, as it were.'

A commonplace request, though it dawned on Alec he was being asked for some kind of enormity.

'If I had done something particular over there, Sergeant...' For all those eyes staring to their front, they were watching, Alec knew, and he could not be seen to recoil, which is what in fact he knew himself to be doing.

'A seasoned man, sir,' whereupon Ferris had roared, the block of fellows had clicked to attention and now awaited this pep talk from the seasoned man.

Here was the collusion. Alec writhed inwardly at the neat, necessary orchestration of it all. How much of it in Ferris was opportunity, how much pure reflex, the seasoned man wondered as he faced the block of recruits. Their khaki shirts were dark at the shoulders where the rainsqualls had come upon them. Facing front, they would not look directly at him as he spoke, yet he knew, reptilian, they watched, had attitude toward him.

'As it happens, nothing very special happened to me after I was dropped into France ...'

And this, true in its modesty, was an outrageous lie too. *I take you from the common experience to that which is for you alone.* How could the thing that had actually happened to him have been more special? In their shirtsleeves the squad stood immobile, yet a glance told you they were cold. Behind their bare heads a milky weather front was bringing a further downpour. Were they not entitled to the truth, in this instance not a dreadful truth but a strange one? For all his instinct, Alec was insufficiently prepared to give a true account of himself, instead concocted his pep talk from such convenient platitudes he could dredge up. He heard himself use the word 'honour', knowing how his own precise experience had entangled him in a conundrum to do with honour, yet here he allowed himself to pass it off casually as an obvious thing.

He watched himself, of course. How fatally easy it was to proceed with the best of reasons, into untruth. How promptly you could find yourself making good-natured noises for the encouragement of others, allowing yourself to be passed off as one thing when happenstance had made you quite another. *In this facile way I outrage the part of myself I most wished to keep intact*, he accused himself.

'Will that do?' he asked Ferris when he had finished.

It would do. The miserable shower had heard the words of a hard-case Australian cousin, the sergeant informed his squad. He turned and shook Alec's hand once more, one eye appraising the hard-case Australian, the other looking through him

In the adjutant's office Alec was told his demob had come through. He could keep a room in barracks for the few days he might need to sort out what he would do next. Return to Australia? Not sure? Well, there were jobs for teachers and officials in the civil administration being set up at Bielefeld in Germany, in case he was interested.

'I'll need to come up with something.'

'I've no doubt you will.'

He sat through the dark afternoon, smoking, drinking tea in the canteen. He should celebrate his demob by going on the razzle, but with the exception of Ferris, the faces around the depot were all new to him. Toward evening the sergeant came and sat down at his table and Alec heard how, having hacked his way through the floorboards of that rail-wagon, the man and his companion had lit out across country, been found by the Frog Resistance, taught those lunatics a lesson in the effective handling of explosives, in time had been overtaken by the Yanks, shipped back here too late for the Rhine crossing show, been drill and weapons instructor since, and was looking for an opportunity if truth be told. Canada, Australia. When Alec suggested they might walk out and find a pub, he learned to his surprise that Ferris was teetotal, apart from the occasional swig to put heart in the lads.

When they stood to part, Alec found his hand being wrung a little more warmly than he thought his intermittent acquaintance with Ferris quite merited.

'Picked you, you see, sir. A seasoned man.' He insisted on this ridiculous view. 'Seasoned men both. We'll bob up safely just as long as we can look each other in the eye. Is that not right, Captain Dearborn, sir?'

'It's back to mister from now, I suppose.'

Ferris ignored this, saluted, and departed. Was Ferris a sentimentalist at heart? Alec wondered, as he listened to the sergeant's boots recede down the aisle between tables. It was still early, but the seasoned man went to his small room, lay on the bed with a book open. He felt no emotion at leaving the army, but what should occupy his life? On the page he read,

It was no dream; I lay broad waking:
But all is turned, thorough my gentleness,
Into a strange fashion of forsaking;
And I have leave to go of her goodness,
And she also to use newfangleness ...

Then he slept, in the morning wrote letters, to Ma and Nance in Australia, to his bank, to Colfax in India, and a wire to Bell in Paris. After that it was a case of returning his kit to the quartermaster, catching a train to Ma's people in Bedford, waiting there until Bell turned up.

15

I COULD TAKE YOU DANCING

Of course it was preposterous. But whichever course he might choose for his life now depended, Alec recognised, on what Bell would find in Normandy. He took walks beside the River Ouse, felt his existence was like a thing locked inside amber, a life withheld while allowing him to see vividly how he was being somehow cheated of its potency. Yes! This was the transformation that was occurring in his being, the spell. He looked, not to how he might act, but how he would be acted upon. And grimly he was fascinated by how his surrender to this fatalist outlook affected him. His health appeared to recover, but he could not say this was quite true of his sense of well-being.

For three weeks Bell stayed away, the only word from her being a plain postcard.

… Have arrived at Caen. Dear God, is there a taxi can negotiate these bomb craters? I'll look into bicycles. In Paris I saw bullet scars on the public buildings. Imagine that kind of thing on Sydney Town Hall! Horrid. So, tomorrow I cycle or march to look for your girl. If she exists, Goose. This is all a bit mad, n'est-ce pas? Love, B.

He read her energised phrases and a week later he had received a wire from her that took him to Charing Cross Station to meet her train. Here she was, advancing toward him at a smart clip, the carriage doors opening and slamming behind her. In his new civilian status, he had put on an overcoat, pulled a trilby down across his forehead and his sense of himself was of someone provisional.

'You look like a secret service person,' Bell greeted him.

'I'm one of those who watch the watchers,' he returned, touching her gloved hand.

'O Goose, I haven't been much use to you at all.'

She handed him her small suitcase to carry, then tucked her arm under his and they walked through the crowds together, sidestepping wherever the crosscurrents of commuters, troops in greatcoats, seamen laden with kitbags, impeded their progress.

'Did you grow so very fond of her?' Bell needed to raise her voice against the terminus hubbub.

'You could say,' he conceded.

Knocked out of his tree might have been nearer, but what right did he have to that self-preoccupation when there was all this everyday purpose eddying around him. Loudspeakers boomed unintelligibly. Here were people hurrying toward destinations, coming off night shift, living between bombsites, with rationing, with empty places at table?

'It was all in the dark.' He tried to make the thing small. 'Perhaps it was too tenuous.'

'We'll find some breakfast,' she suggested. 'Then I can report.'

They took a taxi, to a middling hotel in Chelsea, booked two rooms, then went down into the dining room, and sat at a table.

'The cooked breakfast lovey?' declared the elderly waitress. It was a question of what was available.

Alec lit a cigarette, sat back and looked expectantly at his sister.

'Well,' Bell opened. 'At least your girl is not a figment. She is Vivianne Orbuc. Her house where you went had once been the local priory and is still called *Le Prieuré Saint-Emile*. I suppose this accounts for all its rooms, they were once the cells for the friars. With its buildings it forms a hamlet in the countryside outside a village called Robehomme.'

'You met Viva?'

'I met some farming folk and a housekeeper. When I said I was the sister of an Allied parachutist, the keeper became quite chatty. So far as we could understand each other.' Bell paused. 'Goose, look what I'm coming to is the fact that your girl appears to have vanished. *Elle a disparue en Allemagne.* That was the opinion of *Madame la concierge*.'

'Right,' he said numbly. His first thought was that her dreads of that night had become actual, and Gestapo thugs had come through her house, found the parachute or some telltale of his presence and packed her off to one of the vile camps. 'I should have stayed on with her.'

'She went off to Germany of her own free will.'

'Ah.'

'The housekeeper was adamant on the point. She went *de bonne volonté*. I couldn't tell whether she was scandalised she had gone off with a Jerry, or amazed that anyone would take on all the zone and frontier difficulties attending such a move. Goose, I thought all French people detested the occupation of their country.'

'My girl, as you call her, had her own way of looking at that.'

'It would seem.'

'If she was going to do something it was going to be …' Alec looked for a word, '… cross-grained.' Indeed he could picture *Mamzelle* on some bleak railway platform, suitcase at her feet, an ash-and-charcoal dawn behind her. He looked at Bell and said, 'Do you think I'm an idiot for feeling dismal? I was in her company for no more than a few hours.'

'She saved your life,' Bell replied, 'and you felt happy when you were with her. Of course her bunking off makes you feel wretched.'

The brother smiled wryly at his sibling's crispness. For some moments they were distracted as the elderly waitress brought two cooked breakfasts and placed them down before each. On the plates lay an insipid white shape lapped by a pale liquid and accompanied by a yellow slab of something vegetable.

'The sturgeon, Ma'am?' the brother enquired, rolling a languorous eye and ashing his cigarette.

'Snook 'n' hash, lovey.' And was gone.

'That'll teach you to try on your dandy university drawl,' declared Bell. How deftly Goose could claim her allegiance, as when she used to take him to some swell restaurant during schooldays, and he would put on this suave impertinence for her benefit. Now his purpose was to show her he was his bright self, resilient. How old was he when she first remarked how he would use his flippancy to disguise some injury to his well-being?

'Well, this looks dandy.' He had picked up his knife and fork and was poking tentatively at the fish on the plate. 'So, Germany, says the housekeeper. Was there a forwarding address?'

'I was given a post office number. A town called Detmold. No-one quite knows whether the postal service between countries is effective yet.'

'A town and a number is something.'

'The unbearable thing is, I may have missed her by less than a fortnight.'

'Can't be helped.'

As he picked at the meal, he wondered whether, had he gone to France himself, *Mamzelle* might not have materialised from one of those rooms in *Le Prieuré* with the same sorcery by which she had turned up when he was drowning. That it took his distinct presence to effect her apparitions.

Daydreaming lunacy. People are present by necessity, the plain-thinker reminded the dreamer.

'Goose, this will only make you more wretched, but there had been an incident.'

'Incident?'

'Was your girl notorious?'

'How so?'

'Too flirty with the Jerries?'

'Flirty? They were billeted in her house and used to buy her jam,' he defended. 'What was the incident?' But it was clear enough to his imagining, and sickened him.

'Something cruel. The housekeeper seemed ashamed of it, as did the two or three folk who had gathered where we did our talking. From their faces it was clear I was not to be trusted with the facts. Do you know what might have happened?'

'I can guess.'

'What?'

'If they thought a woman had been too friendly with the occupying power, they used to make a public show of her by cutting off all her hair. Call it the spontaneous penal code, it's one of those conventions in the undercurrents of dear, placid, daily life.'

'It's sanctimonious bullying,' accused Bell.

'The practice goes back to Louis the Tenth. '

'I hate history. You have events and then you have undercurrents. As though no-one could ever make a choice.'

'She had a notion she might cop this.'

'Did she do something unspeakable?' asked Bell, indignantly.

'She fished me out of the swamp,' he said, wanting again to lighten their talk to an easier, somehow more Australian exchange. But Bell, fresh from spacious Portobello, was aggrieved by the idea of people having their hair shorn off in any circumstance of peremptory retribution. Perversely, Alec continued to relate what he knew. '*Une femme au turban* was the term they used for it. The victims would cover their baldness with a headscarf which in turn made them conspicuous in public.' And then, because he could never help himself wanting the roundness of any account of matters he gave, he added, 'My girl got her name Viva from those Germans who were billeted with her.'

'You can call it a convention, but it is still vile.'

'I'm not disagreeing.' He had pushed away his plate, half-eaten, and poured them both tea.

'All the more vile,' Bell continued headlong, 'because those folk were so sheepish about it. They were ashamed!' Momentarily Bell seemed to glare at him. He saw her depth of feeling. And all on behalf of his misused girl. She had not even managed to meet Viva, yet the 'incident' whatever it was, had crystallised for her the war's vileness. Ahead of the Belsen evidence? It seemed so. And it seemed that the currents of her feeling were proper in this, that here was injury affecting the well-being of her own kin. Now Bell was accusing herself. 'I should have seen how they were covering up all their reptile hatreds. Why can I never see the undercurrent of things?'

'You do. You know you do. You're up to the minute.'

The assurance caused Bell to glare in his direction again. It was hard to fathom her evident depth of feeling. She had been living twelve thousand miles away from these reptile hatreds. If he was not careful he might clash with his sister. Abominable things had been done and who was Alec Dearborn BA to say that those who had misused Viva were not compelled by some necessity? And here he was taking an opposite side to his own interest. That was a tolerance, he saw, that roused Bell's impatience. Wrong was wrong, and to explain was to excuse. If a crowd of otherwise fair-minded folk marched some out-of-step poor bastard toward a casual bullet, they were not to be explained away. They were vile bullies. This was different from the reflex of the 'fair go' he inherited from Portobello. It was an attention to even-handedness, learned at Pembroke, and he could see how it had put just a little distance between himself and Bell.

'Could you discover much else?' he asked.

Bell told him how, after the incident, Vivianne Orbuc had kept herself out of the scan of the people roundabout, though was seen occasionally in her orchard or among the canes of berries. The harvest of fruits had occurred in September and October *comme d'habitude*, as the housekeeper wanted to establish. Next thing, *La mademoiselle a disparue en Allemagne!* 'When they shrugged their shoulders, it seemed to sum up their attitude to her. Your girl did not have many allies.'

'Is that what they called her? Mademoiselle?' he asked.

'They said, *Mademoiselle.*' She glanced at him quizzically.

'Ah! You see, *Mademoiselle.* My damsel. That's agreeable, don't you think?'

This was Goose's Cambridge whimsying, and Bell listened because it was Goose, who had been sent away to acquire mystery. But why should mystery count? She knew herself not empowered to quite say.

'You see, when I was in the dark there I couldn't ever give the person an age. Viva could have been young, or old,' and after a moment's reflection he added, 'or both.'

They had pushed their plates aside. Bell now gave a cursory description of her own expedition, by rail to Caen (what was left of Caen after the bombing), by bus to Bavent where she was able to take a room, borrow a bicycle, and go off into the Normandy countryside.

'The floods you encountered were gone. I located your girl's place on the second day and all I knew to look for was a music teacher who lived near orchards and manufactured jam …'

He had neglected to appreciate the trouble she had gone to. 'Bell …' he began.

'Rather pleased with myself, in fact.'

'You've been bonzer.'

But for all his compliments, she could see he was preoccupied with the unalterable fact his Normandy girl had vanished, in short that he was crestfallen. She took her napkin from her lap and folded it again to indicate she had done with the cooked breakfast. 'Goose, when I catch the ship back to Australia, let's arrange a couple of adjacent cabins. I can book. You're free here, from the army and all.'

'What should I turn my hand to in Australia, do you think?'

'I've said. We run Portobello as a team, grow rich from making everyone warm again. You'll run for the Senate and be made minister for something.

'Minister for Daydreaming,' he supplied.

And again it was that sidelong smile but she could see the suavity was troubled. O yes, she had cast him down with her news, as she had when she came down to the school with responsibility for telling him about

The Dad. It was unfair how she had to be the one bringing ill tidings into his life, causing the effect on him.

'It will be for the best, Goose. Your own people,' she countered his flippancy.

'You say you had a post office number.'

Now she looked at him with reproach. He was not going to be swayed toward what was evidently his good. At length Bell rummaged in her bag and produced the slip of paper on which were various numbers and the word Detmold.

'The person she is with in Germany is a Jerry she knew in the war ...'

'An army doctor who likes jam.'

'You met him?'

Alec shook his head. 'Saw him at a distance. Probably.' It was better not to add that it had been in his mind to shoot the fellow. No wonder *Mamzelle* had been a bit short with him when she had come back up the stairs. The bloke had been a lover—except that didn't seem to square either.

'Goose, it's bad luck, but you walk away from it,' Bell tried again. 'I'll make a booking at the shipping office. We'll sail away from ...' she indicated their plates, 'The Land of Snook 'n' hash, lovey.'

He would not be deflected. 'I'm surprised you didn't run into the man she called papa at this priory.'

Bell looked puzzled. 'He was killed in the weeks before the invasion. At least that was what I understood by the housekeeper referring to *le père assassiné*. I assumed you knew that bit.'

'How killed?' Here was more chance illumination. The sheer weight of tension on her that night.

'I didn't think to ask. *Assassiné*? Whatever that means in a war.' Bell shrugged and looked at Alec interrogatively.

'She put me into his nightgown.'

And helplessly he must see how utterly alone in the world she had been that night, dealing with the practicalities, singing herself into her enchantments.

And with helplessness Bell regarded him. During the eight years Goose had been away from Australia the profile of his head had lengthened, she saw, his drawl and manner grown more defined. What did he know now more than he knew when Ma, Nance and she had farewelled him on the ship in '37? Heaps, probably, English poetry and European history, and army business.

'You know, I don't think calling her my girl is quite the proper thing, Bell.' For the moment he could not quite look in her direction, but took another cigarette from his case.

'No.' She stared down at the two plates with their leftovers then directed their focus to immediate concerns. 'Euch! This meal was most unusually awful.' Alec could see she was worn out by it all, the night-trains, the bad breakfast, the low spirits she must cause.

When she looked at him again she saw he had straightened in his chair with a determination to be of good cheer.

'Here's what we'll do, Bell. You catch some sleep then we'll go on the razzle.'

'Is the razzle possible in the land of Snook 'n' Hash, lovey?'

'We'll go to the cinema and look at a flick, then I could take you dancing.'

She gave a smile, agreeing, but not happy that she had gained her larger purpose.

When she met him later that afternoon in the foyer she presented him with a small bottle of calvados. 'I was instructed to present this,' she explained. 'From *Mme la concierge* to *M. le parachutiste*. She wanted to thank your lot for dropping in, I think.'

He put the bottle in his pocket and they went out arm in arm. In the picture house they sat in the back row, passing the bottle between themselves, growing giggly at the over-acted gallantries and over-large faces on the screen. Emerging from the dark into the grey-blue of the late afternoon, their sense of time diffused by the effect of the liquor they sat on a park bench eating fish and chips from a newspaper wrapper, finishing off the calvados. After this they went in search of the Odeon dance parlour where Dearborn brother and sister jitterbugged to the strains of a jazz quintet, Bell allowing her educated younger brother to whisk, fling and catch her efficiently in a dance more acrobatic than intimate.

In the uplift of his spirits, he said, as he twirled her, 'Did you ever see a human knee so restored to take on the world?' and the smile she flashed him in response was a gladdened illumination of her face.

And later, when they said goodnight in their hotel corridor, in the comedown of his exuberance, he confided to her, 'And yet, you see, I have the notion that anyone who looks at me these days must be peering at me through glass, Bell. Do you think that?'

She stood attentive, but gave him no response this time, her profile dark against the small light in the foyer at the end of their corridor.

In the days that followed they spent time with Ma's people in Bedford, made excursions to notable sights. But Alec had the sense that a purpose had weakened in his sister. Wonderful to be with Bell, but why exactly had she crossed the seas? Because in Australia they thought they would lose him? Well, he was back on his feet, if that's what they had meant by 'lose him'. Then again, there was the trouble she had taken on his behalf in France. Generous, but he couldn't quite fathom the intentness of her effort.

He showed her his rooms at Pembroke and afterwards they went to a teashop in Trumpington Street. Here, as though unable to help it, Bell tried again to engage Alec on Portobello, or a ski resort venture, any enterprise that would transpose him from the dark of British streets to the airy Australian tablelands.

'Full marks for trying to reclaim me, sis,' and he grinned at her with his head tilted on one side.

'How dare you, Alec Dearborn!' she reacted, suddenly angry.

'What?'

'Look at me as though I am a creature in the monkey cage!'

'I deny it,' he said, the quizzical smile remaining. 'Categorically.' But he was in trouble, he knew, for she only ever dropped the 'Goose' when she intended to have a real go.

And this she now did. His mental paralysis was self-indulgent. His hankering after the Normandy girl was foolish.

'How can you? What right have you?'

'Drop it, Bell,' he tried, mildly.

'You went away from us with all those prospects! Now, I do believe you wish to destroy your chance in life deliberately.'

'Bell.'

'Why? Because it amuses you to be forlorn.' She gestured toward the colleges visible from the teashop window and accused the university of having brought about this mental feebleness.

He wouldn't answer. Her accusations cast too widely for him to be able to mollify her irritation. Then she raised an aspect of the matter that had not occurred to him. She asked him what was going to become of her.

'You'll marry, of course!' he retorted. 'Some lucky fellow.'

He took her first reaction to be a scowl because this was his expectation. But in fact she was crying, silently crying, and this astounded him. He had seen her tears of vexation in childhood, but never her grief. There was no outward show of grief from Bell at The Dad's funeral. She had been his favourite, and knew it, but as they had stood in the cemetery above the river, cicadas loud in the unkempt grass, Alec had been conscious of her, dark and somehow retracted beside him. How was it possible he could now affect her so?

'You bastard!' She was repeating the word. One or two people on neighbouring tables had heard. Being Poms, they would recoil from the word, but react kindly to her distress. Some one was bound to get up and offer her a handkerchief or, with a soothing cluck, pour another cup of tea for her.

He decided that he preferred to avoid the solicitude of the Poms right now, so quickly he went to the counter, paid some shillings. By the time he returned Bell's grief appeared under control and they left together. As they walked quickly along the pavement he put his arm around her shoulders because he was moved by her emotion and had only this clumsy gesture in his repertoire, which she accepted.

'I don't really understand what I did, Bell,' he said.

'You did nothing. I was stupid,' she replied.

16

MY LOVE, YOU CAME IMPROBABLE

'Stupid,' the older sister accused herself again when she closed the door of her room behind her that evening. Why should preposterous Goose cause her to get so riled?

As she put her clothes away Bell caught her reflection in the wardrobe mirror. Did she take Alec's allegiance too much for granted? Why should she not, given the valley solitude they had shared for the first dozen years of life?

'Goose's well-being is my province,' she asserted to the mirror.

As her own quirky being was his. How could it be otherwise when she could remember, say, a toddler getting to its feet and making first steps from Ma's cane chair to the veranda post, when she knew he was watching her, wincing in sympathy as cook dabbed iodine onto her grazed knee, when she watched him, a gangly boy with his bravura behind the window of the upcountry train, off for his first term at Hume, lonely with his trunk of possessions.

'Save up things to tell me!' she had called, and Goose's twelve-year-old smile, had been undisclosing as an old rabbiter's. Now he nonchalantly tells her she will marry. Perhaps she would. Even so, he had no right.

Too bad, she reflected. She had come across the seas to reclaim him from war and sickness, to return him to the pastoral existence for which she thought his nature best suited. And her efforts hadn't worked. It was as plain as that. If Goose was set on this … this squandering of himself, there was no reason to allow her own presence of mind to slip.

She had conceived of her appointments with wool-merchants in London and Huddersfield as a means of reawakening in Goose a sense of Portobello and its fine wool having a place at the core of their interests and being. The effort, the unsatisfactory talks, seemed paltry now. Very well! She would take an earlier steamer if one could be found, go home and run Portobello for that reward from life she wanted for herself.

Whatever that was.

Or she would sell the station to pay for some likelier enterprise, a ski chalet, a riding stables.

So why should the contemplation of this injure some part of herself? Because (Bell was bold enough to see) the altruism with which she had sustained their Pa's enterprise during the Cambridge and war years now seemed undermined. So be it. If these dealings wounded her feelings, she would accept the injury.

'Because,' she glared at the mirror and accused their childhood pastoral on Portobello, 'to lock myself inside a time of enchantment would be so … so wastrel.'

In the morning she waited at their breakfast table until Alec came down. Was this trimmed fellow, proceeding between tables, her Goose? At some level. She told him her plans, then spent the next few days making arrangements.

'Fair go, Bell,' he protested, seeing how these decisions were a criticism of himself.

Late one afternoon brother and sister arrived at Tilbury, stood at the ship's gangway, he with an overcoat and his trilby pulled down over his eyes. An easterly from the Urals seemed to funnel up the Thames estuary, probe the unprotected parts of their clothing to enter and chill them. Westward toward London the overcast contained rifts of mineral crimson.

'You continue to look like a spymaster,' she remarked carefully, her own collar up against the December weather.

'If only I could be that devious.'

His sidelong smile reminded her of the departing schoolboy, a smile too old for itself. It tore her. Putting her matter-of-fact aside, she asked, 'What will you do, Goose?'

And he answered, 'Do you reckon the Pom Civil Service might put up with me for a while?' his hands deep in his pockets, not quite willing to meet her eye.

'I can tell you are intending to go to Germany.'

For this was her obvious deduction and hardly needed his acknowledgment.

'I can't drop the business, Bell. I want to see where I get taken.'

The last-minute passengers passed them, struggling up the gangway with suitcases, hat-bags. Bell looked at her hands, suddenly shy with him. 'I know what I said earlier, Goose, but…well, your life seems to be all undercurrent and I can't pick up from what I knew.'

For had she not seen from their shared childhood how powerfully on occasion he could take a fancy and follow its subterranean inclinations? *Hey Bell, what d'you reckon if…* As though the unlikeliest notion must eventually come out in daylight and announce itself as the most necessary thing on earth.

'I'll come back to Portobello in a year or two depending,' he assured her, shyly, for her upset in the teashop continued to unsettle him. 'We could look into the resort business. You know, when I've settled.'

'I will probably have sold up by then,' she told him.

'Bell!' For now he must protest, not because the patrimony bothered him, but because in that slip he saw how he had injured her, Bell, his companion from the numinous years. And the injury was not a casual thing as it had been in the past. She was more than stroppy, she was angry. He loved Nance of course, and Ma, it went without saying. But Bell had been there for him, and now must remind him he was at a division of ways.

In this post-war era it became no longer unusual for an Australian to find himself engaged in the schedules of nations that were remote from the interests of his homeland. One such was Alec Dearborn, BA, who was accepted as a personnel officer into the Pom Civil Service to assist in the setting up of the British Forces Post Office (BFPO) as part of the Zone infrastructure in post-war Germany.

Casually Alec had noted on a map of Europe how the German town of Detmold was one of several in the neighbourhood of Bielefeld, and Bielefeld, it seemed, was where the British Zone had its HQ for the time being. It might be convenient to contrive a posting to this garrison, a career move which, by February, he had effected.

Here, he was given a small office equipped with a typewriter and a telephone. He took notes at meetings, requisitioned weighing scales, date stamps and other PO paraphernalia, inspected premises, and managed personnel in the various outlying garrisons of the British Zone. He took a room in a house on Heeperstrasse that had survived the bombing, ate his meals in the temporary officers' mess, was judged effective by the colonels and brigadiers with whom he liaised, while his easygoing 'down-under' manner made him liked by his colleagues. After all, it was a piece of cake, setting up a PO for the Pom military …

'… Compared to chasing merinos round the paddock,' he might stir them mildly. Sometimes he would try to describe his part of Australia, the streaky, silvery, airy, dry spaces of his pastured and lightly timbered country, sheep standing immobile in fog as the crows called mournfully through the whiteness. He tried, after nine years away from it, to capture the remote magic of it for them.

'Can't imagine it, old man,' one or other of them would say discouragingly, at home in these large lounges of dark panelling, the close air smelling of gravy and cigarettes, and tolerated his lyrical attempts as the colonial impulse to offer proof that the underside of the planet was indeed authentic. 'A land brimming with opportunity, they tell me.'

In this way the job allowed Alec a certain amusement at his situation in life, an Australian, not estranged from his homeland, but kept from it because of an outlandish encounter and the notion he had formed as a result. Of course Bell was right. This Germany job was contrived so he could pursue that strangest part of his fortune, one altogether remote from considerations of livelihood. A hopeless notion, maybe, but he had to resolve the business if enchantment was what the notion was.

With his knee now restored for the sport, Alec devoted his Saturday afternoons to rugby, became the tall, bandy-legged fly-half for the garrison side, on a pitch improvised from the neighbouring German town's park. Leap and catch, run and swerve, the game afforded him respites where he could live at the quick of himself again,

But Sundays he set aside for the mystery that preoccupied him. Taking the entire day, he would take a bus to its end-point then wander into the *Teutoburger Wald*, seeking any glade or riverbank in that vast forest where he could smoke, drink Bovril from a thermos and read a book. More than anything, on these walks between the grey and russet verticals of the conifers, under the crooked bare branches of oak and beech, he attempted to find in himself that attentive passivity of mind by which he might regain Viva's presence in his thought. If he could find that passivity, that quality of attention, might he not learn the delicate mental exercises by which he could summon evanescent things? Alec assumed it was necessary he be undisturbed by other human beings in these journeys of introspection, so took trouble to find places that were hard-of-access. In the new year the snow lay lightly on each side of his track, a white sleeve of it on every horizontal surface. In late March the bare black branches of the deciduous trees flickered yellow with the spring's flush of leaves. Sometimes deer would watch him at their distance through the trunks, or a squirrel in the fork of a tree. Rarely did he encounter other folk, indulging his superstition that if he pursued solitude far enough she might, in Ferris's terms, 'pop up,' at least as a voice in his head. But his assumption about isolation proved wrong.

During one of the Saturday games, momentarily, he saw *Mamzelle* amid a clump of spectators on the touchline.

A fine drizzle had greased the ground, turned the ball slippery as kelp. The match was against a side from the French Zone, had been close-drawn, hard-fought, and something electric in the contest had attracted a more than usually large crowd of the off-duty British conscripts, civilian staff, together with a few Germans from the town. The clamour along the touchline in turn heightened the tension and swiftness of the play.

A few minutes before the whistle for full time, the ball tumbled from the back of the pack. Alec at fly-half, was watching for what the scrum-half might do. He saw him scoop it, feint a pass to the left, then take off down the blind side. Alec followed.

Here was that old elation the sport aroused in him. An instant to guess an intention and make a move. Agility of intellect at one with agility of body. A team as though behaving with a single intuition. And here was the complement of his nature, the dynamism in balance with the dreaminess.

He saw the scrum-half clear the French forwards, again feint left, then swerve right. A couple of French backs came at him, would push him over the touchline into that straggly hedgerow of khaki uniforms and raincoats. There he goes, but, timing perfect, he had half-turned and shot the ball back to Alec, who scooped it, heard his three-quarter behind him and to the right, the boots of the pack behind also. Boot-gallop, lovely under-music to the crowd's bellowing. Alec did his own feints, dodges, fended one of the French forwards as he came in, was now being brought down, turned right to shoot the ball to the three-quarter.

There! In that instant of turning!

Unmistakable, surely. In a pale raincoat belted at the waist, a gypsy-patterned headscarf, there was her roundish agreeable person in the midst of the soldiers' rain-darkened battledress and the civilian overcoats.

He went down, boots drumming around his ears. Seconds later came a cheer, indicating his three-quarter had touched down. When Alec regained his feet he looked for the conspicuous pale raincoat but could discover only an unrelieved screen of khaki-clad fellows spilling onto the pitch in order to witness the result of this blind-side dash. Ten minutes later, when the whistle blew full-time, he wandered, muddy, anxious, among the spectators looking for that raincoat and headscarf but again could not identify her among the dispersing crowd. A figment? In all of Germany with its millions of displaced persons, he asked himself, why on earth should the woman turn up here? Because of the presence of this side from the French Zone? No, he had imagined it.

'Your girl is not a figment, Goose,' Bell had been adamant.

In the officers' mess that evening, as offhandedly as he could, he approached a circle of his colleagues and asked if anyone had encountered a Frenchwoman in the district, possibly in the company of a medical man. In these all-male communities facetious banter seemed, to Alec's ear, to have acquired a harder edge since the war ended and now he did not escape the wisecracks, each seeking to out-insinuate the other. Dearborn and his trail of bastards. He began eating at his digs, bringing home items for his landlady to cook and share, the two nodding goodwill at each other across the language gap.

In the ensuing weeks, where his few words of *Deutsch* permitted, Alec would wander among the streets and bombsites of Bielefeld enquiring after a *Französin*. Once or twice he took a bus to Detmold, stationed himself near the post office. *You continue to look like a spymaster, Goose.*

The trail was cold, and his job restricted the time he could devote to his quest. Yet the sight of her, whether real or delusion, had renewed the possibility of her, and given new edge to Alec's longing to be once more in her presence.

His initial job came to an end after eighteen months but he contrived to extend the posting, aware that his tall physical frame and fair looks, when looming in a small office, had a certain power to sway any lone person behind a desk to be obliging.

'You are all undercurrent,' was the other observation Bell had made. Yes, it took him by surprise how devious the purposes within his person were, and with what veiled energy they propelled him.

He purchased a motorcycle and ventured further along the tracks that led through the *Wald,* bumping between groves of beech or valonian oak, occasional spinneys of birch. There were darker tunnels of plantation conifers interspersed by patches of farmland where an occasional burnt out vehicle from the war lay tilted in a ditch, not yet fit for some memorial park nor even a plaything for children to clamber on. Disaffected by the metallic talk of the mess, Alec found a kind of homing instinct wake in him where his eye sought out those contrasts of sunlight and shade that reminded him of the creek-side havens around Portobello in a year of good rains. Put simply, he told himself, he was after peace. Peace from the brittle mess-talk, from the crackly newsreels, bringing what was 'up to the minute', or more treatment of the war outrages.

But this forest would not quite allow the mind to rest. The scene, as he looked at it from behind his motorbike goggles, could not have been more tranquil, yet he knew from his Cambridge history reading that he was traversing that old, immense forest where Roman legionaries of the Augustan era, route-marching along these very tracks, maybe, had watched the Hercynian tribes rise from swamps or materialise from thickets, to come at the Roman shield wall from that density of vegetation with the one purpose of hacking the intruders to pieces.

Can't imagine it, old man.

One Sunday he came upon a stream glittering between tree trunks. Leaning the motorcycle on its side-stand, he followed where the water might lead, ducking for branches or pushing the foliage aside. At length he arrived on the shore of a small lake, hidden from the tracks by the density of the oak and beech trees. The longish tarn may have been less natural than created artificially by some *Graf* or nineteenth-century industrialist as a feature for their forest hideaway. Indeed, as Alec looked about himself he could see a dwelling of some description half a mile or so distant, with a small patch of cleared ground beside it, where a woman in a blue dress appeared to be scything the long grass. Behind the lodge was a jagged ridge of conifers, smoky blue at this distance. But it was hard to sustain his gaze on this, for the sunlight created a green-gold slick on the unruffled surface of the lake that made his eyes water. Dragonflies flicked hither and thither across his line of sight, hovered, vanished.

Alec found a place on the bank and spread his groundsheet, sat munching the *Kleinbrot* and *Wurst* prepared for him by his landlady. The time, he consulted the watch he had managed to hang on to through prison camp, was a little after midday and the day was warm. He took this watch off, and laid it beside the picnic box where he could see it. He would read, he would daydream, perhaps he would swim. There were blackbirds above his head in the foliage. The page presented its lines to him, Wyatt again.

I leave off therefore
Since in a net I seek to hold the wind…

No, the sun was more than just warm, it was hot. Alec removed shirt and singlet in order to feel the benign power of it on his bare skin. He read a few more lines, read them over again because he could feel his attention growing torpid with the heat of the afternoon.

There is written her fair neck round about,
'*Noli me tangere,*' for Caesar's I am,
And wild for to hold, though I seem tame.'

But he found that his head drooped, his eyes closed for intervals from which he would jerk awake and wonder how much time had passed. It was clear his foolish body wanted to drowse. So he succumbed to this urge, curled on the groundsheet and fell asleep quickly.

It was a benign, light sleep in which he dreamt that he had been making one train journey after another, a book always open on his lap. Flickering beside his carriage window at one moment were the airy Australian landscapes of his boyhood, at another the bombed cities and tangled (the word in the dream presented itself as 'tanglered') industrial-scapes he had contemplated as he crossed England between one training camp and another. Sometimes there was Bell to meet him on the platform; sometimes it was a man who resembled perhaps Ferris, perhaps his dead Cambridge crony, Hartigan. At each stop he was encouraged to continue and the emotion attending this advice was an expectation that the purpose of his travel was gradually disclosing itself.

When he opened his eyes he found Viva sitting beside him.

'You are unlikely,' he said to her, mildly.

'Am I allowed to sit with you, Mister Handles?'

As though the problems raised by time and distance were casual when it came to the incontrovertible fact of her being there.

She could be a continuation of his dream, he recognised, a variation on Bell maybe. For a moment he regarded her as she cast her gaze down at him.

'I heard that they hurt you,' he said next.

To this she gave no reaction. Sleep and dream had somehow made her sudden presence plausible. 'I should be dumbfounded,' he said, 'so why am I not surprised that you should just pop up!'

'You can tell me this better than I can tell,' she said, laughing, and spread out a corner of her summer frock in order to demonstrate her material existence to him. The frock was pale blue like the Wedgwood ceramic ware he had seen at the museum in Cambridge before the war, incised with white embroidery about the hem and breast. Her bare arms were brown, her figure perhaps thinner than he could recall from their night in '44. She was probably the woman with the scythe that he had seen in the meadow beside the distant lodge.

'Why are you here?' he tried next.

'I must put to you the same question, I think.'

'A fair cop!' he laughed. For her presence had relieved the burden of anguish in him that had grown so familiar he could hardly recall his existence having been free of it.

'*Et toi? Comment vas-tu, Monsieur le parachutiste?*' she rapped off her enquiry. Was the French to jolt him from sleep and onto his toes?

In his reply, Alec tried to be offhand in how he presented himself to her. 'Well, since we last saw each other, you've been on my mind. Only on and off, you understand.'

It would be important that he discover what was done to her in the days after he left. And how she came here, and who she was with. But he had a superstition she would vanish in the instant he introduced unwelcome material to this astonishing, lovely, fragile situation. Portobello had been part of his preparation for this, he trusted, as he thought about where he seemed to have landed this time.

Clearly she trusted her own presence, for she regarded him, *M. le parachutiste,* whose life she had saved, and he could see she was amused by him, not especially surprised that she should come across him in the depths of a German forest. Why, her attitude was positively sunny, offhand. Perhaps it was this offhandedness that had disarmed what should have been his own astonishment at her sudden materialising. The oak leaves were diaphanous behind her head, the sun glittering through their intervals. Was this the nature of enchantment?

'Then I may sit with you?'

'Do I have a choice in the matter?' he asked her.

For his face could not help its joy.

He sat up and made room for her on the rubberised canvas groundsheet he had wangled from the QM store. But she, with an immediate assumption of intimacy, put his book aside and made herself comfortable with her head resting on his lap, composing her blue frock so that it might not be creased. Her familiarity in this moved him.

And raised a perplexity for him.

For instance, what should he assume about her German fellow? He stole quick glances at her as she settled herself. Despite what he had heard about her treatment from Bell, she looked bonny. Should he touch the delicate round of her cheek? His sense was he had every right and no right. A contradiction that summed up the situation. Her hair was shorter but thicker than it had been when he saw its outline in the dark, he judged.

'So, you've popped up from nowhere again.'

'My home is nearby. You are the gentleman who pops up, I think.'

He considered this, and considered how, once more, here was a species of sorcery existing *within the very crevices of everyday occasions.* He tried to be discreet in how he looked at her for fear she should think he gawped. But he could not help himself. His memory had not misled him during these four years. Whatever had befallen her to bring her into the heart of this German forest, she presented herself as entirely lovely to Alec's sight.

'What am I in?' he asked her.

She had picked up his watch, looked at it idly for a moment, then slipped it into a small pocket in the front of her dress.

'I take it you're still not that keen on the need to know the exact time,' he allowed the small theft.

'For this afternoon we will be together,' she told him. 'When the dark comes I will tell you how it has been with me. Then you will return to your important work.'

'I'll drop all that and go with you to the ends of the earth if I know what I'm in for,' he replied, glad he could be so extravagant in his avowal, glad that she could find his protestation comical.

'How can I tell what you are in for, Mister Handles,' she protested, turning in his lap and looking him in the eye. Then she brought his head close and kissed his cheek, as one who had known him all his life might do.

17

THEY SWAM AMONG THE FIREFLIES

With her eyes closed, she turned her face this way and that on his lap, letting the late sun through the leaves touch each cheek in turn. The radiant yellow air was alive with creatures, a wasp droning nearby, ants marching briskly to and fro just beyond Alec's groundsheet where he had earlier cast the crumbs from his *Brötchen*, birds at their parley in the green canopy overhead. But the effect of this small-scale commotion was to give Alec a deeper sense of the isolation of the two of them in this reach of the forest. He could smell the small perspiration on her together with a sharpish, cottony aroma from her blue dress. It was agreeable, and he hoped his own person was not too rank.

And if he had been complacent at the manner of her turning up, he was astounded by the casual tenderness with which she treated his presence. What gift of insouciance allowed her to take over his person like this? It was as though, instead of leaving her flooded Normandy house to limp off to war he had spent these four years in her close company, the easygoing intimacy between their two bodies growing customary, growing marital, over that duration. Like marrieds. He took quick glances at this dear face, which had cushioned itself so blithely on his lap. Were there the signs upon it of her own wartime suffering, the murder of her father, her humiliation at the hands of the *Maquis*? If he should believe such things had indeed taken place? Yes, bonny was the word for her. Could he caress her cheek, allow himself to lightly comb the dark hair back from her forehead? Should he ask her all the questions for which he wanted answers, or suspend his questioning for the moment?

He waited until she had wriggled her head into a comfortable position, then asked. 'You've made yourself at home, then?'

'Am I not at home?' she replied comfortably, closing her eyes, composing her hands.

'Depends on the extent to which I am,' he wrangled agreeably.

'And are you?'

'Well ma'am,' he took his suave sidelong glances at her, 'I rode my motorbike into an impressive forest, fell asleep beside a lake and woke to find you've popped out of the ground,' he summed up for her, then with mock-affront added, 'so I couldn't tell you whether I was in this world or the next.'

'And I am cutting the long grass, then I am going for a walk to the place where I swim, when I find a sleeping man. Should I not be as astonished as you?'

'Couldn't advise,' he shook his head solemnly.

'I say you look for me.'

'Can't deny it,' he admitted.

'Then here I am.'

'Then here you are.'

She opened her eyes and pressed her finger on the end of his nose as though this clinched their badinage.

'Never in my life have I gone off to sleep in a more exactly right spot.'

'Then you are home, whether it is this world or the next, Mister Handles' she informed him. She had her eyes closed comfortably again.

'Do you believe in a homing instinct?'

'Do you believe in this thing?'

'I'm inclined to.'

They both laughed, delighted by the flippancy they could create between themselves. Then, on impulse he said, 'And I reckon that if you were to tell me you are free to marry a fellow, I would marry you before the sun came up tomorrow morning ...'

But to this extravagance she opened her eyes and gently placed her fingers on his lips.

'Fair cop, what do I know?' he conceded when she permitted him speech again. He had violated some fragile boundary of their being together, and she would vanish if he persisted.

Tender with him, baffling him, it was as if she knew how delicate was this suspension of moments and that it fell to her to guard them both against the bruise of his ardour. He looked down at her and considered the crescents of her closed eyelids, her full mouth and the soft curves of her cheekbones.

'Like the last time we met, I can say how I got here, but I can't say I know where I am,' he said after some moments.

'Ha!' she rejoined.

'And do you know another thing?'

'I know a few things.'

'I've hardly ever called you by your name. In my mind I tagged you as *Mamzelle.*'

'Then indeed, you are no more than an ignorant footballer.'

'I'll say it now. Viva.'

'People give me lots of names. How should I choose?' she deflected his endearment.

'Viva,' he insisted again on the two syllables, then needed at the least to resolve his offer to marry her, 'Do you recall how you gave me your word *joyeux?* Well, that's Mister Handles, right now, I reckon.'

He was in danger of bubbling, he saw.

'If that is so, then for the present I am at home,' she decided, adjusting her head on his lap once more.

Alec's eye was drawn to where a dragonfly zipped across the surface of the lake. Dragonflies were projectiles, could cause a horse to shy, a station hand on Portobello had once explained to Bell and six year-old him. Three hundred million years old, the fellow had said, licking along the edge of his cigarette paper and glancing at the two children wisely. The creature here veered, stopped with wings in furious shimmer. It was spanking the lake surface with its striped thorax, creating small roundels on the water, then darting to a new position and repeating the action. If you concentrated on the creature, the background of reeds and trees seemed to blur into a green-gold honey. No, the long body was not simply striped, but patterned with symmetrical highlights of colour, lapis lazuli, copper, black, and with an extraordinary lapis lazuli head. Was it laying eggs, attracting a male, or simply luring its supper from the micro-life of the lake? The action was mysterious.

So too, he looked down at his love, was this here and now with Viva. He could not forever suspend the questions he must ask her, questions like, had she been at the football that time, how did she come to be here, what had happened to the German fellow she had followed at the war's end? His instinct told him that questions, any questions, would bruise the very lightness of the manner by which he had homed upon her, the delicacy of this miraculous interval where they found themselves together. Yet he must know the necessity of things.

So he took the plunge and tried her on the football. 'Can you remember ...' and he described the gross specifics, a rainy Saturday some eighteen months back, Bielefeld, a team from the French Zone, her own Gallic compatriots.

And promptly he must listen to how she could turn his plodding enquiries back on him, deftly, affectionately he thought.

'Do you then have the knees made good again for the football, Mister Handles?'

He pressed her for a straight answer.

'What makes you wonder that I would come to see such a spectacle of men fighting with each other to possess a ridiculous ball?'

'Because it is what I believe I saw,' he insisted, then needed to allow, 'unless I imagined it.'

'Are you a strong person when you imagine?' she asked in order to foil his insistence on here and now.

The earlier dragonfly had abruptly vanished but had been replaced by a pair locked together in copulation, the male holding the female's head with the pincers at its rear end, leaving its sperm smear on her. The wings of both beat furiously and they created a hovering, furious 'O' in the light above the lake.

'All my questions,' he smiled and looked down at her. 'I can see you want me to put a lid on them.'

She had not encountered this last piece of Australian idiom and was suddenly delighted by the idea that a saucepan lid might bounce and yammer on top of his boiling curiosity.

But free from the facetious after-dinner chat of the Bielefeld mess, Alec had not finished with his bout of seriousness. 'It would be good to know,'

he faltered, 'well, the point at which we seem to connect. I can't tell …'
again he faltered, 'how much you can see into things.' Then resolved to
make his complaint baldly. 'I'm in the realm of the uncanny, and, trouble
is, I don't know how to form the questions I should ask you.'

To which, untroubled, she replied, 'Why should you not know how
to ask a woman some simple questions?'

He must lighten their chat. 'Because I am just a simple footballer,'
and gave her his impish sidelong look.

'Actually, I think not.' (And it was exquisite to his ear, the odd
French way with which she used the English word 'actually'.)

'When I left you on that night in the war, did you continue talking
to me?'

'How can I do such a thing when you have gone?'

'There were choices I could have made where I might have been in
serious strife. I heard a voice in my head, and as a result I am alive. The
blokes I trained with are not.'

'Then it is a good voice, that voice in your head.'

'Is it yours?'

'Hah! *Quelle question!* Are you not complete in yourself?' She opened
her eyes and regarded him.

'Well,' he looked at her ruefully, 'I know I could end up arguing with
you when to be with you again is the most miraculous thing.'

'Then we should not be talking so much. Instead we should swim.'

And quickly Viva had risen to her feet beside him, stepped from her
blue frock and underclothes, then entered the water in a gliding forward
launch. She swam with a strong breaststroke into the middle of the

lake. For some moments he sat watching her because to see her person now in the light of day instead of in that old farmhouse in the dark of '44 was—O yes—*joyeux*. The sun was at an angle where it tinged the uppermost foliage of the trees with a yellow selvedge, beneath which the green deepened into darker crannies of shade. The grassy bank where they had lain together was also lambent where the light caught the seed in a luminous froth.

'Take your clothes off,' she called to him, turning on her back and kicking with her legs.

'All very well,' he called.

'You will show me your teapot knees,' she called again, and kicked with her legs so the green surface of the lake splashed with her commotion.

But in daylight, Alec lacked this casualness when it came to nakedness. He stood wondering at how events propelled themselves. If you found the girl you really wanted, before you volunteered to take your clothes off in her company, was it not more proper to escort her to a dance, to the pictures or to a swish restaurant? Why was it that, with Viva, matters could not proceed in a manner you might expect? Yet he knew he had been transposed casually to some idyll—his English essays during Cambridge allowed him that recognition.

She had swum back to the shore, emerged dripping, and taken his hand. 'Will you swim in these old motorcycle trousers?' she asked. The lake water ran from her shoulders, across the round of her breasts and hips.

So he shed the old jodhpurs, and the remainder of his clothing, then allowed her to lead him to the water.

Ah, it was truly a sensuous shock when you went swimming 'in the crud' as they had called it at Hume Grammar. In sixth form on a Saturday spree once, he had swum in the crud from the Botanical Gardens across to Fort Denison and back. The sharks that patrolled Sydney Harbour were the lesser risk. More dire would have been Truffy striding down the lawns to catch his First XV captain scampering from the waters to recover his clothes. Dearborn the all-rounder, in the nuddy, letting down the school.

Now, with the same leisurely breaststroke as Viva, he followed where she conducted him, the water layered with temperature, warm on top, cold when he trod water and his toes brushed the velvety ooze of bottom mud. She appeared to know the depths and coves of the lake and they followed its intricate contours as the evening came down around them. They murmured observations to each other about the claimant tendrils of underwater weed, the ligaments of branches their feet sometimes came to rest upon, the dusk birdcalls from deep in the tree canopy, the peace above and round them.

'Look.' She indicated where against a bank suddenly there were fireflies congregating. 'Do not speak,' she directed, and moderated her swimming so that she moved silently in the water. 'We will go among them.'

Moving silently so that it was as if they were no more than two heads afloat on the still water, they came among the swarm where Alec could see the coupling of the winged males with the larval females. On leaf, branch, rock face, the small greenish globes glimmered and pulsed from the luminous parts of the female abdomens while the dimmer presence of the male flies flitted with hundreds of wings around the man and woman. Ahead he could see Viva's head, and less distinctly the pale, slowly scissoring blur of her body as it glided silently under the steep, partly brambled rocks beside the water. Unearthly, this concert of activity in the midst of the forest peace.

'Now we will sit and talk together.'

She had stopped swimming and her head was abruptly close to his, her legs brushing his as she trod water.

'If you like.' For a moment he had put his hands on her hips, feeling the movement of her muscles, wondering if she allowed this intimacy. And for a moment she seemed to, then had swum from his hands, leading him again.

It was best to be without volition. It seemed to be one of the conditions of their association and the risk of it provided for him a frisson of delight. They swam away from the congress of the fireflies to where their clothes lay on the slope. The dusk was a pale blue, the canopies darkening to a sharper relief, and in the absence of his timepiece that she had so casually pocketed, he estimated the hour to be, perhaps, after eight. Once ashore she brushed the water from herself with her hands, then appropriated his white shirt to complete her drying. At the end she pulled on the frock, not bothering to fasten the several buttons down its front, and sat once more on his groundsheet. Meanwhile Alec stood by the water's edge, contemplating the distant pinpricking of fireflies on the far side of the lake, conscious how lovely her shapeliness and movements were, unwilling to be seen to gawp at her. What was her status here? He should ask her, and dared not lest ... O hell, he thought she was lovely. He had not taken up his shirt to dry himself and the evening had cooled.

'You are shuddering again, Mister Handles,' she remarked.

'S-s-seems to be a habit,' he answered.

Not a reaction to being swallowed by Normandy mud this time at least. Rather, the cooling night air had combined with his sexual desire and nervousness at her physical presence. He would control it this time, he hoped.

'I will dry you.'

And she came to him and went over his body with the old cotton shirt, efficient, vigorous, jokey. When she stooped to the old injury on the knee she paused and fingered the patella with small circular manipulations. 'It is good now,' she decided. He could look down and see the wet hair parted around the nape of her neck as she busied herself.

And when she rose to face him and give him back his damp shirt, he blurted how extraordinarily fond of her he was and that he probably had the jitters through wanting to kiss her just a little and not knowing whether he should.

To which she answered, 'If you like, we can do this,' and brushed her hand caressingly on his cheek. At this he was beset by the contradictory impulses, to gather her up in his own caress, while inhibited by the thought that his crude smooching and squeezing would disqualify him from that finer, more tender, more resilient regard he wanted from her now they were, against all likelihood, together again.

In any case, what did it mean, *If you like* … Did she feel reciprocal desire for him? Was she really free to be so nonchalant about the matter?

'I have to admit you've got me stumped,' he further blurted, and when her English could not manage 'stumped', he said, 'anguished just a bit.'

'Then we can walk in the woods a little until you are less stumped,' she suggested. 'There are paths.'

He allowed her to lead him, the pale blue of the dusk affording them ample light in the intervals of bare ground between the stands of beech. They passed through a small iron gate and proceeded to climb a slope. As Alec approached the summit of this he could make out a whitish object apparently nailed to a tree, which on closer inspection, he saw to be a skull.

'It's human,' he said.

'It is some outrage from the war.' She dismissed it quickly, and was not inclined to linger. He saw her displeasure with the vile thing, so made to tear it away.

And found she had called sharply, 'No! You will leave this.'

'It's frightful,' he said, looking to where she stood, blue, already some distance further up the path. And that blue of her frock was now an identical tinge with the crepuscular blue of the sky. It seemed to have been dusk for a long while. 'Why don't I throw it somewhere out of mind.'

'You will leave this.' Her head, the profile of her body in the blue frock, they were very still at that moment. Tensed, he thought.

'I thought it might have been a bit rich.' He shrugged, caught up with her on the path, but was thinking how, interloper from the New World that he was, he had blundered into some resilient habit of Old Europe.

'It is an old custom,' she mollified.

Now he had come away from the disgusting thing she grew less tense and narrated for him how skulls nailed to trees had been the manner in which the tribes had dealt with the skulls of Varro's legionaries after the great battle in the forest. 'To let a traveller in the woods know what can pass in the forest is permissible, I think,' she concluded the subject.

'And that bloke?'

'Maybe some deserter the SS killed during the last days. Who can know?'

They walked in silence for a time. Then, worrying a little about finding his way back to the groundsheet and his motorcycle again, it occurred to Alec to ask, 'You'll have a fair idea of where we are, I guess?'

Viva had arrived at a further iron gate and called back, 'We have been on land owned by my husband.' As though a husband were a trivial matter with no particular bearing on anything. 'Now, if you like, you can meet him.'

For some moments Alec stood still, heart-sickened by this disclosure. Had he expected the Jerry fellow Bell had mentioned to turn up in the picture at some point? Probably. If he examined the hours he had spent in Viva's company, both now and on the night of the Invasion, some item of hard reality came out of the dark to jar the enchantment. So how did it work, this intimacy between them? There was not a tinge of dissembling in her nature, he would swear to it.

 Seeing he had not followed, she came back for him, slipped her arm through his.

'This won't do,' he stated. 'The fair thing is I'm told everything that's going on.'

'The fair thing?' she looked at him once, withdrawing her arm quickly. In that glimpse he saw the flare of hostility he had encountered at their first meeting. Then she said, peremptorily, 'You will first see, then we will talk.' She returned to the iron gate and it squeaked on its hinge as she passed through it. When she was some distance beyond she stopped and looked back at him.

'Why should you not have your explanations since you are so keen.'

'I want you to be safe,' he called after her, still unwilling to follow because whenever he heard the unrelenting part of her nature a sense of despair arose in him. 'I want to know that you are at peace.' Yes, he wanted only her good, which was why he trusted his feelings on the matter.

He listened and for some moments heard only the brushing of her frock on the ferns beside the path. Then he saw her stop again.

'It is hard,' she called. 'You will not trust me, Mister. You want to know and at the same time live as if you do not know.' This time in her voice he thought he heard her anguish. Did that make her more real? 'I doodle and you will not trust to it,' she finished.

18

WHERE THE WAR OCCURRED

Even in the decades after he returned to Australia Alec could not calculate exactly how long he spent in Viva's company during this post-war encounter with her. The time composed itself from intervals where the light was profuse yellow, then pearly grey, then the dilute ink of their long evening. There had been some sleep, whereupon he had awakened to that fragile variance between dusk-blue and dawn-blue. By the time he found his motorbike again and returned to the Bielefeld garrison, the sky above the Westphalian plain was overcast and the light neutral. If the hours seemed protracted to him it may have been because his amiable nature had been disturbed beyond his ability to fathom; and Viva's attitude was unfathomable.

She seemed disinclined to restore his watch to him.

And there was, at some level of his perception, a sense of observing the strange fatalism of his circumstances, like watching some grub behind glass where the winding conduits in the earth can be viewed in cross-section by the experimenter.

Now he clumped downhill after her and did not know where to place his trust. Had she not touched his cheek and assured him, offhand, *If you like, we can do this*? Do what? Caress and cherish, luxuriate in the presence of the other in the lovers' privileged trust that closeness to the beloved was forever? Or perform like dragonflies, head blindly gripped, sperm smeared, gone? Ahead her frock swayed as she walked, her hand brushed the ferns beside the path. A husband, she had decided to mention to him, casually as you like.

Yet he did not believe she could dissemble.

'It would be good,' he called out, 'to know exactly where I stand in all this,' his footsteps crunching on the small stones along the path.

'You stand with those who are kind and good,' she called back to him promptly.

'I'm not sure that idea bears scrutiny.' He wanted to keep his tone light with her, but a complex of emotion overflowed this. He wanted her to see what he was, what he could have done. There was a momentary impulse to injure her bound up in this. 'I was got up to be good at war,' he said. 'I could have shot the other fellow merrily,' he paused, then laid it on. 'We were trained to go back afterward and look through their pockets for any useful intelligence. Photos of their sweethearts is what usually gets found, or photos of their kids ...'

She stopped to wait for him. 'Do not,' she laid her hand on his arm.

But he must lay it on because if not to her then to whom? So he made her recollect. 'You disarmed me, and what I then thought was me was being got up for something else.'

She set off again. 'I did nothing. You are romantic,' he heard her dismiss his notion of this role in his life. But how could he swerve from the impression he was inside an enchantment.

'Trouble is, Viva, I don't know what that something is.'

She ignored this plea for elucidation.

'And somehow you seem to have all the answers,' he finished.

This prompted her to turn to him briefly. 'Perhaps you will meet a man you wished to shoot, Mister Handles.' She gave him a glance, then resumed her progress and for an interval they walked in silence.

'Now we approach the house. Mari will be on the balcony with his books. He has managed to arrange the light, I hope.'

'I look forward to meeting the man,' he declared. If he was to be led, laborious bug along the conduits, so be it. At least I'm awake to the fact, he tried to assure himself.

They passed through an archway in a massive cypress hedge that released its astringent aroma to the warm evening air. Emerging from this Alec saw they had arrived at the rear of a lodge, stone in its basement and timber above, dark as though with creosote. Presumably this was the dwelling he had seen from afar off.

'Here,' Viva was holding out her hand. 'We must go through. It is easier if I do not need to feel in the dark for light switches'

He took her hand and was led down corridors and a vestibule to a balcony where, again, all around them was the undulant profile of the forest. Stands of conifer intermingled with the deciduous oaks and beeches, and set down between them, at some distance, the lake formed a gleaming larva of reflected moonlight.

'*Liebling!*'

Viva's call of endearment roused the head and shoulders of a person who, Alec saw, was installed in a cane bathchair at one corner of the deck. The man wore a short-sleeved shirt clinched at the throat by a bow tie, and despite the mellow airs of the evening, a rug was tucked around his legs and feet. He had been reading by the aid of a paraffin lamp set on a small table and the frames of his horn-rimmed glasses inscribed two dark circles on a tanned face with high forehead and scant hair. As the two of them approached he removed his glasses whereupon the disfigurement of his face became evident. Alec saw there was a white puckering of the skin that began on his right forehead and continued diagonally onto his left cheek, interrupted by the ridge of the eyebrow, notching the bridge of the nose. It was shocking in its crudity, once seen then impossible to put out of mind.

Alec scrutinised the man. Was this indeed the fellow who had called on her that night? Viva had indicated that this was what he should expect. The invalid's torso appeared foreshortened by his posture in the chair, as though collapsed into itself.

'*Liebling, sind wir endlich zurück gekommen.*'

The man replied to her German in what was evidently a confident French, and the effect was peculiarly to blend the Teutonic and Gallic syllables into one tongue. This Mari was more senior than Alec had expected, older than his wife by perhaps twenty years. If he could ever put an exact age on Viva. She kissed him, took up his hand and joined it with the visitor's.

'Marius, I introduce Alec,' she identified each to each, keeping her hand on theirs for some moments. She rattled something to Marius in French, from which Alec heard the words, *Monsieur le parachutiste* and *C'est un endormi au bord du lac*. The way they both seemed able to swim between languages, as though swimming between one warm patch of lake water and another, was a little breathtaking. She turned to the hapless *endormi* and translated for him how she tells her husband she has found this sleepyhead beside the lake. Meanwhile Alec's hand is being shaken with some vigour.

'*Endlich, endlich sind sie da!*'

'He says to you, welcome at last!'

'At last? I don't understand.'

Viva shrugged, invited Alec to take one of the other chairs at the table. Accordingly the visitor seated himself and presented an amiable face to his host who, in turn, looked back at Alec expectantly. The puckering of the scar suggested some very makeshift surgery at one time. The war, he assumed. Unnerving to look while pretending the hideous disfigurement was not there. What was the fair thing here? Alec watched as Viva took her husband's book and closed it upon the bookmark, moved the lamp to a more communal place on the table, keeping up her mix of French and

German to which the man listened and nodded meditatively. How long had they been married? Certainly Alec could observe the nonchalance of a marital intimacy, the tease, the mock-gruffness, the insouciance of affection. All this you could tell from the fluid changes of tone in their speech without needing vocabulary at all.

Abruptly Viva had disappeared within the lodge leaving the two men alone together. Marius continued to watch Alec attentively but ventured to say nothing. With the pale of the night sky behind him, his face was in the dark, the scar not so obvious, the expression hard to tell. I am being appraised, Alec saw.

He reached across and looked at the title of Marius's reading matter, and enquired, 'An interesting book?' But he could elicit no response to this. There was to be a language problem after all, it seemed. 'I'm sorry, I just assumed you spoke English.' Again his host was silent, intent in his watching. 'You don't?' Alec tried.

'No,' came the prompt reply. This was accompanied by a resolute shake of the head, which caused Alec to stare at his hands and meditate how he might proceed. With awkwardness, evidently. Then from the dark head had come a qualification to that negative, 'At least, not much,' before the person reverted to his stony silence.

Alec tried his inept French. '*Moi aussi, avec ah … le German …*' He recalled vaguely from school that the French had a more unexpected word for their eastern neighbour.

His host, ignoring this contribution, continued rather crisply with his own excuse. 'I find English a particularly difficult language,' then was silent as though this concluded the matter.

There was a frog creaking in some nearby ditch. But now Alec had been alerted by something deliberate in his host's deadpan manner. He could see Marius was protracting the silence for effect.

'The *particular* difficulty I find with English,' and the German was now rapping out his English consonants with a rather triumphant punctilio, 'is your peculiar use of the continuous present tense!'

'Is that right?'

'"He is coming, she is kissing, we are laughing," and so on.' He glanced at Alec, perfectly deadpan still.

'Quite so.'

'Quite so! Let us examine the following construction …'

Alec waited for the illustration to follow. Something clever, something inexorable. At the same time he had spied where Viva had appeared again at the door to the lodge, and was advancing, a tray in hand, watching this little charade with a knowing smile. When Alec turned again to the husband he found the long, tanned forehead had approached close to his own face. The eyes had crinkled into a hilarity not unlike crying and the effect of the pale diagonal scar on this seemed to split the face into two regions. The guest found his shoulders being gently shaken by his host.

'*Mein lieber Freund,* I say again to you, welcome, welcome to our home. I will play my ruse. Ha ha ha, you can see, I speak English well enough. After a fashion.'

'I'd begun to get a notion you were up to something.'

Marius's face remained in proximity. The expression it contrived was hospitable affection, yet it was impossible not to be distracted by how it was spoiled. Horrific to contemplate the original gash. The entire face must have been opened.

Viva laid out plates and knives. 'He is a naughty man with his humour,' she excused Marius.

'Party trick,' Alec rejoined, thinking, *Everyday she must look upon this fearful thing and absorb it into the run of things.* As he watched the two of them, genially, uneasily, Alec fancied that their collusive intimacy resembled more the indulgences between fond daughter and a surviving parent.

So what was his own place here? Adulterer? *If you like we can do this.* Expected guest? *Welcome at last, liebe Freund.* The guest felt himself to be like someone outside a door unable to decipher the murmur of voices within. Or like the person he found himself to be sometimes in a dream, when he knew he was in difficulties, close to something unspeakable, but unable to put shape to how the unspeakable might present itself.

'We eat a little supper now. It is American and from the tin.'

Nervous as he was, Alec would recollect that, for the most part, the austere meal taken by Viva and the two men who loved her passed off well. They sawed and ate cubes of pink composition meat in its aspic, scooped cold beans onto their forks, drank water and, to finish, an American coffee with a slab of chocolate Viva divided and presented on a patterned dish.

With a genial, if relentless, curiosity Marius probed the Australian guest about his country. The German had an impressive geographic knowledge, knew that Australian swans were black not white and its trees shed their bark in preference to their leaves. Was it true the native people had taken the European arrivals to be ghosts on account of their pale skins? This is really most interesting. And how did his countrymen adapt the English language to their experience, he further enquired.

'People say we go for the understatement a bit.'

'Just so. A dry country subverts the instinct toward self-importance,' Marius stated the rule with a kind of boisterous good will. 'In our era of microphones and arenas this instinct promises well.'

'Can a language have instinct?'

'Do you not say a language can have genius …' he leaned forward, the long scar emerging into focus like a regional division on a map, 'Ha, my friend, I am laying down the law. It is the affair of a host to hear what the guest must make of the world. You must elaborate for me your own opinion.'

The courtesies, this formidable mental energy. Alec tried to picture the texture of his and Viva's life together, the clue as to why she had given him her allegiance against the odds. The wife was quiet, but watchful during their exchanges.

'It's hard to picture instinct without an animal presence,' Alec supplied.

'Of course, of course. Forgive me. Here you have another German who must capitulate to the temptation of conferring animal qualities on abstract things. Which makes him very German, no doubt.' He laughed heartily at what he chose to believe was the national habit.

There was exhilaration for Alec in the discourse Marius offered, an oxygen for the intellect that Cambridge had provided but which the garrison life at Bielefeld stifled. Gladly he told this cultivated, disfigured being about his pastoral upbringing in New South Wales and in turn heard how the forbears of Marius Clausthal had lived in these parts since Hanseatic times. One branch of the family had been margraves. As for this secluded place, it was called *Der Libellensee*, or Dragonfly Water, and had been a family hunting-lodge, now reserved for Marius's use while he adjusted himself to …

'*Meine neue Lebensperspektive.*'

No doubt Viva will have explained his situation.

Alec could see a light at a window where Viva was running tap water over the plates they had used. No, Viva had said nothing to him about Marius's situation.

Marius might now have shed some more light on this. Instead the face and its dreadful crease drew close again, and the host gently put his hand over the younger man's hand. The move was a little stagy, as (Alec could now see) the earlier deadpan had been. Yes, their meal mostly passed off well until this, the second 'ruse' of the evening.

'And you, my friend. I hear you once had a mind to shoot me, no?'

The man was quizzing him, but Alec saw how the face had clenched once more into its extraordinary expression of hilarity and anguish.

'Ah.'

'You do not deny it?' The head must nod knowingly.

'I can't say I was aware it was you at the time. If it was.'

The long forehead had withdrawn but Alec's hand was being patted soothingly and though he could no longer discern it, he had the sense the face was still retracted upon its huge mirth. Should he apologise for … for what? The spell in which war had compelled his actions at the time?

'Tell me,' Marius said next, 'tell me it was not because you wished to steal my girl.'

'Uh?' Alec could see the upper body of the man quivering with amusement at the surprises he was able to bring off.

'Tell, me, with complete truth.' And the hand patted his own again.

'I wished to stay alive and rejoin my fellows.'

'Of course. We were soldiers both.'

Marius's hilarity appeared to subside now. Yet did the enquiry not have its own weird plausibility? The war had been one kind of spell, transforming how a person behaved. Here he was at this man's table, having spent four years thinking about the fellow's girl. Another spell?

'I'm happy the war's behind us,' Alec deflected, and should have anticipated the answer he would get.

'Not so very far behind,' said Marius gently. There was a silence between the two men until Marius called, 'Viva, *Schlafzeit!* My bedtime you see,' he said, turning to his guest. 'She will come now, and propel me to my sleep.'

As Viva prepared Marius for the night, Alec hovered behind her, willing to be useful.

'You will keep clear. I follow my method.'

She manoeuvred the awkward chair down corridors, backed it into the narrow cloakroom, undressed him. Her method, when it came to heft, was that he should lift his arms then, as she gripped his waist, he flopped onto her back in the same moment as she 'rolled' him onto a toilet seat where he groaned operatically. She cleaned him, hefted him back using the same method and, having looped a nightgown over his head, she applied the method once more to transfer him to the marital bed. It was moderately good physics, Alec observed, and lonely strenuous work for her, day in, day out. Marius discoursed all the while, apparently heedless that a visitor should see him naked but for his singlet. If she shared this bed, Alec must repeat his earlier reflection, each morning she would wake to that hideous disfigurement.

And cherish it. In her fashion.

Now she gave her attention to a wireless on the bedside table, turned it on, adjusted the Bakelite switches until she found music. In French she said something to her husband, and then in English, perhaps repeating the same substance, she declared to both men how she intended to walk with their guest down to the boathouse. It was a warm evening.

'O, go away,' he dismissed them, cheerful, petulant.

Viva led Alec down the balcony steps, across a slope of grass to a gate where the path to the boathouse began. This zigzagged down the hill and at places where there was a step, or stones across a stream, he allowed her to take his hand and guide him. A jagged dark of fir trees loomed behind them, while the canopy of oak and beech overspread them on each side, allowing a little light from the pale night sky.

As they walked, Alec was prompted to say, 'I think you are magnificent in how you cope.' But he saw Viva was not one to acknowledge compliments, and she said in turn that she hoped Marius did not rattle him with his mischief.

'He likes to probe around near the bone.'

Yes he likes this. Could Mister Handles understand perhaps how a man who has half his body dead wishes to live vividly with the half he has left? This was why he played his ruses. 'For you it is near the bone, for me it is brave.'

'Yes.'

'I will answer your questions. If you know everything, it can make our doodle a smaller thing than you might like. But you will ask what you wish.'

Still warm from the danger of his exchanges with her husband, Alec began, 'So you told Marius about the Allied paratrooper at the top of your stairs?'

'Of course.'

'Tonight he asked if I was out to steal his girl.'

'And were you?' She had taken his hand as they negotiated a narrow plank across a gully.

'If I was, I didn't know it. Maybe that's not an excuse.'

'None,' she said, responding to his own lightness.

'What happened to Marius?'

The path became predictable again, but she kept his hand in her own. 'You have seen his mind, how it must be always …' she was lost for a good English word.

'Churning away?'

'Churning, churning,' she seized on his word. 'Can you believe he was …' and this time she preferred the words from her own language, '*un homme vital et tranquil.*'

'I see a disabled bloke whose vitality is unquenched, and must escape from him somehow.'

'He is more than one year in Russia, then comes to France. With other soldiers he is billeted in our house. We do not like how this is placed on us, papa and I, but we do not suddenly close our eyes to where the life is,' she defended. 'France is better for the German army, he tells us. We find he is a pleasant, educated man who speaks to us in French. When it is late in the evening sometimes Marius and my papa can talk about languages and about subjects they find interesting. It is all innocent. They drink a little calvados. In wartime even this can happen. When the flooding is made, the Germans leave our house, but Marius visits, to buy jam, to have conversation with papa, to see me.'

'There grew an attraction between you?'

'He is aroused; I am aroused. It is to feel alive. I live where the Boche are detested and I feel joy in the presence of this man who is a Boche. It is joyful to listen to the conversations between this man and my papa, to see the skill of two men who can make the best of what they have in bad times. Perhaps, with my papa, I live too long outside France to have the best feelings for *La Patrie*.' Alec saw her shoulders shrug. 'It is joyful to see this friendship.'

'*Joyeux.*'

'Exactly so.'

'Did you marry Marius in the wartime?'

'No Mister Alec, a prudent girl does not marry an enemy in wartime.'

'Were you seen together very much?'

'Of course! I am a stubborn woman. I say to myself, *I will do this.* Then my papa is dead.'

'What was it happened?'

'He is murdered in the woods. I assume it is by the patriots. His body is found under leaves by the dog belonging to a Boche officer.'

'Why was he murdered by your own people? Because of you?'

Again Alec saw Viva shrug. 'Papa has been a teacher of languages. Twice the SS take him from his school to interpret at interrogations. He is big, he is gentle. He comes home and is unhappy.'

Alec recalled her images of torture in bathrooms. 'He told you what went on?'

'Why should he need to? I have imagination.'

'Was Marius a sympathetic enemy?'

'When we all talked together, we chose pleasant subjects. Always. We make a spell. Sometimes with the music, for he plays good piano.'

Viva paused while they once more traversed the little brook, then resumed. 'Papa is at the lycée in Caen and he takes the bus. One evening he does not return and by the next evening I know the truth. The *gendarme* shows me a letter from a typewriter, which says how papa is ashamed and so takes his own life. If that is so, where is the gun? They are stupid. Who knows the reasoning in the head of a patriot?'

'When I was with you, I had not guessed you were so hurt.'

Alec felt helpless in the face of this, wanted the facts but saw they did not help. 'When did this happen?'

'What does the date matter? It is done.' And after they had proceeded some steps down the path, she reversed this pronouncement. 'April 19 1944. To this date I sign my name on the papers.' It was the first time he had heard her attach herself to an actual point of time.

And six weeks later, June 6 1944, she was putting me into her papa's nightgown, Alec calculated. You might have thought she would have preferred to stay out of the way of a fellow bent on loosing off with an automatic weapon. As she narrated these things his image of her seemed to grow more emergent, like gazing at some pattern, a fern leaf, the markings on a bird or dragonfly, that yields its finer filigree only as one looks into it with increased fineness of attention. Only with her it involved both a physical and a moral manner of being. O, she was one to cope, profoundly loveable in this.

She went on. 'We find a small joyous possibility and they think we are on the side of firing squads.' The protest was stated dully. 'At this time the Boche soldiers behave well toward me. My countrymen do not. Do I say this is a rule for the Boche and my countrymen? No. I say only what I see.' They were walking on the last leg of the path before the waterside and she had dropped his hand.

'What happened to you after I took off?'

'The patriots come.'

'Did they hurt you?'

She dismissed this idea. 'They are three, not from my district. They have weapons supplied by the Allies. They are young men, you know, who like to have the cigarette drooping in the mouth. They take me to a table in the street where a fourth man asks me whether I have kept the Boches in my house and I reply yes. They ask if I have been allowing a Boche to court me, and I reply yes because I know it to be true. The man at the table tells me that because of this I must be shot. I see some of the people of my own *hameau* standing around the table. They are very curious; they do not like me because I say the things I think, but I believe they are not on one side or the other.

The man at the table nods and I hear the three young men working the mechanisms of their popguns. But this is their ruse. For someone has found a pair of big scissors. I have one patriot on each arm and the third patriot cuts off all my hair. One of them pulls at my clothes a little, one spits on the ground at my feet, but they do not have a heart for this. I can see in their smiling they know they are not in their best lives.'

'If I had stayed put that night, I might have done you some good.' He must voice his anguish, for all that it was helpless, sterile.

'I think you are a good man, Mister Handles, but you think backwards too much.'

'Could you not have told them you had sheltered an Allied paratrooper.'

'Why should I plead?'

They were silent for a period until he said, 'So you weren't shot?'

'I am put into a lorry with other bad girls and we are driven through the streets of Troarn, Bayeux, some of the villages. Then we are allowed to go away. I go to my house and live in the upstairs until the river is restored and the flooding is down. I wear a scarf on my head until my hair grows again, but I feel no shame. I will look for my love, I say. Perhaps, if I am not being punished, I will not be thinking like this.'

'I could have seen you right.'

Viva ignored him, continuing her account. 'There is no one to come to my music lessons during this time. In that first autumn I can do some of the harvest myself, by the next year there are a few people willing to help me again. Where the flood leaves a mark, I clean the mud from my rooms. I am busy. In the next year, after the fruit harvest and jam making, I go looking for my love and so I come here where I find him. But of course he is not as he has been.'

They were now at the lakeshore. On their left was a roof held up by posts, half-planked along one side and enclosing a small wooden jetty beside which there was a punt similar to those Alec had seen during his Cambridge days. Viva kicked off her shoes, sat down with her feet dangling in the water, and lit a cigarette from a pack in the pocket of her frock. Alec seated himself beside her. Presumably his watch was still in that pocket.

She dragged on the cigarette then passed it to him. 'We will share,' she said, and leaned back on both bare arms, her face illumined by the strange paleness of the night. O yes, she awed him. The oddities of Invasion night, her rigmarole of enchantment and musical doodling, all this was becoming clear to him now in their extraordinary necessity.

'The tension you were under must have been colossal,' he said.

She shrugged. 'Making a doodle with you at the piano on that night keeps me from too much thinking, Mister Alec Handles.'

They sat. There was still one part of the substance to cover. 'Marius seems to have run into some bad luck before the war ended.'

'It is on the morning of the invasion,' she supplied. 'You have your aeroplanes very busy on this morning. One uses its bullet to make damage in the spinal cord of my love. His driver is killed, the vehicle destroyed. My Mari lies in the ditch without pain but with no powers.

'Should I be thankful I knew him before this happens?' she asked herself, then continued.

'A soldier finds him in his ditch. He takes his money. He takes his watch, he takes his army ration, and this includes the jam that he has collected from me that night when you see. Then he understands that Marius is alive through all his stealing and watches him closely. This man is a deserter. So he does not like this close watching. He still keeps his bayonet, and he uses it as you have seen.'

'And you must live with these consequences,' Alec stated.

Her response to this clinched the picture of her he had been forming.

'I am ashamed if I do not.'

The lake was very calm in the windless night. A fish broke the surface nearby with a brief ruffle of waters; occasional night noises came from the forest behind them; otherwise the long intervals of silence might have suggested a huge simplicity to the world. And yet within his own being it seemed to Alec there was an intractable puzzle locked away, one that was not amenable to approach or to be disarmed with words.

At length he had to divulge, trying to sound casual. 'I was also attacked by a fellow and as a matter of fact I took him for a Boche deserter.'

'It is a dangerous countryside on that day,' Viva took back the cigarette and drew on it, then passed it to him again.

Alec described for her his desperate fight in the shed as the bombardment had been coming down around them, the German words that had popped up in his head from nowhere.

'Miraculous really,' he looked at the fine profile of the head beside him.

Viva appeared unimpressed by the miracle of it.

'My point is this,' Alec persisted. 'We got very close together, this bloke and I. In a scrum like that you get a fairly intimate whiff of the other fellow. Jam was what came to my nose. I kicked over the jar he had been licking. Common enough article I suppose,' he led her, 'but you had been showing me your own wares not long before. Anyway …' and he looked for her responses closely, 'I got out of it. I even took away a memento because the bloke's watch broke its strap in our tussle and, needing a watch, I kept it.'

For an interval the silence of the woods was unbroken, pent, Alec wondered afterwards, for he could not even hear her breathing or any rustle in the movement of her clothes. But Viva had put her hand into the pocket of her blue frock and taken out the watch she had so casually appropriated in the afternoon.

'This one, Mister?' she said, quietly, holding the dial out that he might see it in the moonlight 'If you like, I will restore it to its owner.

'It seems to have stopped,' Alec observed this. Having come so far into the spell, he could not in retrospect say the ownership of the watch was unexpected.

19

I WILL CARRY THIS CHILD

For a long time they sat together meditatively. The moon, now high above the lake, diffused its light as through a pale gauze. Perhaps a zephyr had touched the lake for there came the small sound of water licking at punt and jetty, and from behind them in the trees the careful footfall of a deer, or perhaps a boar, edged at a prudent distance around them. From the higher woods came the owl-call they had heard earlier during their meal.

'I'm not keen on coincidences,' Alec broke their silence. 'Some kinds at least.'

'What kind?'

'The uncanny kind. Something bizarre pops up and you ask, what's going on here? You think you can pick a pattern that will tell you more about your life than the moment you inhabit. It's as if you can say, Why look! Here's my birth and here's my death, and here's the little curve between. Am I making a speech?'

'Keep making your speech, Mister Handles.'

'Well, you know you are glimpsing more than you want to know, and yet the fatalist idea of it holds you fascinated. So your attention shifts from getting on with the job in hand to an idea that your life is on a glass slide and if you only stare at it long enough you'll understand the pattern. And then, likely as not, your attention gets distracted, the glass slide has gone blank, and what you're left with is a queer sensation a bit like dread. That was a speech,' he tried to disarm his earnestness.

'Dread?' she pinpointed.

'I think so.' After a pause, he decided to say that part of his fascination with her was the peculiar notion that she might have exercised some pull on what happened to him after he left her that day.

'You have dread when you are with me?' she asked.

'Love and dread,' he replied. He would not have guessed this to be true before he made the admission. 'It might not be a whole feeling without the two.'

'You are romantic.'

'So you've insisted.' He contemplated her for some moments then looked away, pursued his thought on the idea of fate.

'Australia is called New World, you know, a land of opportunity. I suppose what this should mean is that if you go at a thing, you make the story of it yourself as you go along. You are what you do. We call it having a promising future. My old headmaster used to say I had one.'

Viva took time to reply, then came to the point. 'It was you, Mister Handles, who insisted you should know how you stand.'

'Yes.'

'Now you can see how it is with me?'

'Yes.'

'I will not give up this difficulty. It is what I have chosen. But I could not have chosen otherwise.'

'I have never known a person so downright brave.'

She dismissed this extravagance and continued, 'Perhaps in a few weeks it is best for you to go back to your own country.'

He would not answer for some moments.

'Look for opportunities, eh!'

'Yes.'

'Give you up.'

'Yes.'

'That's going to take a bit of hard work, I reckon.'

He wanted to downplay the strength of the emotion he felt. What is it happens when your thoughts centre on a girl? Your self goes behind a glass. He had passed four years contemplating the kind of delicious, casual intimacies he had seen pass between Viva and Marius at their supper table. Could he have been said to have been contemplating opportunity, he asked himself bitterly.

'Where do you think it is,' he looked at her sidelong, tapped both his head and the region of his heart, 'that bit you can fix if you've got the know-how?' He had wanted the reaction to come out suavely but, stupid of him, had let himself down with his overstatement.

Viva regarded him steadily. 'You have the tears, *M. le parachutiste.*'

'A bit,' he conceded. But the spasms of bitterness rose in him, the way one moment he seemed to be her subject, the next her object.

She watched his emotion, made no move to comfort him. Instead she chose her approach to his unhappiness and her voice had that especial clarity he had fallen for from the start.

'In English you have the word lovely. You know? Lovely, loveliness, when the body presents a picture that is in agreement with the person. In French we say, *charmant* or *aimable,* but it has not the conviction.'

'I'll take your word for it,' he managed.

'You are the bad-timing. I cannot manage in my life two loves,' she put her argument methodically, 'but I say to you even so, Mister Handles-Alec. I think you are a lovely man.'

Through his distress he grinned at her. 'You must be your father's daughter when it comes to the languages, I reckon.' He was using the back of his hand to deal with the moisture from his foolish eyes and nose.

'It is true. I have thought that you were very lovely since I found you in the mud.'

Found him in the mud. This, for all his misery, caused Alec to laugh with outright joy. However fraught, here was the tilt of her humour. And an affirmation he meant something to this person he cherished. Something.

'If I went back to Australia,' he was already trying out his second-best options,' maybe later you might take the steamer out there and see Portobello for yourself. If, you know …'

Generous of him, to offer the spacious, lunar paddocks of his country to her. She could bring poor old Marius out there, if he could be got into a state where he might travel on a steamer maybe. 'We could all of us have some fun, I reckon.' It must be obvious to her, he reflected, how he was now trying to salvage a part of her for his future.

Yes, she might come out there one day, she replied. But her plan, it appeared, brutally, was to remain in Germany a year or two more. Then, if the emotions of *après guerre* in her own country became more stable, she would take her Boche husband and her child back to the orchards in Normandy. Here they would make their livelihood from *la confiture*, from the calvados. If the season were bad or the people roundabout remained too … *antipathique* … to help with the harvesting, she could perhaps teach some music at a school in Caen, or Cabourg. She looked down at her hands, then felt she should correct Mister Handles with respect to Marius who would neither be poor, nor old, if she had anything to do with it. She was a force.

But Alec's attention had snagged on her word 'child.'

'So on top of it all you are a mother?' He had to clear his throat. 'You have a kid in the background some place?' Momentarily he saw how, if it was possible to love a person tenderly, you could also hate them tenderly.

And yet what right did he have in the matter? Could he say she had been dissembling toward him? Not ever. So, was his ignorance about her state in the world simply because he hadn't asked her the right questions?

'Boy or girl?' he added to his enquiry, wanting the full measure of despair. But she would not respond to his black mood. When he grew calmer he said, 'I think I see you, then I don't,' and the sidelong smile he gave her was trying nothing on this time. He was conscious how, that afternoon, her head had lain in his lap, and now she had requested he remove himself to the far side of the world. It was an odd message, if taken as a whole. How could their moments of intimacy, beside this lake, or four years ago in her Normandy attic, be so exquisite for him, so offhand for her?

Again she would not answer immediately. Then she said, quietly, 'I think I am not very hard to see through. I have no child.'

'You said …'

'But I want.'

He gazed out on the water, eventually said, 'Understandable.'

'Once upon a time I save your life,' was the reminder with which she began. 'Now there is something I want you to do for me, Mister Handles.'

'Apart from remain in the complete dark about you?'

'It is delicate.' She waited. So forthright all along, he could have sworn there was hesitancy in her manner now. 'With my life being as it has been, do you think I know many people, Alec?'

'I've no idea.'

'There is no-one else in my life I can ask the thing I will ask from you.'

'It must be my loveliness.' He looked away from her.

'You will not be bitter!' she scolded. His mood made her falter for some moments, but she recovered herself, turned to face him, placed a hand on his cheek that he too should turn and look at her. 'Now you will listen to me.'

'I will.'

'I say I have no child. Marius is with me. He is practical.'

'Then you're well-matched,' Alec complimented her gloomily. And all at once he could forestall the thing she was asking.

'We will be together, you and I. I have said so.'

She wanted him to father her child then forget his role in the fathering. Simple. Presumably the performance of dragonflies was not possible for that vital, broken man she had married. So Alec Dearborn, BA (Cambs) was the stand-in. *Dearborn and his trail of bastards.*

'I ask you to make this thing possible for me.'

'A fellow likes to be useful.'

'Please, do not make this attitude with me.'

Her proposal was entirely characteristic of her, practical, altruistic, fraught. Out of the war-havoc she was set on creating a family for herself and that poor damaged bloke up there who was going to get his measure of life no matter what. And she was going about it with charming directness.

'The way you go at a thing, you'd make a fair fist of running a sheep station,' I reckon, he told her, then in a more subdued tone, added, 'I had the fancy we might make a whole life of—you know—you and me.'

Viva said nothing for a while, and then he found she had kissed him, clumsily, somewhere around his eyebrows.

'You are the lovely man. If we have two lives, this fancy is possible.' She was looking back at the water as though nothing had happened.

And he could feel, minutely, the disarranged hairs of his eyebrows prickling back to their places in the wake of her impulsive kiss. He asked her, 'If Marius were not in consideration, do you think you might have cared enough to take me on?'

'Yes. Of course. I think so.'

'We're looking at a lifetime?'

'I cannot tell. I find you lovely. You come down into the mud too late for me, just a little. It is the Invasion. You should make it sooner.'

He looked at his hands, and then the profile of her face, her hair shorter and thicker, her rounded cheek.

'Funny,' he said, 'but you've just brightened me up. A little.' And an instant later was surprised that his face had once more been the site of one of Viva's ill-aimed kisses.

Now she was on her feet. 'We will be on the water. It is my wish.' She roused him up. 'You are Cambridge, Mister Alec Handles. You can pole us.' Was she ever able to make a suggestion that was not in the imperative voice? And why did this innocent, peremptory manner so beguile him?

Having taken his hand she led him into the boat shelter, busied herself arranging the canvas cushions on the thwarts, while he, with a rusty tin, baled the water that had collected in the well of the flat-bottomed craft. Together they handled the punt from its shelter out onto the calm lake-water.

'You trust this thing, I suppose?' he asked, as he took the pole and tried to recall the knack of punting from Cambridge days.

'Not one bit,' she said, using the small paddle to correct his steering. He poled for some minutes until the bottom mud became too deep and soft to provide for his thrust, whereupon he attached the pole to the mooring rope and allowed it to dangle overboard while the punt drifted between the trees on either shore. 'Let's hope we can get ourselves back.'

From the forward thwart he heard her say. 'If we have success, Mister Alec, I will hide nothing from this child. You understand?'

'You're straight as they come,' he told her. His statement seemed to be a blaze of his ardour for her, because somehow she could accommodate being undisclosing with a quality of astounding candour. And he could make a fair guess as to why she had wanted to come out here onto the water. She had an enviable detachment toward the business, more than he could say for himself. The lovemaking. Could he call it that? He believed he adored her, so what did that entail? If he allowed himself to go along with her plan there would be fleeting consummation to this passion, that casual copulation of a dragonfly, O but not that ampler, longer adventure that had teased and spurred him.

'Is it adultery, do you think?' he asked from his end of their craft

'I have said. Marius is practical.'

She came forward and arranged one of the cushions so she could sit immediately before him. 'Give me,' she requested taking his fingers. He saw she had taken from her frock pocket a small sachet from which she removed a pair of nail scissors. Now she held up his hand so that she might see well enough to trim his nails. He regarded the concentration on her face as she went about the task, the eyes with their very slight cross-eyed look, that round of cheek that might grow plump one day but now was, and even in that rounder future, he knew, would be lovely in his sight. *When the body is in agreement with the person.* One part of him looked into his being to seek confirmation of this. There was the image of his elder sister.

Bell, I have never been sure of anything. It was why he loved the football. With the ball in your hands you had certainty. Which put aside the need to look for certainty.

And another part of him, pedestrian, prudent, voiced the objection to her, 'I am expected to show for work tomorrow.' Even as he voiced it, he knew this impediment to their lovemaking to be meagre. 'By rights I should tramp off and find my motorbike.'

Viva demolished it promptly. 'It is dark. Later you may find your belongings; I will show you the path. You may tell them you were lost in the woods.' She concentrated on her manicuring for a moment, then gave him an arch look. 'If you tell them this you will say no dishonest thing.'

'Straight as they come, you.' And he in turn must give her an arch look.

She used one blade of the scissors to clean out the crescent of muck behind the trimmed fingernail, her head bent and close to the hand. She had a good eye when it came to using a sharp instrument in the dark. Setting his hand down, she appeared to assess his face. 'Be very still, Mister Alec,' she instructed, and began to snip stray sprigs of his hair from his brow. 'Very still!' she warned. So he placed his hands on her waist that he might have a bulwark against which he would not sway. 'You have the good bones,' she complimented him, touching the ridge of his cheek with a finger. Her face was very close to his own. The proximity, the tease of her finger on the structure of his facial bones, in turn made him long to caress that rounded cheek with his fingertips, kiss her slightly imperfect eyes, her lips and throat. But the practical risk was to be stabbed by her darting little scissors if he did so. He kept very still indeed, wondered how she intended to actually proceed upon the business of their sexual congress. She would be wonderfully practical, of course.

'Do you want this child very much?'

She leaned back from her trimming of his hair. 'But yes!' And after a pause, asked him, 'And you? If this is to be the best we can have together, do you not also wish for it?'

He surprised himself by how little he needed to think through the question. 'If it is the best, then I wish for it.' And to his moral credit, Alec believed he knew what he was agreeing to. Here was need. Here was a person with her eye on renewal. Here was the good. And yet.

And yet he would return to his own country leaving a child in the world that was his own but was not his family.

'I am glad,' said Viva.

'Will you grant three conditions?' It was mildly surprising to him that he was able to put a number to his needs from the confusion he felt as to what she had sprung on him.

'What conditions?'

'If a child comes and it is a girl, you will call it Bell.'

'After the big sister? This I grant,' she agreed immediately.

'If, when it grows older it wishes to meet me, you will permit this.'

'You will be on the far side of the world.'

For a moment her face had clouded. He needed to think. She was scrupulously fair-minded he believed. Her anxiety lay in the distance that would be between them. Then he tumbled to it, and must add,

'You will have to trust me that I would not have it in mind to steal your child from you if you were far away.'

She hesitated, so he said again, 'You would need to trust.'

After some further moments she said, 'I grant. What is your third condition?'

He thought about how he wished to express this wish, for it was intimate to his own desire for a fulfilment in this life.

'If we'll be going different ways after this … this event,' he began, 'we will have our distinct lives. I accept that. But I would like, before the end of our years, to have the chance to be once more in your company. For a little.'

'Why this?'

'It will help me to know the value of what has happened here—with you and me. A fidelity.'

'Of course I grant,' she said, and snipped a further stray sprig of his hair, then stopped and restored the scissors to their sachet.

He could see the dark of her cleavage where her frock had come forward. He had felt her breath on his cheek when she spoke, had breathed the distinct air of her neighbourhood.

'What happens now?' he looked at her, expectantly, surprised that his words seemed to wobble rather. His hands had remained on her waist.

'Now we can be together.'

Yet she was clumsy in her intimacy, business-like. First she must slip from his hands to arrange the canvas cushions along the well of the punt, then she must turn back to him with a small look of desperation he had not seen in her countenance before.

'You see,' she thumped her front, 'I have in here *la tendresse*, but I do not know very much how I should behave now.'

And here was another illumination of her atrocious plight. For had she not felt the first stirrings of love for a man in those abominably unhelpful circumstances of the Occupation, and the next instant her love had been most horribly spoiled. She had not made love to a man before.

'I'm no expert, Viva,' was the best answer he could make.

'Is this droll, do you say, for a married woman to be like this? So ignorant.'

'It is very droll,' he told her, and was kissing her face, quickly and everywhere, with anguish, with joy, with fear she might vanish.

They were equally naïve in the motions of their sexual congress, possessing neither cleverness in their kisses nor knack in how they should slide, ebb and flood their hands over each other's bodies. When Alec was clumsy unfastening the buttons on the front of her frock she assisted him, yet when they lay, caressing, body against body, the shock of her nakedness, the wholeness and trust of it, Alec could not say he had ever experienced the vibrancy of his well-being more exquisitely, nor ever wished it for another person as he wished it for Viva in those moments. Where was her own well-being? He wished he could have held it in his hand and caressed the abstract thing expertly and with entire devotion.

When, in the course of their caresses, she held his face back to look at it, and they exchanged some banter, humorous and private to them, she responded with kisses more enthused than accurate as to where they fell. Alec, in turn, had elbow and hipbone that bumped her, surges of passion that were crude in how his hands and mouth roamed about her person. It would be true to say their first act of coition overtook them rather than obeyed any prior idea they might have had about the business. But his anxiety that she would not come to the reach of her pleasure was quelled when he heard, besides his straining, and the lapping of the water beside the boat, the catch, and catch, and catch of Viva's breath as, whatever physical mystery it was, her orgasm passed through her person. They lay together, calm.

And may have slept. But woke again, and with their mutual sense of the term on their love, recommenced their lovemaking, calmer now, more searching, more intelligent to the urgency in the other. As they moved with each other, where, on the still water was their flat craft drifting? Occasionally the woods crashed with some animal movement. 'It is the pig,' she advised. 'It is being disturbed somewhere.' When their desire was at peace, again she slept while he remained awake. He had no means of counting the hours but could share that sense, ancient as Stone Age man, that the night was at its stillest. There was little animal movement from either bank now, but a valley off Alec heard, pok-pok, and then perhaps three minutes later, pok-pok, pok-pok. Shotguns?

'It is some of the English soldiers from the town.' She was awake, and explaining dreamily.' They are in the forest for their sport. They look for the pig which are mostly gone from here.'

He covered up her ears with his hands so that she might drift back to sleep. Once I was a soldier in a grand and fair enterprise, he said to himself, yet never in my life have I so wished to protect a person from the violations of the world as now.

Pok-pok. Pok-pok.

In time Alec also slept. By the time the sun woke them the popping of the sporting guns had ceased. In the early rays the forest canopy seemed to steam, the light like slivers of glass through the gaps in the leaves. Birdsong contended, a dragonfly, as though pursuing some grid pattern a few inches above the water surface, arrived, vanished, reappeared.

When Alec looked at her person beside his, uncovered, still rising through the layers of sleep, his instinct was to cover her against the slight dawn chill with whatever was to hand, her frock, his cotton shirt. Upon her opening her eyes, he saw her instinct was to draw his head close and kiss bits of him, and the complex knot of feeling in his person, which for convenience must be called passion, propelled him toward their third coition.

From one of these unions their twin children were conceived.

They lay in each other's arms. If the punt had drifted in the night, the profile of forest on either shore appeared much as it had when they had set out.

'I cannot be thanking you, Mister Alec Handles,' she murmured against him.

'Why can you not?' he asked reasonably.

'When we are both *avec une joie égale*? This would be very droll.'

'Droll,' he echoed. 'How can a word bear so much?' And again he must kiss her, the eyelash, the nipple, the already vanishing person.

By plying the paddle on alternate sides, they took the craft into shallower water where Alec could use the pole effectively. Their interlude was at an end, and his response was to disguise his pain with cheery inanities as he ducked to avoid the branches of trees that overhung their course through the water. Viva was subdued, replied to his chatter with monosyllables, brushed aside the tendrilly boughs as each loomed.

When they were on dry land once more she would not quite meet his eye and said, 'It is best if you are not in the company with Marius again, I think. We will take a path so I can show you how to find your motorcycle.'

'You told me he was happy with this.'

'Not happy. Practical,' she reminded. 'If you return to the house you will hear him make his ruses. This may not be so agreeable. We will take a different track.'

'If it is what you wish,' he agreed.

He would have liked, on this last walk, to have placed his arm around her shoulders or her hand in his, their bodies brushing together as they walked. But she preferred not to be so encumbered. They took a track to the right and were soon ascending the ridge they had come down on the previous evening. When they passed the skull nailed to its tree trunk Alec stopped. The ghastly relic was dirtier, browner, more perished than he had remembered it from yesterday evening's moonlight.

'You know,' he turned to her, 'I'd really like to be told this does not belong to that deserter fellow we've been talking about.'

She backed away, hostile to him. 'How could this be so?'

'Because of the spell,' he persisted.

'This is crazy idea.'

'It is not that man?'

'Did I ever have my eyes on him? Why are you foolish?'

'Because I cannot rid myself of the notion you can ...' he faltered for the idea was indeed foolish.

'Can what, Mister Handles?'

'Pull things out of the hat just a little.'

'There are five million German soldiers in this recent war.' She would acquaint him with facts.

'Point taken.' He was crestfallen, but perplexed. 'Last night I did not understand your ...' he would have preferred a different word, '*attachment* to it. Sorry,' he said, giving her a pained smile, setting off again down the path.

'You will wait,' she said, and was now a little above him on the slope. 'You will see how you stand. We have been together. You will see what I am like now.'

Briefly she touched the death's head with her fingertips, then began with great calm.

'When the war closes the SS come among the Boche soldiers and shoot deserters and the fainthearted ones. Can you say how much thinking happens in a person's head between I shoot, I spare? It is casual. There are many killed. This,' she touched the skull again, 'is one, I think. He has the bullet hole here,' she indicated to Alec a place behind the skull. 'Come, you may see. It is neat.'

She paused. He did not move, and Viva resumed.

'I come here to *Der Libellesee* because it is where my darling is. I find him as you have seen. Your aeroplane has destroyed his body. One of his own people, a deserter, has hacked his face to make of it a hideous thing. Each morning in our bed I wake to this. I make the promises to him and to myself that you know. I walk in the woods with my troubled mind. They are generous what they can hide, these German woods, do you not think so?

'One day when I walk, I see, where the pigs have been snuffing, there is a human corpus,' she pronounced the English 'corpse'. 'It is more military uniform than corpus, it is more buttons than uniform because your tough military fabric is … unstable like this,' and she descended the track to pinch his flesh.

Now, as she spoke she was close. 'It is in bad state, this corpus, but I am still only two years from my haircut, and from the patriots who kill my papa. So my thoughts are in bad state also. Can you understand? I am able to look at the thing in this ditch.

'You are soldier in this war, mister. You tell me you are trained to look through the pockets of the dead soldiers. I can tell you, after one year being dead, the strong soldier body collapses very much inside its uniform. I have good nerves when I am in this ditch with this corpus. I look through pockets for papers and pay book. All are eaten by the insects. I cut off the buttons,' she took from her pocket the sachet so he might see, 'with these same little scissors I trim your hair. Why? Because I am mindful there is a mother or a wife who will wish to know who this one is among the five millions. Do you think Viva has no heart?

'But for my own need I take away the head. Mari will not see this; it is my need. The head detaches easily because this corpus has been long enough in the ditch for its parts to lose interest in one another. I take it to the water and I clean it. I travel to the town and tell the authorities in Detmold I have found the headless corpus of a German soldier on my husband's land, and I give them the buttons. They come and take it away, and when they have gone, I bring a hammer and a nail and I make this place for it.

'But I do not understand why.'

'Because,' she rejoined fiercely, and seemed reluctant to supply more details for the macabre shrine.

Then, recovering her calm, she justified herself. 'Because I want my darling with his body as whole as yours is, his face the fair thing you have and as it is when first I talk with him. Do you understand how you are in this now?' She gave him a level stare. 'You come to me on the last time I see my darling whole, so you are lodged here…' she tapped her forehead, 'because you are how I can compare with the thing I cannot have. And this makes me angry. So when I am angry I come here and look at this and try to think about what you have called the fair thing. I must take the course that helps me.'

'Yes,' he agreed. It numbed him, how she must put herself in the way of the dreadful.

'Can you still think I have the loveliness?'

'O yes,' and would have gathered her into his arms, but she wanted none of this, and set out briskly down the track. 'Now you know how you stand,' she called back.

He followed her through the woods for what may have been two or three kilometres, the lake appearing intermittently between the foliage below them, the crunch of their footsteps echoing.

So it would effectively end as it began, Alec reflected, his following this person through woodland. She was formidable. To have come up against her was the profoundest experience of his life. Would she abide by the three conditions? Straight as they come. But he felt injured that she should have recoiled from his wanting to hold and comfort her just now. She was so fierce when it came to guarding her power to cope.

At length, where a muddy track lead down toward the water, she stopped and waited for him to catch up. 'If you will continue another kilometre you will recover your motorcycle, Mister Handles. I go here and walk home beside the water.' She held her hand out to shake his hand in farewell.

'Could I not hold you?' he asked her, shy, anguished.

'It is worse if we do this,' she said, looked at him quickly. 'For both.'

He shook her hand. It was very formal. 'I hope it goes well with you,' He could only bear to take quick glances at her face.

And she was shy with him. 'Perhaps if we have success, it will seem less strange this thing we have done.' And she was already picking her way down the smaller track, steadying herself on branches.

'It will be good,' he called after her. 'I hope it will always be strange.' Then the branches of an oak tree obscured her blue frock, and Alec continued along his own track to where he had left the motorcycle an aeon ago. She had kept the watch.

When he reached his room, he washed, then slept for the remainder of the day, went to the garrison canteen to eat. Recognised by a group of his colleagues he was asked where he had been that day and he gave them the excuse that Viva had supplied. Lost in the forest.

'It's the itch for walkabout,' observed one who knew a little more about Australia than the others. 'Gets to the young males when they're in season, this need to wander off on their own and have a good think about their popsy.'

Alec smiled amiably at the chiacking, made his excuses early, went home and wrote his letter of resignation from the Pom Civil Service. In the days after he separated from her, Alec continued to wonder whether Viva would abide by his three conditions and thus prolong some level of their relationship. Straight as they come, he insisted to himself, but could recognise how their intimacy would recede, her interest in him lapse as the years passed.

 He lodged a postcard at the Detmold post office giving Viva his forwarding address at Portobello. Within a few months he was on a ship to Australia from where he had been absent for twelve years. As he sat among the Dutch and Italian migrants in the ship's canteen, abstracted by the music of languages he could not make out, or as he sought solitude to smoke a cigarette at the stern rail, he tried to free himself from the idea that his life had been a trapped thing since the moment he had escaped from his transport over Normandy. Certainly Viva had now freed him, but as the weeks passed and the oceans of the world churned whitely, briefly back from the ship, Alec Dearborn (BA) was oppressed by the thought that once you have looked upon yourself being acted upon, it became exquisitely complex to recover that frame of mind where you could entertain the idea of a promising future. If he could recover that, he could free himself.

20

THE LANGUAGES OF THE LAKE

So Alec returned to Australia where he lived out his days, and in his last conscious moments was astounded by how lightly the purchase on time of his sixty-six years appeared to his mind's eye.

For a few months in 1950 he stayed with Bell and Ma on Portobello. Now, from Smoko Hill, you could see the newer southern suburbs of Canberra being constructed. He assisted on the property where he could, repairing a fence or the iron on the shearing shed roof, yarding the mob at drenching time. And at dipping time, he stood at the plunge dip with his ducking stick, shoving the heads of the merinos into the dipwash as they thrashed through the trough.

But Alec just needed to glance at the authority in Bell's eye when she gazed across a pasture to see how far his own feel for the land had withered. Bell's authority lay in the economy of effort with which she worked her sheepdogs, the set of her mouth when she went straight at some temporary difficulty, the quiet decision with which she classed or culled the flock. He could see how, in the years he had been away, Bell's being had become concentrated around this pastoral life. Sinewy, tanned, her movements, say loading or unloading the tray of the vehicle, were more brutal, than the gracile sibling he could recall from the rocks at Ulladulla that time, or her arms along a chair back in the softly lit dining room of the Metropole after a game. Something lost, yet it was enviable, this focus to which she had committed her nature.

As he pushed the heads of the sheep under the arsenic tri-oxide mix, he looked up to where she was working the two-way gate that let the emerging animals onto the two draining aprons.

'Do you miss all that pre-war razzle-dazzle from town, Bell? Hunter's Hill, The Metropole, and all that?'

And she had looked up with a quick smile, then returned her attention to the sheep as they tottered, streaming, from the trough. Her face under the hat brim was now middle-aged, he saw.

'I can tolerate the *odd* spree!' she called out at length, though to watch her eye moving upon the flock you might wonder if her attention could ever be distracted for such a leisure.

Sometimes during that winter of 1950 Alec took the twenty-two up into the further reaches of the property where he would sit with his back against a tree. One level of his attention watched for rabbits and foxes. Another was adjusting his sympathy away from the strange scenes of foreign places and back to what was immediate to him. How, for instance, a Monaro mist would transform a big brittlegum into a delta of pale grey veins against the white. Or how the last hour of sunlight in this airy woodland could angle so searchingly under the foliage to suffuse the planet's surface with an aureolin gold.

'In your mind you're adrift,' Bell gave her opinion, having coming upon his place of retreat in the vehicle.

'Surely not.' He licked the paper of his cigarette.

She sat down on the earth beside him and scuffed at the bark litter with her boot for a while, then broached her topic.

'Look, I want to sell up here and get a smaller place.'

He knew her interest had been homing on the fine-wool end of the industry for some time. She had done some looking into the breeding that Merriman and others had done, had heard a rumour how one might breed the world's finest stud rams and ewes in those cloudy sub-alpine valleys beyond Cooma. If you set the mind to it, she had opined once or twice.

Meanwhile here was the government paying good money for land on which to build Canberra. With luck they could set Ma up in a bungalow in town, divide the residue with Nance.

'Goose, I know it was Pa and our uncles who set this all up, which makes it historical ...'

He regarded her steadily, holding the lighted match away from the fag. Truth to tell, his difficulty with The Dad's expectations of him had never won him to The Dearborn Pastoral Enterprise.

'You're the history-minded one. Would you be very sentimental if …?'

'With respect to that,' and he looked at her solemnly, as though about to utter some vital objection, then flashed her a smile, 'I have to say I wouldn't raise a hair, sis.'

A tease. But Bell, impatient with the put-on, had worked out the details of his own moving on to a finer pitch. 'Goose, I think you should go school teaching.'

He adjusted himself against his tree, drew meditatively on his cigarette and said, 'I think you could be right.'

'It would rebuild your … well, presence of mind.'

'It would do that.'

Indeed, quite clearly he could see it would give him the useful mental jolt people seemed to think he needed. Classroom jabber and squeak of chalk on blackboards, the surge and ebb of shoes on stairwells and in corridors, the taking charge, the being on watch for what turns up from moment to moment. 'I can just imagine it,' he said.

Besides he was thirty-one.

'But you know, Bell,' he crumbled a strip of the bark in his hand, and gave her the look, suave, troubled. 'What I can't work out is …' He faltered, looking for the words that would cover his perplexity, shifting his gaze from her to the prospect north.

'Can't work out what?'

'Well, how a person knows whether the existence he's been given has been of value to anyone else.'

By the New Year these changes in their lives had been accomplished. Bell acquired eighteen hundred acres behind Berridale where she created her sheep-breeding program. In the early days she hired a rabbit and dingo trapper named Claude, a man younger than her who had fought in New Guinea. With his assistance she fenced, laid down superphosphate by hand wherever she judged a patch of her pasture required improvement, nurtured the stock and would suffer no intermediary to do her buying, selling, or classing. She was reckoned to have a superb touch when it came to judging the quality of wool, and to be a tartar when it came to chasing vehicles from her paddocks that might bring in the seed of noxious weeds in their tyre treads or on their trays. Casual shedhands who allowed their dogs within the precinct of the shearing shed where they might spread infection went in fear of her scolding. Fussy, heedless if she gave offence to neighbours or shire officials when it was a matter of applying her ideas to her breeding program, nonetheless she was bounteous at auction time when the buyers would find a damask tablecloth on a trestle furnished with many bottles of whisky and rum against the drizzling weather of the sub-alpine spring.

As the boom in wool continued Bell began to make money and her stud rams and ewes acquired a reputation at the Annual Sheep Shows held at Moore Park. Claude the trapper stayed on because it was practical he should do so, first as a station hand, later as a husband and background figure to his wife's clarity of purpose.

'How are you managing?' Alec asked her on one of the late night phone-calls that became their habit over the decades.

'As always,' she replied, then twigging his more searching purpose, said, 'I'm fine, Goose. He calls me Sweedie. It is very strange.'

Their marriage was childless; Bell survived him, living on into deep old age.

In that same New Year of the half-century Alec took the post as English and History master at the Anglican grammar school in Canberra. He became a housemaster for the boarders, coached the First XV on their practice afternoons and pursued this vocation for the next thirty-three years.

With his large frame and appraising manner he was liked and in turn found he was suited to the demands made upon his temperament by the hurly burly of classroom and dormitory. There was a knack to the authority that required at times a certain staginess, yet allowed for more affection. In time he became adept whether it was a matter of bringing four hundred fellows to order with a stentorian bellow, or identifying the one child in their midst who was lost in some personal grief.

During these three decades he exchanged occasional letters with Colefax who had a series of headmasterships in the English grammar schools. But Alec did not apply for advancement in his profession because it did not occur to him to think he was involved in a career. When, at his retirement, he heard his colleague describe Mister Dearborn as a natural teacher he was genuinely surprised to hear it.

'A colleague who, I can say, belongs with those who are kind and good.'

The sixty-five-year-old one-time paratrooper sat in his academic gown listening to this tribute and supposed it might be true. The school hall was packed and when the speech ended, certainly the fellows, thumping their shoes on the floor in a thunder like sustained gunfire, appeared to think so. Miraculous rather, Alec reflected, to have once tumbled from an aeroplane, not into deathly mud and asphyxiation, but to the course in life that led to this applause.

As though one's life was attended, not so much by persons as by figures. There was Ferris, for instance, to see a fellow through the doorway from life into death, there was Viva, archetype of those who effect rescue and renewal, Bell the same. What did that make Alec Dearborn?

Fanciful stuff (as the shoes drummed and the cheers roared).

Yet these figures persisted in the patterning he construed for his life. He could recall how, ten years previously in Hobart where he had come with his fellows for an inter-schools rugby week, he thought he had glimpsed the wall-eyed jumpmaster crossing a road

'Sergeant Ferris?'

The man, compact, a muscularity in the face as Alec could imagine would be preserved in Ferris's face, had looked round, briefly, uncertainly, hurried on. Could have been the man. And here was the applause for his farewell at last subsiding. Could Mister Dearborn say his existence had been valued?

Merely for the things a fellow learns to rattle off in a classroom or on the sports field?

During all these years Alec did not marry.

'I seem to have slipped through my prospects,' he once remarked at a house party for Bell when she was staying overnight en route to the Sydney Show. The amiable brother was taken aback when, even after all these years since the Cambridge teashop, she recoiled from his levity, unwilling to deal lightly with the subject of his bachelordom.

'Goose!' How Bell could pin the seasoned teacher with that old childish nickname! Her glass of claret undulated as she scrabbled for the emphasis she wanted. He watched her, this sibling who, of his two, had turned out to matter. It was a rare thing to see her put a few glasses away, yet these infrequent sprees were as inalienable to her nature as anything else in it. 'Goose,' she had gathered herself. 'When you used to walk among people everyone thought you were a young ...' and she must hesitate before she would utter the word, '*god!*'

'Come off it, sis.'

And he coughed a little, having become a bit in the way of these bronchial complaints during the course of his fifties.

There was something in Bell's over-the-top reminder. Across the years, Alec's debonair looks, amiable nature, attracted to his welfare the good will of those with whom he worked and played. There was always someone to organise an anniversary celebration, prepare a plate of food, make a speech. As though he were someone whose role it was to release the good will in others. He found himself at these occasions, grinning a little too broadly, smoking a cigarette or, as the years passed, trying to give the cigarettes away. Was it really him to whom the humour, the plaudits referred? On occasion it seemed to him he skimmed at this level of his consciousness, like an ice-skater or a surfer along time's cusp.

And that hidden lake in the mind where the doodle could inhabit, how did that persist? He would go up to the suite of rooms he had in the boarding house after finishing for the day and sit at the second-hand piano he had installed, allowing his ear and his fingers to find some agreeable, evanescent progress of notes, his mind to release itself from the day's hurly-burly. As the decades slipped by, he was pleased that this idle pastime did not pall. It was not that his thoughts always turned to Viva on such occasions, but when they did it was at this twilight time before he needed to switch on the lights and prepare a simple meal.

Of the three conditions Alec had asked for, Viva fulfilled the first two with some exactness. She named her twins Bell and Marius. At each birthday she posted a letter to Australia describing their lives over the twelvemonth such that, in the course of the decades their natural father learned of their play, their schooling, travels, occupations and marriages. These letters were efficient, but stiff as though she had no skill in translating the quick and charm of her talk onto a written page.

'Dear Mister Alec,' they began, and ended '… yours sincerely, Vivianne Clausthal,' with her own surname, Orbuc, in brackets.

That 'Clausthal' caused him a pang. Why could she not sign herself simply Viva, or keep up the tease of her nickname for him?

She gave no news of herself beyond what could be deduced from the description of her children. There were periodic movements back and forth between Germany and France. He sat in his darkened room and thought how she would experience merry hell hefting that bumptious, broken man around the rooms of her Normandy farmhouse. Would she install a piano for him somewhere that the two could arrange themselves together for duets; she mentioned he was musical. She would presumably have that secret attic as a place for her own retreat.

By the mid sixties Marius's name slipped from mention. If the correspondent was stiff in her written English, she was adroit in deflecting Alec's enquiries on the subject of his rival. Perhaps now was the time to take a trip to France, turn up at her door? But the big ignorant footballer found he had become foolishly nervous when it came to putting himself in the role of a suitor now that he was forty-seven years old and immersed in the education of young males. Besides, that blunt surname in her signature deterred him from such a plan.

In the blink of an eye eighteen years passed, her twins finished at their lycée. They would try their English in Mister Alec's country, Vivianne Clausthal wrote. She had not lost the imperious manner. As the twins came through the airport barrier at Sydney, gangly, wan from the long flight, speaking French to each other as a defence against the raucous strangeness into which they had arrived, Alec saw with a stab of pleasure the new quantities he and Viva had brought into the world.

'They've copped your fair looks,' observed Bell with equal immediacy, having accompanied Goose on what anyone could see might prove a dicey encounter for a bachelor schoolie in his forty ninth year.

Circumspectly the father and the twins studied each other during the succeeding days. Veritably there were inherited physical characteristics from their Australian side, and perhaps a certain mildness of temperament too. But the vital attitudes, the nuances of feeling and gesture, the decisive lift of an eyebrow, the inimitably quick slant in the corner of the mouth, these enlivening mannerisms were all from their mother.

Within the limits of language their visit went off satisfactorily. They spoke just a little more English than Alec or Bell spoke French. In the first instance they went up to Bell's mountain acres where, for a fortnight they bumped between granite outcrops behind the tractor, distributing superphosphate or a roll of fencing wire. Sometimes there was snow; sometimes there was the most exquisite bronze sunlight in the Alpine scrub. At times, watching how they seemed to act in accord with one another, they seemed strange to the father as a pair of outer planets. Nonetheless they liked working with the animals and among the sheds. Then Alec took them down through Nimmitabel to the ocean where their enjoyment was a more conventional thing. From the beach they returned for some days to his rooms in the newly built Grammar boarding house, and abruptly there was no time for more.

His children, his own twins, were well mannered toward him, but foreign. They possessed a most impenetrable nonchalance toward all he could show or ask. They would disclose little information about their mother. Their interests, Alec soon perceived, carried them away from his own life. There was a kind of impatience in them he could not fathom.

Maybe it was a good thing, he rationalised, to be free of that centrifugal pressure which had brought them into existence. On their first arrival at the airport, he had discovered, their birth-names had been dropped in favour of the nicknames they gave each other, Belo and Zelik.

'Now everyone says these. *Maman, les professeurs.* You may too, it is cool.'

They provided one illumination as to the fidelity of Viva's interest in him. On their last day the three drove down the highway to Sydney Airport, Alec's Kombi enclosed in the squalls of rain that had caught them after Marulan. Belo (she pronounced it 'Bey-lo') who spoke the better English, sat beside him in the front, Zelik (Zel, Zeluc, Zelly, his nicknames being the tribute of affection he evidently attracted to himself, whether in Normandy, Germany or wherever) was recumbent on the bench seat behind. The rags of cloud across the Southern Highlands, the gusts of rain and the grind of the kombi windscreen wipers had the effect of making the three remote from each other and they had not talked for some time when Alec, concluding some train of thought, glanced at his daughter.

'Are you close to your mother?' he ventured, hoping he could get away with such a direct question in an eighteen-year-old person-and-daughter.

'*Maman?* Yes, I adore.'

'Me too,' the forty-nine-year-old made the avowal to his chancy child. 'Bowled over in fact. By the force of her. The loveliness of her.'

He feared the distillation of his feeling for Viva that he wanted to communicate to these, his for-the-moment children, was coming out too formally. For them certainly, for his own sense of things too. The formality would cause the intimacy of what he wanted to make reside within their lives misfire. But if he did not say the thing through, what would they make of this burly, affable schoolteacher on the other face of the planet?

'I have never known anyone else who had such a necessity and yet such a mystery in her person.' He should have tried to get that complicated thought into French for them. '*C'est ma bonne chance,*' he finished lamely, not certain he had got the idiomatic palaver right.

The girl was thoughtful for a while and Alec assumed she had taken in his explanation in her offhand way. But at length Belo said, '*Maman*, when she wishes to think of you, she plays the English tune.'

'What tune is that,' he asked.

'You teach her this one,' the girl turned, eyebrows lifted, and in that lift, a surprise that verged on the indignant, heartrendingly the mother.

'Moreton Bay,' he supplied. 'It's Australian.' He recounted how he had only needed to finger it once and she could play it back to him. 'I bet she still has a splendid ear,' he probed.

Then Zelik was audible from the back seat, the contribution at once formal and rapid. '*Maman doit être une femme trés occupée mais le jour de l'anniversaire elle est découragée. Quelquefois nous en voyons cela.*' He rapped his French too heedlessly for Alec to comprehend it. The parent wondered indeed if it was intended that he should.

There was a moment of sympathy in the look Belo gave him. 'Did you understand?'

'Something about *découragée*,' Alec floundered.

'Zel says that our mother has to be always busy, but on the anniversary day we sometimes see that she is sad.'

'Discouraged,' Alec modified, to which the girl shrugged. 'What anniversary is that?' Alec asked next.

Again she gave him a look of slight surprise, as though he should know more. 'Your big day! The invasion.'

He allowed the information to settle in his mind. He could conclude that she thought about him on occasion. By arrangement almost. It was fidelity. Enough maybe. They drove for an interval in silence.

'Will you be sure to give her my love?' he made his request, content if the power of feeling could be disguised by the conventional phrase.

'Sure,' Belo gazed from the car window at the stormy landscape. 'It is no big deal.'

As he entered his sixties, the knee injury converting itself into a nuisance arthritic pain, it was the chest infections that would put Alec into hospital for a day or two. In one of his letters to Viva he had mentioned tests. It was chat, yet behind it was the acceptance she should partake of the wholeness of his life.

A letter from Colfax provided Alec with the cue to this quiet watch he had kept on the idea of his life's wholeness. The letter, routine enough, contained a clipping from one of the British newspapers, with a scrawl across its top in biro, 'Pals of yours?'

The picture showed several Parachute Regiment fellows gathered in Normandy for the fortieth anniversary in 1984. The press photographer had evidently knelt down to take his shot of the group from below and the man on the right was Ferris.

Roy Ferris, now of Hobart, Australia, the caption read. Alec took in the aspect of the man, the once spiky hair largely gone, the head more like a tree bole than anything, yet the expression on the face attent, still suggestive, despite the blazer and tie, of energy, of 'Go, fuckya!' Perhaps the pressman's ploy was to have the veterans looking down on all who surveyed the photo.

How casually the cue arrives. As Alec placed the letter under the paperweight on his desk and drove from his new suburban flat to the clinic to receive the results of the tests, his sensation was like that when he used to proceed down the corridor locking up the classrooms at the end of the summer term, a timeliness, an impulse to leave things orderly, completed.

'We found rather more than we wanted to, I'm afraid.' The specialist compressed his mouth, glanced from the patient to the envelope of X-rays.

'I had the notion you might.'

Of course the diagnosis also caused that flare of animal dread in him, the shrillness along the bone. But the patient sustained his lopsided smile for the sallow specialist whose voice had the soft intimacy of some radio announcers. For my own dread I can bear responsibility. *Do you see*, he might have informed this bloke who was evidently decent and dutybound to pass on bad news, *how life is a matter of learning the exact point where nerve is required.*

He was told the number of months he might expect, what the trajectory of the pain was likely to be. Mr Dearborn was a man of impressive physique still and that strength would be a bonus. As Alec drove home he asked himself what else he would like his life to have included. It might have been nice if she had managed to fulfil that third request. That thread confirming fidelity. But of his three conditions, it was the foolish one, to expect an allegiance to persist against the tide of renewal.

I will be with you for this, Mister Handles, she said at a traffic light.

You are released, Viva. We both live too stubbornly in a place and time.

It will be simple, she closed the topic.

He applied himself to the arrangement of his worldly goods, this to Nance and her new grandchildren (also twins), that to Bell, the books to a Queanbeyan second-hand seller. The soldier, who had once worried whether he had the nerve for bayonet work, found he had the nerve to face his own death cheerfully. He could not avoid the rigmarole attending a personal extinction, the further tests, the intervals of treatment at the hospital, the barbarous programs of medication. None of the consultants appeared to consider his case to be operable. Between lambing and drenching, drenching and shearing, Bell came down to drive him back and forth to his appointments, to sit with him, to arrange his lawn be cut or his gutters cleared.

Day by day almost he could register the progress of the cancer, how walking or rising from a chair could seem absurdly burdensome, how trying to manipulate a simple tin-opener on a tin of asparagus could topple his big foolish body over from the effort it required. The small hours of the morning were worst. Sometimes he pictured the dark interior of his physiology as a counterpart to the terrain of his night in Normandy, new sites of discord breaking out here and there, his cells loosing off automatic fire at each other, the new outbreaks never quite calculable. As though he had taken the war into himself.

To counter this ill reverie he tried consciously to join up the two parts of his life, the part that had been on view—footballer, teacher, and the tender part he had guarded from all except Viva. In the end could the two be made whole and said to have been of value to anyone? Nance, her sons and grandchildren came once to see him. Bell sat with him, talking sometimes of everyday things, sometimes of the past and both brother and sister felt that strange unease at how banal conversation could be when there was so little left of it to run.

Once, interrupting her spiel, he said to her, 'I think I allowed my life to get distracted, Bell. I think you had cottoned onto that the time we were in Cambridge after the war. It's why I upset you then.'

She looked at him, shaking her head slightly, but not willing to contradict. Her idea was that he should win this match against disease, as he had done before. But she watched all his lovely hair fall out and the generous musculature of his body grow gaunt. Her good cheer broke just the once.

'O God, Goose. This is frightful.'

They looked at each other, his smile aslant, courteous, one of his eyelids drooping a little absurdly on the altered face, Bell no longer of an age where she could cry, but regarding him as though with a reproach that he could think of making an exit from her life.

She touched his bald head and said, 'I'll bring you a hat,' and left for the week of shearing. As Alec listened to her steps down the ward he could see from the window the lake with a shoal of sailboats upon it, the suburbs half hidden in their lustrous October foliage. Beyond was Red Hill, still looking more paddock than nature reserve. Charlie Russell who had been their neighbour on the Narrabundah Run had continued to pasture his sheep there long after suburbs surrounded those thinly treed slopes. Alec knew that if he could be bothered to slip from the bed and shuffle to the window he could look in the other direction toward the shawled hunch of Black Mountain. Could he call this southern prospect his own country? No. Between going off to Hume and returning from Germany he had lost his tenure here. Yes, he had been distracted, so that when he had come to live in it, near it, he never quite recovered an intimacy with the place. And in that Cambridge teashop, Bell had looked down his years and sensed he would become alienated from it.

Poor Bell. If the time spent with him was to be bearable she had to keep up a practical patter, and get him talking, turn time into a spell of forgetfulness. When she brought up the past, he supposed she wanted to conjure an agreeable glow. From his present perspective, those remote experiences seemed airless. Given the sleep of the night was so elusive, it would be good to snooze now, which he did.

Bell never did meet Viva, but the two women passed each other in the foyer of the Community Hospital as one departed for the shearing, and the other made enquiries at the desk.

'I wondered whether you might turn up,' he came up through his light doze and turned his head to her mildly.

'You will die this time, I think, Mister Handles.'

She gave him her level look and again he was struck by the fine tones of intimacy with which she could regard him, having seen him so infrequently. Why was forthrightness the means she used to express her love? Yet that is what she meant, he could see. Well, good on her. And he saw how her working life had made her body solid rather than plump, but she wore her clothes well, a blouse of simple design, a longish travel skirt. And there was the slight skewness of her eye, the face subtle, appraising, different from when he had kissed it. Ah, her own still, and dear.

'Not before time, eh.'

She smiled at this, then pulled from her bag a red woollen cap and placed it rakishly over his bald dome. '*Le voilà!*'

'You have forestalled something my sister was planning for me,' he said, as she adjusted, stepped back to look at him.

'It is practical.' But she continued to experiment with the hat, her eyes lively, attentive to the effects she could create.

'You know, it has always done me good just to look at you.' How easy it was to say this to her, as though her presence had been a regular event in his life. He would need to be careful how much he talked if he wanted to get by without the oxygen bottle.

Conscious that routine conversation had never been within their range, he nonetheless asked her the routine questions. How were their twins? Belo was happier in her second marriage. Zel may have found someone at last. Did the priory flourish. She would let Zel take over the Priory because it was too painful in her legs to mount the ladder into the apple trees now. It occurred to him he could ask her about the details of Marius's exit from the world, but at the extremity he knew himself to be, events located in exact time were not of especial interest to him, were banal even.

So instead he said to her, 'You know, we exchange news on everyday matters like an old married couple,' and then, after a pause, and wise to his effect, he added a respectful, 'Ma'am.'

'In these years it is better we should have been occupied,' she dealt with this.

I worry you'll vanish in a puff,' he said. For the joy, the completion, was her presence, and the talk was strangely superfluous. Yet by convention they did talk from some region of mind where the words did not especially matter but the proximity of the person created an entirety of being.

If any question from the old days survived in his dying body, it was the question he had asked her in the forest. 'What am I in?' Had she, from the first, set up a watch on his life, some psychic palaver not to be explained? Were both their lives watched by immaterial interests, barbarous or benign, that could arrange and create self-consciousness? Palaver too, maybe. Perhaps their lives were like all lives, not watched, but contriving the watch on themselves as though it were a watch from a removed viewpoint.

What did she think, he wondered as he looked at her, his eyelids drooping with fatigue, keeping up his sly smile that must look inane to her. And what right did he have to tax her on the matter? She was going into the life beyond him. Even before she made their situation plain, he had recognised the fact.

'I can think of no more to say to you,' she said.

For this was the plain fact, yet she had crossed the seas to be present.

There was an interval before he said with his sly, sidelong look. 'We need another piano, I reckon. Doodle ourselves into the next existence.'

And she nodded, as though in collusion with the vain, comic idea.

'It does me good to look at you,' he repeated, hearing his own voice that was not his voice, so exhausted, as though every word, every notion had been worn out, like shoes, like a toothbrush, like every material thing. And yet the presence of her, as the last hours of his life ticked away, agreeable to contemplate, her face, carried by decades beyond his last look at her, not puffy but fuller in its curves as he had once supposed it might become, the eyes set back more, blacker perhaps. Yes blacker, definitely. He would have been a good husband to her.

After a time she left and he submitted to the routine, the discomfort from within his foolish body, the unbelievable weakness that seemed to pervade his limbs. The nursing shifts changed over, lights went out, he was sometimes asleep—ten seconds? An hour? The night watch was very long. He was still able to manipulate the oxygen mask when he needed it. A nurse administered morphine—Was he awake or asleep when this occurred.

Then, in the dark, Viva was at his bedside. The sheet was being untucked, his legs pulled over and placed on the linoleum floor. 'You will trust me Mister Alec,' she said, and raised his body from the bed.

'I doubt I can support my own weight this time,' he told her in the morphine lightness that seemed to possess him.

'You have a foolish body, Mister Handles' she soothed him, taking his arm around a shoulder, carrying his oxygen bottle in the other hand. How could she hope to walk him past the night nurses?

'Are we going on the razzle,' he asked, as they shuffled.

'You will trust me.'

'If you like.'

There were corridors, there was a lift, there was a darkness and odd caches of neon light as they made their progress. Why did the nursing staff leave them unchallenged? There was a room. It had carpets, children's plastic toys scattered about the floor. And a piano.

'We will doodle,' she informed him.

'But I am calm,' he said.

'I am not,' she replied.

And for this reason, it seemed, she would place him opposite the bass notes while she took the high, plaintive keys. To get started she needed to place Alec's hand on the ivories, but once there he found he began a doodle of bass notes quite promptly, and soon they were playing as they had, the weakness in his foolish body, the intractable bole of regret in her person offering no impediment to the fluency of a music that came into existence and vanished almost immediately. They played, and sat silently, occasionally exchanged remarks.

'When I came to you I had seen a man lose his face,' he said to her at one point. 'It was Lance Corporal Brown, I realise. You see, they taught us to live alongside our fellows. I accepted this completely. Yet I could not recognise the man till now.'

In her turn she replied, dandling a fivesome of notes. 'The face of papa is unspoiled. They shoot from behind the head and there is blood in his hair, but his eyes are narrowed in the liveliness when he must translate some interesting phrase for his student. His eyes smile a little. He is on the kitchen table, his body too long so the feet and shoes hang in space.'

'These things have a quiet place now, Viva.'

'They are placed, but they are not quiet, Mister Alec,' she said.

Twice she needed to hold the clear-plastic mask over his mouth and nose and turn on the oxygen supply. They played some more, and when the darkness in the room began to grow paler, she took him back along the watery floors to his bed.

She would come in the morning, she said.

When she came in the morning she was mistaken for Mr Dearborn's sister by the nurse on the morning shift and informed that Mr Dearborn had been moved to another room. On being escorted here Viva saw he had died some hours previously. To accommodate his extinction Alec had been swathed in white sheets, the red woollen hat like a ridiculous cherry on a cake. The parts of his face and throat she was able to survey were yellowish and awful in their complete peace.

'You will leave,' she requested the nurse who had escorted her.

And when she was alone with him the Lakewoman stood beside the corpse and found she could not keep her emotions under any practical control. Here was the fact as she had stated it to him. He would die. Absurd that her body must stiffen, must quiver around the desperation this fact released in her. Yet she went with her emotion. Because this person had been her Other. Because she had known sorrow for things that had been, but could not have calculated how wild was the sorrow for the thing that might have been.

She sat in the sunlit room for some time, and after the first onset of her sorrow was spent, she went away and returned to her own country.

Alan Gould is a poet, novelist and essayist. His recent publications include *The Past Completes Me – Selected Poems 1973–2003)*, his novel *The Schoonermaster's Dance* (2000) and a collection of essays, *The Totem Ship* (1996) He has won the Grace Leven Prize for poetry (2006), the 1999 Philip Hodgins Memorial Medal for Literature, the 1992 National Book Council Banjo Award for fiction and was co-winner of the 2001 *Courier-Mail* Book Of The Year Award for *The Schoonermaster's Dance*.